TWILIGHT OUTREACH

A Story of Love and Redemption

A novel
By

JAYE

ISBN: 098626170X
ISBN–13: 9780986261701

And the light shined in darkness; and the darkness
comprehended it not.

-John 1:5, King James Bible

Prologue

"**All rise!" bellowed** the burly, female bailiff in a stern voice that echoed loudly through the half empty courtroom.

"The Honorable Judge Judith Hawkins presiding," she went on, as the Connecticut family court judge entered the courtroom and ascended the bench. The diminutive justice shuffled a few papers on her desk before quietly perusing her computer monitor. She then lowered her bifocals to carefully survey all those assembled in her courtroom this rainy afternoon; her eyes coming to rest upon the throng of professionally attired adults flanking a neatly dressed, angelic-faced girl.

"Please give your name and relationship to the case for the record; starting here on the right, counsel first," instructed the court officer.

An elderly, silver-haired African American woman modestly dressed in a simple black pantsuit spoke up first in a soft but clear voice. "Rachel Ward, law guardian for the child Dominique Glavin," she said and then promptly took her seat at a long, horizontal oak table festooned with three perfectly aligned black mounted microphones pointed upwards. The petite, young girl was left standing beside her.

"James Ratti, attorney for the mother, Mrs. Joyce Glavin," offered up an impeccably attired man in a tailor made suit. He spoke with an Italian accent and he occupied another part of the table with a small stack of legal papers in front of him. Beside him was a conspicuously empty chair where his client should have been.

"Jefferson Smith, counsel for the father," proclaimed a short, racially am-biguous, middle-aged man in a baritone voice. He too, then took his seat at the table.

"And you, sir?" the officer said dismissively to a tall, African American man with a stern countenance, and warm brown eyes; his stout, muscular frame and arms threatening to bust through his police sheriff's uniform.

"I am Robert Glavin, father of Dominique Glavin, my daughter," he said proudly in a booming voice before taking his seat by his attorney.

Then after a brief silence, the court officer moved toward the young girl standing beside the seated law guardian.

"Young lady…your name, please," the bailiff gently prodded the beatific, freckle-faced youngster. The girl was striking in a simple pleated grey dress and shiny black patent leather shoes. Her sleek black hair was pulled back in a severe ponytail.

"My name is Dominique Glavin. I-I am the daughter," she responded, like a question, in a soft-spoken manner. She then quickly took her seat, her eyes darting about nervously.

The mother, the former Mrs. Joyce Glavin, was not present. Judge Hawkins took careful note of that disturbing fact. She then paused to con-sider the request for a change of the custody order that she had presided over some eight years ago, the reason that had brought them all there today. Judge Hawkins spoke directly to the one who had made the request; the twelve-year-old child Dominique.

"Dominique, I read the letter you wrote to this court, to me. You are a very intelligent girl, I must say. But, am I to understand that you want me to change the custody arrangement that gave physical custody of you over to your father and to allow you to reside with your mother instead, the very same mother who is not present for this very important hearing?"

Not sure if she should answer, Dominique turned to look at her law guardian for guidance. The venerable law guardian, who had served the court for over 19 years, nodded her approval for Dominique to respond directly to the judge as she had coached her. Dominique slowly rose to her feet and found her voice.

"Yes, y-you're Honor," Dominique managed. She was incredibly nervous; still she succeeded in controlling her tendency to involuntary twitching as the law guardian had trained her. "As I said in my letter, I want, want to live with my mother. My father is too strict and abusive. I-" she said.

Judge Hawkins raised a hand in a gentle but stern manner that caused Dominique to stop suddenly in mid-sentence. The slight echo of her small voice hung in the air of the otherwise silent courtroom, adding to the gravity surrounding the proceeding. The judge spoke low and softly, focusing her eyes directly on little Dominique.

"Dominique, when you say your father is abusive…does he physically punish you or, does he otherwise… hurt you in any way?" the judge asked carefully.

Dominique paused for a moment. Her young mind struggling to understand the manner in which the Judge asked the last question. At that moment, a jolt went through her and she stood straighter, rushing to answer, as the inference of the judge's question became clear. "No, no, nothing, like that! It's just…he doesn't let me do anything. I can't talk to him. I just want to live with my mother in Stamford. I need my mother. She wants me to live with her too," Dominique finished.

"But she's not here, Dominique. What am I to assume from that?" the judge returned. "Where is your client Mr. Ratti?" the judge demanded, directing her ire at the mother's attorney.

Joyce Glavin's attorney sprang to his feet and answered up, his black slicked back hair glistening brightly in the overhead courtroom lights.

"Your honor, my client is an investment banker. She had every intention to be here, but could not make it because of the demands of her job. She had to fly out of the country at the last minute, but she is available by speakerphone, if necessary. But, we have all the reports from the social worker who interviewed my client and went to her home in uh, Stamford. The report clearly states that my client is more than a fit mother for her child," he declared then sat back down.

The father's attorney, Mr. Smith stood up and chimed in.

"Your honor, we have all read the report and the letter Dominique wrote, but the mother's absence at this important hearing speaks volumes of her true willingness to be a viable custodial parent over young Dominique. Remember why, my client was awarded physical custody in the first place, because of the mother's drug use and…"

"There was no finding of neglect, your Honor and besides my client voluntarily entered and completed a drug program," quickly interjected the mother's dapper attorney.

"I am well aware of the history of the Glavin family and their divorce proceedings, like everyone in this community, gentlemen." the judge stated. "That's not what we are deciding today."

"Well, your honor, her father has been a great parent. Even if, by his own admission, somewhat stern." the father's attorney continued. "He has provided his daughter, Dominique, everything a father could give his child. She is doing very well in her private school. As the school reports show, she's among the top in her class. She is the captain of the school soccer team. Why take her out of the private school she has been attending for the past four years? As the county sheriff, my client is a pillar of the community. We ask that you take into account the mother's absence here today, and keep the custody arrangements as is," he concluded, taking his seat.

The mother's attorney fired back. "Your honor, we have adjourned this case three times already. My client was present the first time the case was heard. We adjourned the case the second time because the father's job as town sheriff precluded him from being present. Which if I may add, my client graciously understood. I am here speaking on behalf of my client today. If need be, she is available by speaker phone now. The child is 12; she is old enough to make an informed decision regarding with whom she wants to live. Since the divorce, she has resided with her father for the past eight years and she is unhappy although privileged. Now she wants to live with her mother. The father can still have liberal visitation," he said, before sitting back down.

Judge Hawkins was torn. She knew the Glavin family in happier times. They were pillars of the community, a shining example of a happy, productive, African American family. She didn't know how to proceed. She turned to the law guardian, who was also her longtime friend and whose opinion she greatly respected. Judge Hawkins was known for always siding with the law guardian in cases involving the best interests of children. She decided to make no exception in this case.

"Law guardian, what do you have to say?" she said.

Mrs. Ward stood up slowly, opened her mouth and spoke with authority, well aware of her influence in the court with this judge.

"Your honor, I have interviewed the child on several occasions and her recent experiences with her father are troubling, if not disturbing," she began. "He doesn't seem to understand that she is becoming a young woman. Dominique has expressed a deep desire to live with her mother. She speaks highly of her mother even though she is fully aware of why her father was initially awarded custody of her. Dominique is an intelligent and mature child. She is of the age where she needs her mother as she blossoms into womanhood. I believe that she should be allowed to live with her mother, your honor. To force her to stay with her father would only further traumatize her."

Judge Hawkins, inspired by the words and wisdom of the law guardian, was suddenly emboldened to make her ruling. "I am going to side with the law guardian. Physical custody of Dominique Glavin is hereby awarded to the mother Joyce Glavin with liberal visitation granted the father. All other orders to continue." the judge hammered her gavel to signal the end of the court proceedings. Dominique was beside herself and giddy with happiness and excitement. She hugged her law guardian tightly around the neck.

"All parties are excused," commanded the court officer.

Everyone made their way out of the courtroom expeditiously except for Dominique's father, who walked out slowly behind his attorney, his powerful, strapping frame now bent under the weight of the judge's ruling. He was unable to shake the feeling that he had lost his daughter forever.

PART 1

CHAPTER 1

Bronx, New York City; Six years later

The early Sunday morning sunrise revealed a bevy of scantily clad women still working the streets of the notorious South Bronx corridor commonly known as the "The Zone." Young women of all shapes and sizes, colors and complexions, proudly flaunted their partially nude bodies for all to see, strutting around in audacious stilettos and ultra-trendy pumps, wearing thongs and skimpy leather outfits; halter tops and tight miniskirts; spandex tights and shimmering hot pants; poom poom shorts and booty cutters, showing off fleshy butt cheeks, buxom breasts and shapely long legs, all for one purpose: trading sex for money.

A bustling caravan of luxury cars trailed behind the throng of enticing prostitutes. The vehicles rumbled and weaved their way down every street corner, boulevard, road and avenue where the women could be found plying their trade. The men in the flashy cars strained to catch the attention of the women, lusting after their bodies, hungry for their time. They blared their horns, shouted obscenities and screamed lewd comments at the prancing whores.

"Hey, you with the fat ass, Come here," a surreptitious man in a sporty green Mustang bellowed as he stopped abruptly and without warning in the middle of the busy intersection to pick up a slender, young prostitute in tight, low rider jeans, an assortment of colorful tattoos cascading down the small of her back. The horny john sped off with the object of his desire.

A few blocks away, another prostitute casually stepped out of a silver 325i BMW, only to quickly get into a black late model Suburban with black tinted windows. Just up the block, a voluptuous, dark-skinned prostitute in a florescent mini-skirt flagged down a tan Cadillac and bargained its driver for her services. A white Mercedes Benz with gold trimming pulled up to a group of prostitutes milling about; the men in the car aggressively engaged the women in illicit conversation before the women jumped in the luxury sedan. Another juvenile prostitute in short shorts was walking away with a lone male john to a secret rendezvous, her curvaceous body sashaying in the emerging daylight.

The "Zone" corridor stretched interminably for miles, north and south, like a foreboding road to some faraway place from which there was no return. The Zone was this God-forsaken neighborhood's unofficial red-light district, a once bustling, expansive industrial area, now renowned only for its blatant street prostitution. It attracted pimps and sex workers from all parts of the city and country. Word had spread over the years that any prostitute could make a good living working "the Zone" as long as she got with the right pimp and looked halfway decent. Men flocked to the area looking to indulge their sexual fantasies, having their pick from a large variety of sex workers. On a busy night it was often hard to tell if the men were preying on the women, or the women were preying on the men.

Not far away from the horde of alluring women, a silver late model Cadillac Escalade sat parked between two cars on an obscure side street. The luxury SUV rocked erratically every so often. Its tinted windows were fogged up.

Inside the high-end vehicle, a very attractive, freckled-faced prostitute outfitted in a black laced bustier and wearing a thick 18 carat white gold chain, was going down on a large, handsome, well-dressed, middle-aged man. The john who had picked her up off the street early just minutes ago was stirring, riveted by the sight of the attractive young woman taking him in her mouth. She filled the SUV with loud, titillating, slurping and sucking sounds aimed to heighten the man's illicit experience.

"Come on, baby, come for me. Come for me" said the svelte seductress in a sultry voice.

"I'm- I'm almost there, honey. Just keep, keep on doing what you're doing. It-it won't be long now..." the man managed to say, breathlessly enjoying the woman performing on him, tantalized by her technique, delighted by her skills. He ever so gently, patted the woman's black hair, stroking it softly, endearingly, watching her head bobbing up and down incessantly, in his lap, blowing him. She sucked him like a vacuum, pulling him in with her sensuous lips, deep-throating him, bringing him to the edge of ecstasy then back again.

After several long minutes, the stylish john could contain himself no longer. Seized by a paroxysm of pleasure, his sweaty hand suddenly gripped the back of the woman's head, forcing it down on him. He was about to come. Undeterred, the prostitute, sensing what was about to happen, continued ever more rapidly and enthusiastically determined to make the john come. The man belted out a half scream, a hybrid of relief and orgasmic joy. He came. A large pool of ejaculation quickly formed at the top of the condom. Satisfied at her conquest, the young woman stopped and squeezed firmly on the john's engorged penis, forcing more of his release into the prophylactic. She reached for a tissue in her purse, removed the condom, before quickly tossing it out the window. Dutifully wiping the man down, she watched as he became flaccid.

Satisfied, the john paused to catch his breath and collect himself. He was spent. He basked in the tension leaving his body. Slowly reaching forward, he pressed the ignition button with his thick index finger. The engine roared to life.

"Grrrl, you sure got some skills. I forgot how good you are. You're something special," the heavy-set, African American man remarked, a wicked smile snaking across his face. "You really are."

The disheveled john was still trying to catch his breath as he was out of shape and gain his composure, exhausted from the illicit activity.

"What you said your name was again, baby girl?" he said as he tried to navigate the SUV out of the tight space they were parked in. "I won't forget this time, I promise."

The attractive prostitute felt unusually comfortable with this man, as he was by now a regular customer, this being their third encounter. She was flattered to be in his company. The man was elegant in a silk cobalt blue suit with a light blue silk shirt and matching tie. Gold jewelry could be found all over him. She thought that she could confide in him.

"Passion," she said, casually. "My real name is Dominique but everyone calls me Passion," she returned with a wry smile. She sat up now in the plush, white leather seat, fixing herself in the flap down mirror. Exposed on her right thigh was a large tattoo of the cartoon character Betty Boop, holding a small bouquet of flowers. The prostitute quickly applied lipstick to her succulent lips before she tucked her perky breasts into the bustier.

"What's your name?" she said, smiling, fully expecting the man to give her a false name as most johns do. "You asked me my name the last time but never gave yours. You married or somethin' or you got some big secret? I won't tell," she said slyly.

"You can call me….Roger," he said after some thought, clearly lying. "Well, Passion," the man said, "I sure hope I see you again; that's for sure! But I got to get going now. I'm running late, is what I mean."

"I know; I will see you too, Daddy-O," the attractive prostitute said, staring at the gold rings squeezing his fat fingers. "Just call me and I will be waiting for you on the corner as always. Where you going with yo fine self? Looking all Gucci-down. What kind of cologne is that?" she said.

"Oh, the cologne, it's uhm, Christian Dior; but listen, I enjoyed this a lot but I have to go. And don't you worry your pretty little self where I'm going, just know that I will be seeing you again, Passion," he said.

The dapper gentleman slowly drove his Cadillac Escalade up the block, just within sight of the parade of prostitutes still milling about on the main street in the early dawn.

"Stop right here," Passion said, pointing to the spot he had picked her up at. "Ok, bye, Rog-er, Hope to see you again," Passion managed with the same smile on her lovely face. She climbed out of the SUV and walked in the direction of the other working women, stopping to count the money the man had given her. She appreciated that he never tried to cheat her or try to bargain her down. He always gave her what she asked for. She stuffed the money in her designer clutch purse.

Passion stepped purposely past the dwindling gang of prostitutes, stepping lively in her translucent patent leather pumps. She went past eager johns striving to get her attention in a vain attempt to solicit her for sex. Passion ignored them all. She was good now. In her mind, she had made her money for the night.

She quickly arrived at a rundown tenement building on the corner of Prospect Street where she lived with her pimp. The front door offered no resistance, the front door lock having been broken long before she started calling this decrepit building home. Passion took the urine-soaked elevator to the fifth floor. Arriving at her apartment, she knocked three times on the unmarked door.

"It's me, Passion," she said.

A tall, dark, hulking figure of a man slowly opened the door and allowed Passion just inside the apartment vestibule where he confronted her. It was her pimp, known on the streets as Lavender. The apartment was almost completely dark. Only the light from a flat screened TV in a back room beat back the all-consuming darkness. The pungent smell of marijuana choked her nostrils. Strains of Rapper Wale's "Bad" played in the background.

"What you got for me, P?" the man said in a deep, raspy voice, his flaming red eyes piercing with hypnotic intensity.

"I made good tonight; here," Passion said, pushing a roll full of fifties and twenties in the man's large, calloused palm.

The large pimp took wad of money and barely counted it before shoving it in his pocket. He was furious.

"Bitch, this ain't shit! You steady short-changing me," he growled. "You should be making more than any of my hoes out dere, not this bullshit! You need to get yo dollars up, fo real! Didn't I tell you? I want at least $600 from you every fucking nite! I'm tired of this shit! What you think, you too good fo this shit? Huh?" the pimp said, his voice rising, his fury intense. "Did you forget your bitch ass ole man brought you here already owing me money, huh? You know what? I'm going to humble that pretty ass. Watch! You might as well be giving my pussy away! Fuck this! You can't stay here no more, not until you start makin' the money you need to be makin'! You hear me? You been fucking evicted! Go find somewhere else to stay, bitch! Get the fuck outta here!" he shouted. "And don't come back till you got it right! And you betta not make me have to come find you either!"

"But Lavender…" Passion started, trying to quell his rage; but before she could finish her sentence, he opened the door and shoved Passion back out into the hallway, pushing her so hard, she fell back against the wall, hitting her head hard before collapsing to her knees. The door slammed shut. She could hear the lock turning in the door. Passion remained on the dirty hallway floor a long time, racked with stabbing pain. Tears smeared her mascara and stained her cherubic face as she drifted into unconsciousness.

⬥

Dominique arrived early at her mother's half a million dollar palatial condo in Stamford, Connecticut in the summer. She was bursting with anticipation and excitement. Her mother's two white and black pit bulls, Cloak and Dagger, trotted out to greet her on the winding cobbled walkway with beautifully manicured lawns on either side. Dominique bent down to hug each dog eagerly.

Erik, the Ecuadoran doorman, gracious and welcoming as always, greeted her kindly.

"Hi Dominique," he said, tipping his hat. "It's been a long time. My how yous grown. The missus, uhm, is waiting for chu. She said for yous to make yourself comfortable. Let me take yous luggage," he said as he easily shouldered her bags, leading her into the luxury high rise building.

Her mother's condo was lavish with its four bedrooms, three bathrooms a large, open kitchen area with a marble island, and a living room full of antique furniture. Freshly polished hardwood floors glimmered attractively. Expensive, vintage paintings of the countryside and seaside adorned the walls. A dazzling chandelier bought in France, hung majestically from the high ceiling in the living room. Light filled every corner of the condo through the custom-made windows. An 18th century handcrafted bookcase filled with books on every subject related to finance and banking, stood in a private study. Beside the bookcase her mother's academic awards hung in elaborate custom frames. The small patio deck was also fully furnished with, a modest grill and plush deck furniture. A glut of house plants from ferns to Philodendrons, filled almost corner of the condo, adding a sense of relaxation to the otherwise stodgy decor.

Dominique found her own room readymade with a full sized bed, a computer table for her Apple IPad, flat screen television mounted on the wall. She was so happy to finally be able to live with her mother again. It was a dream come true.

After several hours of Dominique waiting, the former Mrs. Jocelyne Glavin, finally emerged from her bedroom, casually dressed in an elegant, black, off the shoulder tee and form fitting yoga pants. Her mother's age-less beauty made her seem more like an older sibling.

Dominique jumped off the couch at the sight of her mother, "Ma!" she said, and ran to embrace her.

"Come here, my dear," her mother said blithely, a bright smile painted on her face; her slanted eyes the template of her daughter's. The former Mrs. Glavin's slender, muscular arms were spread wide to give her daughter a big hug as if she were trying to embrace the sun. Joycelyne Richards stood six feet tall with an athletic build honed from countless hours in the corporate gym and a strict diet regimen.

"This has been a long time coming," she said. "We did it! We did it!"

They embraced each other, mother and daughter heartily. They both cried as if they had overcome some terrible storm and were now basking in the calm weather.

"We have a lot of things for us to do," Dom!" her mother said wide-eyed with excitement. "Get yourself situated first, ok my darling then we are going to celebrate a new beginning."

True to her word, Jocelyne Richards-Glavin took Dominique to Broadway plays and teen concerts. They vacationed in the Poconos, Miami's South Beach and took a five-day cruise to nowhere. Dominique talked exhaustively with her mother on every subject she could think of, from boys to school and everything in between, until the wee hours of the night and early morning and continuing on until the next day, something she could never do with her father. They spent countless hours in the kitchen with mother passing on to her daughter all her cooking recipes. They posed for silly pictures together at the mall, and shared a Facebook page. The thrill of being with her mother, having her available to her at a moment's notice, was a constant high. Dominique would often fall asleep in her mother's bed, reliving the joy she felt when her mother and father were still together.

It was so much different than being with her father whose stoic, stern manner often alienated her and his lack of affection creating a distance between them.

Dominique's world was wonderful again, and she couldn't be happier. But her idyllic joy still couldn't hide her mother's often erratic and inexplicable behavior. Dominique didn't say anything about the long hours her mother often spent holed up in the bathroom. Dominique didn't mention anything either when her mother missed her first teacher's conference at her new school, or her first high school soccer game; or the all-important conference finals; nor did she mention when her mother's late nights out spilled over into the afternoon of the next day, and she was sprawled in her bed. Nor did Dominique voice concern over vacations that were abruptly cancelled without warning, often the very same day. And always the excuse was because her mother was working or had to go to the office—even on the weekends. Dominique ignored it all, simply because she was reunited with her mother again. Besides, her mother always apologized profusely for her behavior and made amends by staying up countless hours with her daughter going over homework; or putting Dominique through exhaustive soccer drills to get her ready for the next game her mother promised not to miss. Or buying Dominique the latest smartphone; or taking her on a shopping spree. Her mother would do all those things only to then again lock herself in the bathroom for countless hours, disappear unexpectedly or miss another important event in Dominique's life. And then the apologizing, and making up would start all over again.

"Dominique, come in the living room. I would like you to meet someone," her mother said, one cold winter day when Dominique arrived home after school. Dominique stepped into the living room, stomping the snow off her boots. She found a short white man standing beside her mother, looking more like her son because of the height difference. He had a tanned complexion and wild blond hair and the hint of a moustache. His teeth were badly stained and in need repair; he avoided direct eye contact as if he had something to hide. He was handsome with green eyes but he gave Dominique the chills.

"Dom, this is David. David this is my daughter Dominique," her mother said beaming with a big smile. David is my fiancé, Dom."

A cold vice closed around Dominique's heart upon hearing the word 'fiancé. She could barely hide her disappointment upon hearing the news. After all, Dominique secretly held out hope that her mother and father would reunite. She believed that her living with her mother again would be the catalyst to convince her parents that they needed to be a family again. Now that hope was gone, vanished like the wind.

"Nice to meet you, Dominique," her mother's boyfriend said in a deep voice, his eyes undressing Dominique. "You are as beautiful as your mother, here. The same eyes and…"

"Oh, oh hi Mr. David," Dominique said, cutting him off. "Con-congratulations! Nice to meet you!" Dominique said in a whispered, hurried voice then she made a dash to her room, hiding her anger in the form of tears.

Her mother's fiancé David was from that day forward a fixture in the house, like one of her mother's house plants. Dominique would come home and he would be sitting on the couch in the living room or out on the patio deck smoking his cigarettes, never saying much, just smiling. Her mother catered to him like she used to cater to her father so many years ago, preparing his breakfast, making his dinner, picking up behind him. It made Dominique cringe. David would come in the morning and leave only after Dominique had fallen asleep late at night. Dominique could never get over how he made her feel, uncomfortable and uneasy, like he was some monstrous wolf in sheep's clothing.

Her relationship with her mother changed as well as David absorbed all her mother's time and attention. Rarely would they go on mother-daughter dates and when they did, her mother would cut them short once she got a text message from David that he was coming over; no more late night chats in her mother's bedroom. No more vacations unless David was tagging along. Now it was all about David. David, David, David. Dominique felt lost. She felt betrayed and resentful, like a promise that was made and broken. She found the two dogs, Salt and Pepper were now her only companions, her only confidantes.

Dominique woke up in the middle of the night, awakened by the sound of the front door opening and closing. It was four in the morning and David was finally leaving the house.

Dominique roused herself to go to the bathroom but found the light already on and the door slightly ajar. She opened the bathroom door and peered inside. Dominique was horrified to find her mother sitting at the small table bent over, sniffing white powder up her nose with a tightly rolled hundred dollar bill off a vanity mirror.

Dominique had long known about her mother's cocaine addiction and how that was the deciding factor that helped her father win his custody battle during the divorce proceedings. But her mother had successfully completed a drug treatment program, and had told everyone she had kicked the habit. But now Dominique's was witness to the terrible truth.

"Dominique!" Her mother shouted, startled at the sight of her daughter in the bathroom mirror standing just outside the bathroom, staring at her in disbelief. Cocaine powder *sat on the tip of her nose. "What are you doing up so late? And why didn't you knock on the door?" her mother said, by turns embarrassed, and ashamed to see her secret revealed and angry at herself for not locking the door.*

"Ma, no! What are you doing?" Dominique whispered at her mother, her heart breaking, sinking in a hole of despair, ignoring her mother's useless questions all the while. "I-I we thought, you said you had stopped! You-you told Dad and everybody, everybody you had stopped! You said you had stopped! What, what are you doing?"

Her mother looked at her daughter mortified, feeling her daughter's pain and disappointment but unable to stop herself from finishing what she had started; her addiction was like fire in her veins. She continued to snort in front of her daughter.

"Dominique, I'm sorry you had to see this," she said, talking with her head turned, still preoccupied with the white lines on the vanity mirror. "I truly am but, but I can control it now. I won't let it control me anymore," she said, hardly believing her own lies. "Look, you have to understand," her mother said, now turning to face her daughter. "I work a very stressful job. I'm a black woman working in corporate America with a bunch of white men who treat me like I don't belong there. This helps me cope."

"But ma, no..!" Dominique said, unable to process what she was witnessing, the whole scene seeming surreal, like waking from a dream into a nightmare. But now it all made sense, her mother's behaviors all made sense to Dominique now.

"This helps me, relax ok, Dom! Now go back to bed and close the door. You have school in the morning and I have to go to work. I'm going to be all right. I promise. And, please don't tell your father or he'll come back for you! You know how he is," she said, with derision in her tone.

"But ma, let me help you..." Dominique began to plead, moving slowly toward her mother. "I can help you...you can't..."

But before Dominique could take another step, her mother quickly stood up and with a suddenness that halted Dominique in her tracks.

"I said close the fucking door and go back to bed!" her mother roared in an authoritative voice and tone Dominique didn't recognize and took her completely by surprise. She shoved Dominique back out the bathroom and violently slammed the door shut in her daughter's face with a forceful thud.

Dominique stood shocked and frightened for a long while, crying without tears, the closed door now just inches from her face. She stood frozen in place for some time before slowly, mechanically, doing as instructed and went back to bed, very sad and very afraid, sensing dark clouds beginning to dim her future.

Chapter 2

The Reverend Avery Emerson Jr., senior pastor of Grace Baptist Church, was a big man. He stood about six feet tall and had a big girth and wide frame to match his outsized personality. The stocky pastor was an unusually friendly person with a forceful manner, a firm handshake and an instant smile. Light complected with an immaculately trimmed mustache and short haircut, the fifty-years-old pastor always filled up a room with his presence. He was a handsome man, given to wearing expensive, bright colored, tailor-made suits, silk ties and gaudy jewelry. He had diamond studded earrings in both ears and a gold, diamond encrusted watch with a similarly studded pinky ring. He wore his cologne heavy and many times the smell of his favorite Christian Dior musk fairly choked those standing in close proximity to him. The pastor had a fondness for the finer things in life, including nice cars, manicures and fine food. He looked every bit a pastor/pimp.

Reverend Emerson flirted with all the women in the church, making each one feel like she was the most special person in the world. But surprisingly enough, he remained free of any scandalous rumors. Many of the women in turn felt free in expressing their fondness for the portly pastor and more than a few tried to spread rumors about him but none successfully. The women adored him, captivated as they were by his engaging personality and smile.

The pastor lost his wife some four years ago in a car accident. When she was alive, his wife Mrs. Gloria Emerson was the envy of all the women in the church, not only for her status as the First Lady of the church but for her own beauty, intelligence, compassion and grace. When she died, the women of the church lined up to comfort the pastor during his time of mourning and let it be known they would be more than willing to be his new wife.

Like Candace Martin, who took to imitating his wife's trademark wide-brimmed derby hats and pointy toe pumps. Then there was Sheila Jones, a twice divorcee who copied his deceased wife's short, immaculately coiffed hairstyle to get the pastor to choose her as the new Mrs. Avery Emerson. And Joy Grant, a shapely older woman who wore the floral print below the knee dresses his wife was fond of. But the pastor remained a widower, never hinting of trying to find someone to replace his departed wife.

Everyone always came out in droves in their Sunday best to hear the good pastor preach. They admired Pastor Emerson's good, lively and powerful sermons. He wasn't a fiery preacher; he was a smoldering one, the power of his sermons building to a soft crescendo. His voice, heavy and deep-throated like a radio deejay always kept the females enthralled and always inspired orgasmic hallelujahs and amens. Pastor Emerson studied at the Divinity School at Howard University. He delivered his sermons in the tradition of the best Southern, African-American preachers, with all the vocal pyrotechnics and related effects.

Grace Baptist church was located just off of Story Avenue in the Bronx about five miles from Prospect Street and the "the Zone." It stood three stories high. Its striking Gothic architecture caught the eye of the casual passerby with its pointed arches, vaulted roofs, buttresses, large stained glass windows and spires. The church steeple was tall; its spire reached to the heavens. A large cross stood at the very top. The base of the church was adorned with stained glass windows, illustrating various scenes of the Creation. The church facade portrayed God commanding light from the heavens. The side of the church depicted God breathing life into Adam and Eve. And near the back of the church, there was illustrated Adam and Eve being thrown out of the Garden by the Archangel Michael under his flaming sword with the Serpent lurking nearby.

Grace Baptist was a pillar of hope in this downtrodden community. It was a sanctuary for those trying to escape the harsh realities of living life in "the Zone." Prospect Street and its adjoining streets and avenues, for many, many years suffered from rampant crime, lawlessness and poverty. Drugs flourished in the area and many drug addicts lived in the community. In recognition of this, Grace Baptist church was involved in almost every aspect of trying to improve the neighborhood, from providing free and low cost day camps for children in the summer, to their own meals-on-wheels program for the sick and shut-in.

Before her untimely death, the pastor's wife started a refuge for runaway girls in the community who wanted to escape life on the streets. The fledgling program was housed in a small wing of the church. It started off well and was instrumental in saving many lost and wayward young women. However, since her death, the program lacked leadership and resources to keep it going efficiently, causing its doors to close.

It was half past eleven when the Pastor Emerson finally arrived at the church. He was late for the morning service. Several church members often complained how unbecoming it was for the pastor to always be late for his own service. The good pastor couldn't come up with enough excuses as to why he was always late for Sunday morning service. He forgot to set his alarm, he explained often. He caught a flat, he would say, other times. He stopped in on an elderly congregant who couldn't come to service, he would say more than once. He used the last excuse so often until one of his diligent deacons started asking which congregant was sick and volunteered to make the visit for him. Then he had to come up with another excuse. It was too much. He wished he could help himself.

As he walked in the church, after parking in front of the church but entering the sanctuary from the rear, the Reverend Emerson set his mind to deliver the morning service. He began to focus on the Word he was about to preach to the congregation of Grace Baptist Church.

The Associate Pastor, Mr. Richard Eisley, spying the pastor at the door, politely waved him in. Mr. Eisely was accustomed to his pastor being late. The congregation looked up and saw the pastor, head bowed, take his seat behind the pulpit. The 20-member church choir, resplendent in their bright red gowns continued singing softly, clapping and swaying in unison.

The chorus finished the preparatory hymn, "Holy, Holy, Holy," the last hymn before the sermon. The pastor rose to his feet now, his arms raised above his head.

"Lord, bless us this day, the day that you made and give me the strength to deliver your Word." He approached the podium. Silence pervaded in the church sanctuary, interrupted only by a woman's feeble coughing.

He began.

"Forgive my lateness today but my car simply would not start until I bought a new battery," he said.

The congregation sighed loudly as one, always ready to forgive their beloved pastor for any infraction.

"Anyway, let us begin the reading of the Word," he said, opening a huge gold colored Bible.

"The Word is taken from Acts 21:14-18. Let us read it together," he beseeched the congregation.

When they had finished eating, Jesus said to Simon Peter, "Simon son of John do you love me more than those?
He answered, "Yes, Lord, you know that I love you." Jesus said, "Take care of my lambs,"
Again, Jesus said, "Simon son of John do you love me?
He answered, "Yes, Lord, you know that I love you,"
Jesus said, "Take care of my sheep,"
A third time he said, "Simon son of John do you love me?"
Peter was hurt because Jesus asked him the third time, "Do you love me?" Peter said, "Lord, you know everything. You know that I love you!"
He said to him, "Take care of my sheep."

"Thus ends the reading of the Word, amen" the pastor said and composed himself before going on.

"If I might put this in some context: This exchange between Jesus and Simon took place on the third day after Jesus had already risen from the dead and was spending time with his disciples before he would ascend into heaven.

"Now, Jesus kept asking Simon 'Do you love me? Do you love me? And each time he asked him to do something. 'Take care of my sheep,' The reverend's voice became an even deeper whisper drawing the audience forward to pay attention, like he was telling them a secret.

"He didn't want Simon to just talk the talk; he wanted him to walk, the walk. If you say you love me, then take care of my sheep, take care of the lost, the wayward, the weak, the least of these; take care of your brother, your sister, and take care of one another. He's talking about love acts, to show your love, not just to proclaim it. We as Christians like to say we love Jesus and proclaim him as our savior, but we need to also show our love for him by our deeds, by our actions, by how we treat one another, to love one another.

"So as we leave here today, let us commit to taking care of his sheep, which is our neighbor. Let us show our love for Jesus by loving one another and taking care of one another," the reverend said smiling broadly, his arms lifted high over the heads of the congregation.

"Let us bow our heads and pray." The pastor spoke loudly to the congregation in prayer.

"Good Lord, make us instruments of your peace. Where there is hatred, let us sow love; where there is injury, let us show pardon; where there is doubt, faith; where there is despair, hope; where there is sadness, joy; where there is darkness, light;" the pastor finished, and the congregation said, amen.

"Now, I believe we have some babies to christen. Let those families come forward," the pastor announced.

And those with babies in their arms quickly rushed the pulpit for the good pastor to lay his hands on their newborns.

Chapter 3

In a posh, co-op apartment, in the North Bronx, three prostitutes cooled their heels after a hard night's work. Passion, sitting lazily on a beige butter soft leather sofa loveseat, was soaking her sore feet in a tin bucket of iced water.

"So how did you make out last night, P?" asked a very stylish prostitute, known on the streets as Mercedes. She was partly looking at Passion waiting for an answer, partly admiring her own fire engine red Gucci platform pumps.

"I did pretty good; y'know, the usual," Passion remarked, evasively. She noticed the smirk on Mercedes face and knew that she knew all about their pimp putting her out in the street. She was aware that Mercedes was simply being sarcastic. Passion pretended not to know that she knew.

Passion was, by far, the finest young woman in Lavender's stable of prostitutes. Tall with model features, flawless complexion, shapely long legs and svelte figure, Passion's intoxicating beauty made her the envy of the other working girls. She had a singular loveliness that only a few women in a generation possessed. Men found Passion's delectable femininity irresistible and drooled over her stunning good looks. Even still there was a suggestion of hidden strength and street grit in the 18-year-old that let people know she was more than just another pretty face.

Passion was uniquely talented and crafty in satisfying her customers sexually needs. Johns who paid for her services always got their money's worth and never left feeling unsatisfied. Men admired Passion's innate ability to appear to be genuinely interested in being with them, gratifying their needs and wants, never forcing anything or being demanding, the most accommodating of all the women. Her tendency to take people as they are and not be the least bit judgmental, whether they were an out-of-work construction worker or a well-heeled Wall Street stock broker, put nervous johns at ease, was much appreciated and made them feel special.

Most of the other prostitutes looked up to Passion. She wasn't only smart and good-looking; she was real and down-to-earth, too. Passion cared about the girls she worked with, always looking out for them, running errands, helping any way she could. Passion was quick to caution about certain johns who looked dangerous or shady—to stay away from them; warn others that an engaging john was actually an undercover cop. Passion advised the other girls on what to do if they weren't sure a client was a cop: "Make him touch you, especially in your private parts. Ask him if he is a cop. He has to tell you the truth or its entrapment. Make him do all the talking," she would say, never explaining how she knew this. The girls listened to Passion; too, after all, she had never been arrested for solicitation.

Yet, for all her good looks, street savvy and charm, Passion was among the lowest earning women on the stroll, making less money than other prostitutes far less attractive than her. She seemingly didn't know or care to learn how to turn her fetching looks into cash money. For one, Passion often negotiated prices with her clients, something her pimp expressly forbade her to do; Passion wasn't addicted to hard drugs like most other prostitutes and so wasn't hard pressed to support a demanding habit. Either way, Passion wasn't earning her keep and this frustrated her pimp to no end. Lavender was of the opinion that she was either too stuck up or too stupid to hustle money and so he never tired of humiliating and degrading her at every turn. Putting her out on the street was just the latest in his guerilla pimp tactics.

"I made about three hundred dollars last night," Passion said, still avoiding the subject of her being put out in the street by their pimp. "The last trick I was with was a very classy guy. Nice ride and everything. He's been a regular," she added, speaking of the dapper, middle aged man. "He says his name is, Roger," she said, feeling proud to have been with a classy, well-heeled and generous client. "I know that's not his real name but who the fuck cares?"

"Oh really?" Mercedes responded, playing Passion's game. "Tree hundred, yeah, that's about your usual take," she said in her on again, off again West Indian accent. She was still preoccupied with her own platform pumps, now imagining seeing a smudge on them and wiping it with her licked finger.

"Yah should be making more than that with that sweet, innocent face of yours and nice ass, y'know," Mercedes said, coyly, with the slightest hint of envy. "I know Lavender done told you that plenty ah time."

"Yeah, whateva," Passion responded, so tired of hearing that. "He doesn't sell his ass, either. He's not out on the street like us," she returned.

Mercedes laughed to herself, quietly amused by Passion's true predicament of having nowhere to stay.

If Passion was the best looking of all Lavender's women, Mercedes was the best dressed. Whatever she lacked in natural beauty, compared to Passion, Mercedes more than made up with her ultra-flamboyant style, rich ensemble of expensive, name brand clothes, and pricey designer shoes.

A proud Coolie, whose mixed Indian and Caribbean heritage bestowed on her a captivating, exotic look. Mercedes dressed to impress and enhanced her sex appeal with her high fashion style. The 22-years-old Trinidadian-born but, Brooklyn-bred Mercedes was no more than five feet three but stood tall in six inch red bottom heels. Prada ankle boots, Christian Louboutin pumps, Jimmy Choo wedge sandals, Lanvin stilettos, Coach Booties, Sergio Rossi sling backs were just some of the designer shoes Mercedes stepped out in on any given night. She turned the ho stroll into her own personal fashion runway.

Mercedes underwent plastic surgery in the Dominican Republic to give herself booming buttocks with more eye catching appeal. She had breast implants to achieve the buxom look she craved. She was fond of wearing expensive weaves and dyed to match whatever outfit and shoes, now pink, now electric blue, violet, blonde or her personal favorite copper red.

Brought to the United States when she was nine years old by her doting aunt, Mercedes immediately took to high couture from reading popular magazines, watching TV shows and music videos. She quickly started imitating what she saw and did anything and everything to satisfy her expensive tastes. By age 11, Mercedes was stealing her aunt's credit cards to purchase name brand clothes online for herself. By 13, she was turning tricks.

"I made about $1200 and I had to quit early," Mercedes boasted. "My last trick wanted me to stay with he the whole night, talking about he couldn't get enough of me. I told him, I had to go. I told him he needed to find himself a girlfriend," Mercedes laughed to herself. "Plus, he had no money. He ran out," she laughed. "Sorry ass!"

Mercedes consistently made the most money of all the other girls. She made a quarter of a million dollars last year, which was remarkable given that Mercedes was a part-time prostitute, working only on the weekends while attending a private college as a full time marketing student during the week.

"Anyway, it's all in a day's work," Mercedes sighed.

Mercedes was Lavender's bottom girl. She ruthlessly, recruited new girls, managed the other girls in Lavender's stable, collected money from them, provided them with birth control, matched clients with girls online through her Lonely Hearts website and kept Lavender abreast of any police activity that might affect the business. Lavender could always count on Mercedes to handle his affairs when he was out of town recruiting other girls or locked up in jail

Mercedes had the words, "Bottom Bitch" tattooed in large, elaborate script across her artificially enhanced butt cheeks. She had another bar-code tattoo on the back of her neck with her body measurements, 36, 26, and 38.

"You got that right, Mercedes," said Desire, a white prostitute taking a drag on her cigarette. "Tricks ain't nothin' but scumbags," she said.

Desire was one of Lavender's older white prostitutes and his first bottom girl. Desire was a hot number when she was younger and in her twenties, but now, after years of drug abuse, four pimps and three children, she was more like a hot mess. She had ruby-red lips that spiked beyond the lip-line and penciled-in eye brows. Her pasty white skin hung on her like a wet rag. Her breasts were full but far from perky and her once proud figure was misshapen and bloated. Desire's full blonde tresses and sexy legs were the only thing that kept her in the game. Desire decorated her body with colorful tattoos of the faces of her three children. She also had a large tattoo of her pimp Lavender's name scripted on her left breast, matched with her own name tattooed on her right breast. Other small but decorative tattoos like butterflies and flowers could be found on her wrists and ankles and forearm.

A blonde, South Carolina native, Desire was a prostitute-turned-stripper-turned-prostitute. She was notorious for allowing Johns to go raw or have sex without protection if they looked 'clean enough' and paid extra. As she got older in the game, she used that habit more and more to pad her upfront fees; she had to in order to compete with the younger girls in the game. Desire had three kids, two of them from turning tricks or trick babies, the third and last one belonged to her pimp Lavender.

"A lot of these tricks act like they want to make you their girlfriend or somethin'. This is business, right here, nothin' personal," Desire went on with a distinct southern drawl. "I had my share of datin' johns or havin' trick boyfriends. They get all close to you, want to marry you and then forget how they met you—on the skreet. Then they want you to cook and clean for them. Later for that, shit. I got to get my hustle on, honey," she concluded.

Desire struggled to earn her keep on the stroll, but not for lack of trying. Where once she was a magnet for johns on the stroll, she now made most of her money on the off nights, during the week, when there were fewer girls on the tracks to compete with. She usually left the weekends to the younger girls, so as not to embarrass her herself, unless she was really pressed for money.

"Can't change a ho into a housewife, right Desire?" Mercedes put in.

"That's what they say," Desire responded. "Trust me, I know." Then they all started to laugh.

"You never said, how much you made, Desire. I swear I saw you getting a lot of attention out there," Passion said, smiling. She liked Desire and counted her as a real friend. She saw her as the big sister she never had. She admired Desire's ability to laugh at herself. Desire's feelings for Passion were mutual.

"I ain't even going to embarrass myself and tell you," Desire said. "Let's just say, my fat ass done broke even."

"Broke even with what?" Passion questioned.

"Broke even with this gottdam leather outfit I bought for last night. Now, my fat ass, can pay for it," she started to laugh at herself.

"Check this out," Desire said, always ready to share a story of her nightly escapades on the stroll. "This nigga picked me up, wanted to get everythin', y'know, suck and fuck, for like only $50. He said that was all he had. Now I know he had more fuckin' money than that. Shit, the mutherfucka was driving the new Acura."

"So you told him to fuck off?" Mercedes assumed.

"Fuck no. I ain't stupid. My fat ass had to take what I could get, what with all you young bitches out there. Shit, I was surprised he even stopped for me." Desire said laughing even more. "He fucked the shit out of me too; almost killed me with that big fuckin' dick of his. I think he was married cuz I saw a big fat ring on his finger. I always get the married niggas lookin' fo white meat," she bragged to herself.

"Well, that could never be me. Ain't nobody getting all this for no 50 dollars," Mercedes said, emphasizing her body with a funky up and down gesture.

"Never say, never," Desire returned. "I was the shit back when I was your age, too."

"Really?" Mercedes said, mockingly, hardly believing it.

"Yea, I could give Passion a run for her money, too" Desire said.

Mercedes paid Desire no mind. If anything she felt sorry for her and saw her as a washed up, pathetic ho--ratchet, with nothing going for her but her natural blond locks; she often wondered why Passion associated with her. Mercedes thought she and Passion were the best looking prostitutes on the strip and believed they could easily become high paid call-girls. Mercedes had aspirations of becoming a Madam for high end call girls and was only working the street until she could make the right connections. Mercedes was of the opinion that strong minded women like her can become high class prostitutes as successful call girls and porn stars which, in her mind, is a respected form of prostitution. She just couldn't get Passion to share her vision.

"Well, let me have it, girls, I need to get my rest, school t'morrow, y'know." Mercedes said, putting her hand out to collect money from the women.

Desire handed her money to Mercedes who promptly put the cash in a small safe to give to Lavender later. Passion didn't offer up any money. Mercedes took immediate notice.

"Oh, you already gave your money to Lavender, P? Was he happy?" Mercedes said, still trying to get Passion to talk about being put out. Passion ignored her and turned her attention to Desire.

"Desire, how are your kids? How is Tiffany? I missed her last weekend," Passion asked Desire. Passion usually visited Desire on her days off and often babysits two-year-old Tiffany, Desire's second child.

"Oh she's fine. Gettin' on my nerves. Oh, what time is it? I got to get home so that I can let Star go home. Lavender told that new bitch ho to baby-sit for me," Desire said, referring to the new prostitute named Star, recently recruited into Lavender's fold by Mercedes.

"Listen, Passion, honey, so where you goin' to stay now that Lavender done put you out?" Desire, said, letting it be known that everybody already knows she was put out and homeless. And putting it so matter-of-factly like it was no big deal. "You ain't the first ho Lavender done put out in the skreet and you not gonnabe the last, trust me. Y' know it's not gonna be forever, just for a short while cuz he didn't throw yo clothes out, otherwise you would be fucked." Desire said. "Anyways, y'know that Lavender wants you to bring in twice what you were bringin' in before he will let you back in. But in the meantime you have to find a place to stay. You got any place to go?"

"I don't really know…" Passion said, looking forlorn and pitiful. She was failing miserably to withhold a stream of tears.

"You could stay at 1385," Mercedes offered, referring to the vacant apartment on Prospect Street that the girls use for some of their tricks who don't have cars.

"That rat infested hole in the wall? Oh please," Desire shot back at Mercedes, shocked that she would even make such a suggestion to their friend.

Desire leaned forward and grabbed Passion by the hands. She bent down to stare her dead in the eyes. "Listen, girl, I got a two bedroom apartment and it's a big place. Ima keep it a hundred, it's not the cleanest. You could stay with me; ok? I need a roommate and someone to stay and watch my kids when I'm working the skreets during the week. Ok?"

Passion started to cry, but, overwhelmed and beside herself with Desire's generosity.

"Oh, Ok, thank you, Desire, I mean it," Passion said, crying, wishing she didn't need anyone's help.

"And you could work for me in the meantime," Mercedes offered up as if she were being so benevolent. "Up your street game, show me that you could make money out there like you should and then I will speak to Lavender about taking you back," she said. "You don't want to go to another pimp anyway. Lavender would find you and beat yo ass."

"Oh, ok!" Passion said, feeling better.

Desire stood back up now. She turned to leave but not before asking Passion for a favor.

"Listen Honey, could you do me a solid and stop by that food pantry on Beck Skreet and pick up some food for me? I'm real low and I don't have time to go shoppin' now. I need my beauty rest. Besides, they cut off my food stamps again 'cause I missed my certification appointment again. I was tired from workin' the skreets the night before. And if my social worker finds out that I don't have food in my house, that White bitch will remove my kids again," Desire remarked, speaking as if she wasn't White just the same. "That white bitch made me go clean for nine months before I could get my kids back. She is always trying to catch me out there. So can you do that for me, Passion, baby?" she said. "Besides, I can't see myself goin' to no pantry beggin' for food, kids or no kids."

"Ok, sure," Passion stated, wiping away her tears. "I will stop by over there on Monday. That's not a problem at all," feeling grateful that she has a place to stay now.

"Thanks, Passion. You're the best-est. And please play these numbers for me," Desire said, handing Passion a note with a list of numbers. "And don't forget to bring your clothes. We ain't sharin' no underwear. I gotta go." At that, Desire left out the apartment.

Soon after, Passion got ready to leave. She reached out to give Mercedes a hug. Mercedes hugged her back.

"Ok, see you later P. I will tell Lavender to lay off of you, alright hun," Mercedes lied, knowing she had no intentions of doing anything of the sort; she got her kicks out of seeing Lavender dog Passion out. "Just take care ah urself. I have to get my rest so I can work on this midterm paper," she said as she powered on her Apple laptop, the trademark logo illuminating on the back of the monitor. "And here's some money to get your hair and nails done. You look tired," Mercedes said peeling off a hundred dollar bill from a roll of bills. "Just consider it a loan."

"Ok, bye. And thanks," Passion replied, gratefully taking the money. Passion removed her feet from the bucket of lukewarm water and wiped them dry before putting on her see-thru pumps. She then started heading out the door, feeling ever so thankful for having Mercedes and Desire as friends.

Chapter 4

Saint Ann's Food Pantry was located on Beck Street on the corner of 141st Street in the South Bronx, not far from Prospect Street. It was about 4:30pm on a cool Monday afternoon. It was closing time. For twenty-three-years-old, Jameer Creston, running the neighborhood food pantry was something of a dream come true, a way to give back to the community he came from but also a goal he had set for himself on the way to becoming a church deacon. Jameer had volunteered to start the pantry some three years ago to respond to the overwhelming need in the community. Poverty was real in the community. Many families struggled with putting food on the table. It was Jameer who brought the issue to the attention of the pastor and the congregation. With the support of Pastor Emerson and the church deacons, he spearheaded the effort to open the food pantry in an old rectory long closed by the church. It was rough going at first. They had a hard time keeping up with the demand for free food. The small team of deacons, lay members and volunteers would often give away too much food at a time. Over time, they learned to ration the amount of food they gave out and increased the donations. In the two years that the food pantry has been open, it has been recognized as a success, even by the local media.

But that was two years ago and Jameer was getting restless. He would never admit to being bored with the food pantry but he wanted another challenge, even though many times long lines would accompany the opening of the pantry and they often ran out of food. Jameer felt he was being called to some new project, some new outreach to bring glory to the church—and himself. He just didn't know what.

Jameer had come a long way from the, skinny, troubled kid with the speech problems no one wanted. Abandoned by his father before he turned five years old, Jameer was raised by his mother Danielle Martin and his mother's girlfriend, LaShay Richards. As he became older, Jameer started acting out. At the urging of her girlfriend, Jameer's mother turned him over to child protective services, saying she could no longer manage his unruly behavior. The trauma of being sent away only exacerbated Jameer's already out-of-control behaviors. He was shuffled from foster home to foster home, often testing the grownups in his various placements. By the time he was 14, he had seen five foster homes placements.

It wasn't until his case landed on the desk of a young and industrious caseworker did things change. The caseworker located Jameer's long lost godmother, Mabel Denise Creston, who had lost favor with the family for her holier-than-thou attitude and outdated beliefs. Mabel Creston was a nurse by trade and the best cook ever, famous for her oxtails and breakfast rolls. Godmother Mabel went to church four times a week, not including Sundays. She was an active member of Grace Baptist Church, in charge of preparing the Sunday dinners which generated considerable revenue for the church. Mabel opened her heart and home to her troubled godson. She dragged Jameer to church with her not the least bit intimidated by his scowling face and angry demeanor. She let Jameer know that she was going to set him straight or die trying. She introduced Jameer to meet the Pastor Emerson and his wife. They helped him deal with his anger and him find peace within himself. The pastor introduced Jameer to the Bible and encouraged him to study and grow in the understanding of God. Through mentoring, Jameer eventually learned about love and forgiveness. He tattooed The Lord's Prayer on his right forearm so he would always remember it.

Godmother Mabel adopted Jameer when he turned 16, right before she died at the age of 70 from diabetes. She left Jameer her apartment and a small inheritance. On her dying bed, Jameer promised he would honor her life by dedicating himself to a life of faith.

The chimes over the door to the food pantry jangled loudly, announcing a late arriving customer. Jameer had forgotten to put up the "Closed" sign and lock the door. He was annoyed at himself until he saw a tall, very attractive young woman, scandalously-dressed in skin tight hip hugging designer jeans and pricey stilettos, saunter into the pantry. Her hair was immaculately styled and her nails were done. She had a sexual appeal that was palpable, a profound carnal magnetism that left Jameer gawking and staring open-mouthed. It was Passion.

"Can I help you, ma'am," Jameer greeted her with much humility in his voice. "We are kinda closed," he said, failing miserably to hide his admiration for Passion.

"Damn, but aren't you a food pantry, here to help people?" Passion said defiantly, while furiously chewing down on Spearmint gum. She had come straight from the beauty salon intent on bringing Desire the food she asked for. "How the fuck could you be closed?" Passion seldom cursed or used profanity unless she was provoked or angered or frustrated. She had her mind set on helping her friend. Passion sucked her teeth and was about to turn and leave before Jameer stopped her.

"We are a food pantry, Ma'am, but we don't stay open all day, and we do have posted hours on the door. But how can I help you?" Jameer said ignoring the woman's expletive, hypnotized by her stunning beauty.

"Well, I need some cans of food. I need some food, that's all," she said, her mind set on wanting to help her friend, Desire.

"Ok, I can help you there," he said. Jameer was smitten with Passion. His eyes, traced the soft, curvaceous contours of her body. He took careful note of her worn but expensive high heels. He also couldn't ignore her beckoning cleavage.

"Ok, that's not a problem," Jameer said, while pulling down a food basket to give her. "By the way, my name is Jameer," he said by way of introduction. "What's your name? What brings you in here, other than the obvious?"

"What?!" Passion shot back, incredulously. In her mind, she only came here asking for food and didn't think she had to explain anything. Passion wasn't sure of the young man's intentions. She was used to men trying to pick her up. She looked Jameer up and down, taking time to study him. Jameer was dark and handsome, with beautiful eyes. He had a modest gold chain hanging from his neck and his clothes—a patterned Polo shirt, cuffed designer blue jeans that blended well with his Timberland boots--flattered his slim, athletic frame. Passion was especially intrigued by the biblical scripture tattooed on his forearm, peering out from under his rolled up shirt sleeves. Jameer had a soft swagger that she found inviting. She decided to play his game only because she thought he was cute. She wanted to know where this was going.

"Well, if you must know, I'm here to help a friend. She's very sick and asked me to come here. Is that good enough for you?" she answered. She had made up her mind she wasn't giving him her name. Last thing she needed was people talking about her going to the food pantry because she was homeless *and* hungry.

Jameer smiled. She was quick-witted. He liked her attitude and didn't take offense to it. She was used to taking a lot of stuff from men, he thought to himself. "I understand, "he said. "But it's also part of my job to ask people what brings them to a food pantry so we can better serve the community."

"Ok, well my friend is broke, and she lost her job and she needs food for herself and her six years old daughter Diamond. So I'm helping out," Passion explained.

"Oh, no problem; that's fine," he returned. "I'm sorry, Ms, I didn't get your name, just so I know who I'm talking to."

"Ms," is fine, "Passion returned, now getting a little bored with the small talk, convinced that the young man was just boring and not interested in anything else. She didn't have time for conversation unless he was paying her for her time.

"Well, 'Ms,' for a family of two, we usually measure about 50 pounds of food items. You can choose from what we have on the shelves. I know it's not much but we will get more at the end of the week if you want to come back. Feel free to help yourself," Jameer said and handed her the basket.

Passion quickly took the basket and went through the aisles quickly grabbing some cereal boxes and cans of food and vegetables. Once she thought she had enough food, she handed the basket back to Jameer.

Jameer weighed it on the scale, smiled reassuringly. He then placed the food items in two plastic bags. He tried to engage Passion in small talk, again, unable to help himself.

"Your friend is really lucky to have somebody like you to help her out like this," Jameer said.

Passion was unmoved and kept wondering what he really wanted from her. Over the years she learned not to trust anyone, especially men. Everyone had ulterior motives, she learned.

Jameer continued. "Y'know, at Grace Baptist church we could use more people like you in our congregation who are willing to look out for the sick and shut in. Do you have a church home?" he said, while handing her the bags of food.

"No, I don't Mister Jameer," Passion responded. So that's what this is all about. He's trying to get her to join his church, Passion concluded to herself. She knew that no one is ever really genuine. No one is to be trusted. Everyone has game. Her family life taught her that. Her time in the streets confirmed it.

"I appreciate you inviting me to join your church but I'm a working girl. I don't have time to visit people unless I'm getting paid for my time, but I thank you for helping me, ok? Bye," Passion said, playfully winking.

"Well, think about it. We certainly could use someone as smart and pretty as you," Jameer returned flirtatiously.

With that Passion turned and left the pantry, with the bags in one hand, looking back at Jameer only to smile.

Jameer locked the door behind Passion and put up the 'Closed' sign this time. He never did get her name, he surmised regretfully.

Several minutes later, on his way home, Jameer was still thinking about the attractive streetwalker. As much as he wanted, he couldn't quite get her out of his mind. There was something about her that fascinated him, even beyond her good looks, something tragic that made him want to know more about her and why she chose that path in life, the life of a prostitute. Jameer struggled with his tendency to fall for women who've been through difficult times like him, broken, wayward women. He had been disappointed before. Still, he couldn't help himself. Where were her parents? Do they know what she's doing? How did she end up on the streets? Did some sweet talking pimp introduce her to that life? Is she supporting a drug habit? All these questions and more went through his mind. Prostitution has been blight on the neighborhood for so long that people in the community have come to accept it. No one has ever made any attempt to clean up the streets or the women who prostitute themselves, the aspiring deacon kept thinking. A light bulb suddenly went off in his head as he arrived home on the bus. He would pray on it first, and discuss it with his mentor, but he had found his new calling.

Chapter 5

It was late in the afternoon when Passion finally arrived at Desire's apartment from the pantry run. Desire lived with her three children in a two bedroom apartment on Randall Ave, on the other side of Prospect Street. Passion brought Desire the bags of food she picked up from the pantry.

"Hey, D, it's me," Passion said, after knocking on the door. Desire let Passion in and then just as quickly ran back to the bedroom.

"Hey, D, I got the food you wanted," Passion said as she placed the free groceries on the dirty, stained-filled kitchen counter. "There was a cute guy at the pantry place. I think he wanted to get with me, but no money, no honey," Passion shouted over the loud music playing, laughing to herself.

"Ok, thanks luv. I'm comin'," Desire shouted back. "My baby done messed hisself."

Desire's apartment was messy and dirty, a pigsty. The furniture was old and dilapidated and in various stages of disrepair. The beds were always unmade. Dirty dishes regularly stood in the sink for days, weeks and sometimes months at a time. The trash hadn't been taken out and remnants of fast food and cigarette butts were everywhere.

"Damn, you need help cleaning up?" shouted Passion

"No, I got it," Desire shouted back from the back room.

The bathroom door was off the hinges and rested perilously against the wall in the hallway, waiting endlessly for the building super to repair it. Missing bathroom tiles pockmarked the bathroom floor. Dirty clothes were strewn about the apartment floor in piles as Desire was always meaning to take the clothes to the laundry but never really ever did, just like she was always meaning to clean the dishes.

Desire's three children slept with her in the master bedroom. The other bedroom was for extra clothes, kids' toys and to entertain tricks in the event she picked one up on the way home for a quickie. Grey standup Bose speakers stood in the living room blasting Beyonce's "Drunk in Love" off of a mixed tape. Desire reluctantly turned down the volume of the music.

"Thank you, girl for the food. I'm down to my last..." Desire said as she emerged from the bed room, puffing a cigarette while cradling her son Marquis in her arm. Her other two children, Tiffany and Diamond came running ahead of their mother, wearing trendy but dirty clothes. Desire cherished her son Marquis, just barely one year old, over and above her other children, mostly because of who his father was. Marquis had a head full of black curly hair. His light brown eyes seemed to come out of face. He was the image of his pimp father.

Once she made her way to the kitchen, Desire started stirring hot grits on the stove with her free hand, while holding Marquis in the other. Tiffany and Diamond eagerly rummaged through the bags of food, desperate to satiate the hunger in their stomachs. Desire ignored them, for the most part.

"Did I hear you right? You turned a trick at the food pantry or something?" Desire said.

"No," Passion laughed, not used to seeing Desire without her eyebrows penciled in. She couldn't help marveling how it made Desire's forehead appear bigger, making her look like an extraterrestrial. "I said this cute guy at the pantry was trying to talk to me. He was tight cuz I didn't give him my name. That's all. He didn't have no money though. He wanted me to join his church."

"Oh," Desire returned, somewhat disappointed. She continued stirring the grits. "My husband was cute too, but he wasn't in no church. The cute ones never have no money but they always believe in God. "

"I guess so," Passion replied. "What happened to your husband? Does he know what you do?" Passion asked while sipping on a soda she found in the refrigerator, hidden behind the dozen or so cans of beer.

"He knew. But what could he do? That's how he met me. Girl, listen, I started turnin' tricks when I was 14," Desire proudly proclaimed. "Trust me, he knew what I was doin' when he married me. Let me tell you, I was raped when I was 12 years old by this girl, Leslie and her 17-year-old brother Kevin, one night when they were staying over my house. My mother had gone out somewhere. Leslie held me down, while he raped me. I never told my mother."

"Oh my God," Passion exclaimed. "I'm sorry that happened to you. I didn't know."

"Yup, they then pimped me out of my own house to men in the neighbahood." Desire laughed to herself. "They threatened to kill me if I said anything. They brought tricks o'er to my house at night while my mother was out earnin' extra money by sellin' her own ass to the navy servicemen who worked at the naval submarine base in Goose Creek, South Cah'lina.

"I mean, she and her brother weren't all bad; cuz they let me keep some of the money I made; that's another reason why I didn't say nothin'. Plus, we used to all get high smoking weed and shit. With the money they gave me I was able to buy things for myself, my mother couldn't get me. But, girl, when my mother found out that her teenage daughter was also her competition, she flipped. She had them both arrested, Leslie and her brother, and then put me out. I was only 16 at the time." Desire paused, teary-eyed.

"I wound up with a fast talkin' pimp; a black dude, Bubba much older than me. He had a thing for white girls. He gave me a place to stay and got me hooked on some good shit; best coke I ever had. I swear. He made me work for it though. I stayed with him 'til I met Jeffrey."

"Who's Jeffrey?" asked Passion. "Another pimp?"

"Yeah right, hardly," Desire shrugged as she put her son Marquis to sit at the table getting ready to serve him the grits.

"Jeffrey was a horny sailor who fell hard for my fat ass. He was a trick who ended up becomin' my boyfriend, then my husband. After one night, he fell in love with this pussy and damn near begged me to move in with him. I loved him but didn't like him chasin' off my pimp, like he did, because he had some real good shit. Anyways, we ended up gettin' married n' all. He proposed to me in a bar. I think we were both drunk. I took his name, Cassidy.

I was goin' to be a sailor's wife like my mother. He was my first love, if you could call it that. I was 18, I think. What did I know? After he was kicked out of the navy and couldn't find work, Jeffery started beatin' on me like I was to blame for all his problems. But I made up my mind to help him after all, he was my husband, so I taught him how to be my pimp. We started workin' out a local strip club in Charleston. It wasn't a lot of money but it helped us make ends meet--and stay high, y'kno wha I mean?"

Desire and Passion both started laughing.

"How'd you meet Lavender?" Passion asked, always captivated by Desire's storytelling.

"I met Lavender at the Doughboy, this popular strip club in Charleston, "Desire continued while lighting up a cigarette. "He had come to South Cah'olina lookin' for girls to bring them up to New York. The minute I laid eyes on him, I knew he was big time. I mean he had crazy swagger and those clothes and jewelry, was nothin' like they had in Souh Cah'olina. I had never met a New York pimp. I wanted him to like me. I know I was the best lookin' bitch in that club. He wanted me to dance for him, gave him a lap dance and blow job in the VIP section and sure enough Lavender took a likin' to me. I was twenty at the time. He told me he could take me to New York City and make some real money. I said, let's go then. You know me," Desire said, reminiscing. "So we left and the rest is history. That was 13 years ago." Desire said wistfully, blowing cigarette smoke in the air.

"And what about your husband?" Passion asked, naively.

"Oh, Jeffrey? What did happen to his ass?" Desire paused to think. "Oh, I heard when I left him he got with some ratchet ass ho who stabbed him to death when he tried to put his hands on her. Desire said, matter-of-factly.

"Wow, that's some story, D.," Passion said. "I feel so bad that happened to you."

"Y'know, I was Lavender's first bottom bitch when he brought me up here. I helped recruit a lot of girls for him. But that bitch Mercedes came along and convinced the other hoes not to listen to me. And just cuz she knows how to use computers, y'know, type real fast, Lavender put her in charge. That crackhead bitch!" Desire said, angrily. "I can't stand that bitch, crackhead ho. Anyway…so, you could sleep in the other bedroom, P." Desire said to Passion, coming back to the present. "Just move all that stuff out of the way," she said, referring to the mountain of dirty clothes piled up on the bed. "I'm goin' to wash them."

Passion was adept at making herself comfortable any place she had to stay. It was a habit she learned working the streets, moving from place to place. Passion was a clean person and hated dirty things around her. She couldn't understand how Desire lived the way she did, but didn't let it bother her too much. She was just grateful to have a place to stay. Ever since she started working the streets, finding a steady place to live has always been a problem.

"Don't worry about me," Passion, replied to Desire. "I lived with Lavender for a year and a half and it was far worse than this. At least, I know you will keep the lights on in here. Lavender would always forget to pay the light bill and we would be weeks in the dark," Passion said.

"Can you believe that crackhead bitch, Mercedes?" Desire said loudly. "She makes me so sick! She knew that Lavender had put you out into the street and she has that big ass co-op apartment to herself and she wouldn't even offer you a place to stay. What a selfish bitch! I hate her bourgie-ass! I mean when I was Lavender's bottom bitch, I always looked out for my girls. That's what a bottom bitch is supposed to do. I don't care how much money she makes, you don't do that to people. Don't worry though; she's goin' to get hers. Just watch my words come true," Desire said. Desire always reminisced about the time when she was Lavender's bottom bitch, the head girl in charge, bringing in all the money. She never really got over being demoted, especially as she was Lavender's baby mother. She longed to be returned to her old status.

"Did Lavender give you the money to get your hair and nails done, baby girl?" Desire asked.

"No, Mercedes did. But she said that it's a short-term loan, and I have to pay her back." Passion said, somewhat downcast.

"With interest, I bet. Yo! You watch that bitch, Mercedes! Desire said. "She ain't no good."

"Yeah, of course," Passion said.

"That's why you have to make more money while you're out there on the skreet, girl. You're a very pretty girl. Three hundred a night ain't goin' to get it. I really don't understand why you don't make more money than you do. You could make more money than Mercedes if you really wanted to," Desire said. "You want to make enough money so you could do your own thing one day."

"Well, don't sweat it too much, girl. At least Lavender is a real nigga. Not like that fake ass pimp you called your boyfriend. What you said his name was again?"

"CJ," Passion said, sadly.

"Yeah, CJ. But don't worry, you should be back with Lavender soon," Desire said. "When I was his bottom bitch, I was makin' good money almost as much as that bitch Mercedes. But anyways…," Desire, often had to stop herself from reminiscing because it made her miserable, and angry.

"Thanks for going to the food pantry for me, anyways. I think I'm goin' to work this Friday night. I have to pay the light bill before they cut my lights off, again. C'mon boy eat this shit," Desire shouted as she noticed Marquis just playing with the food. She then pushed the bowl of hot, lumpy grits closer to him. "And you betta eat it all cuz, I'm not cooking t'night; I gotta work," Desire deadpanned.

A loud boom, followed by a violent crash woke Dominique abruptly from her sound slumber. Pandemonium descended on her mother's luxury condo in an instant. The sound of several thunderous footsteps trampled through the place, breaking glass and knocking down anything that wasn't bolted down. She heard bookcases falling and antique vases smashing on the floor. She could hear loud voices giving commands as they charged into every room. Salt and Pepper were quickly muffled, their loud barking gave way to pathetic whimpering. Dominique was terrified. She hid under her bed covers. The heavy footsteps found her mother's room. Dominique could hear her mother screaming for her life. Dominique then bolted from her bedroom and opening the door ran to her mother's room, hoping to save her.

"Ma! Ma! What's happening?" Dominique screamed. She saw what seemed to be dozens of armed police officers in dark armored uniforms and goggles with rifles and guns drawn and aimed high. Police drug sniffing dogs were roaming freely throughout the luxury condo held in check only by strong armed police officers and a sturdy collar. The once beautiful condo was ransacked, with broken glass and broken furniture everywhere. Dominique fought through the police who were now gathered in her mother's room turning up the bed and anything that was in their path.

Dominique saw her mother, huddled in a corner, her hands handcuffed behind her, her knees at her chest in a corner. She was wearing red see-through negligee; her breasts were exposed. Her pupils were dilated and glazed over. She was high and strangely quiet now. Dominique joined her mother on the floor.

"Ma, what's going on? Why do they have the dogs chained up?" Dominique said baffled by all the chaos.

"Stay with me, Dom," her mother said, eerily calm despite the riot of police officers.

The police officers followed behind the police dogs who were sniffing voraciously at the walls then barking at them. The officers had found what they were looking for.

"It's in the walls! It's in the walls!" shouted one of the officers.

The police began smashing the walls, causing sheet rock to fall and splattered onto the Persian rug and hardwood floor. Soon spilling out were countless neatly folded plastic bags containing white powder. *"Jackpot!"* shouted one of the officers. *"Check the girl's room!"* an officer commanded.

"Come on! Get them out of here! Read the woman her Miranda rights outside," another police officer said who seemed to be in charge of the drug raid.

Three officers grabbed Dominique and her mother and led them outside. Dominique's arms were pulled violently behind her as she was forcibly handcuffed; cold steel clamped down hard on her wrists.

Once outside, the cold autumn air slapped Dominique hard across the face and her white cotton pajamas did little to keep her body warm. Dominique was shocked to see a garrison of police cars in front of her mother's condo; their siren lights flashing red and white, lighting up the whole neighborhood. Crowds of people in the tony neighborhood lined the streets watching wide eyed as the whole scene unfolded.

Dominique spied her mother's boyfriend, David, handcuffed and prone against a police car as officers rifled through his pockets and, shouting expletives at him.

'Hey, Mitch, the girl is sixteen. She has to go to child services!" shouted a female officer. "I'll take her," she said, forcefully separating Dominique away from her mother and the officer. "Hold on dear," the petite female officer said as she removed the handcuffs from Dominique. "I don't know why they put these on you. I have a daughter your age. You didn't do anything wrong but we have to find a home for you now. Is there anyone we can call for you, sweetie?" the officer said.

But before Dominique could answer, the officer's attention was diverted momentarily by another officer calling her. She turned back to Dominique.

"Stay right here, ok?" the officer said. "My sergeant is calling me. Just stay right here and think about who you want us to call for you otherwise you have to go to Manhattan. Just wait for me. I'll be right back."

The officer left Dominique standing there alone amidst all the busy activity. Dominique ignored her and ran to her mother.

"Ma!" Dominique screamed to her mother. "Ma!" She screamed again. "Don't let them take me!"

"Dominique, I'm so sorry, baby. I love you, baby. Call your father, call your father, baby," her mother said as officers led her to a police car, forcing her head down into the car before pulling away.

Dominique was left standing by herself, amid the chaos and confusion and flashing lights, trying to make sense of her world now that it was turned upside down.

CHAPTER 6

It was a chilly Friday night in the city, not uncommon for late March. The Bronx streets were slightly less busy than usual. Few cars could be seen rumbling down Prospect Street. It was one of those rare nights in the neighborhood when there were more prostitutes on the streets than johns looking for a good time.

Passion was posted at her usual designated spot on the corner of Prospect Street, two blocks away from a bodega known for selling drugs. Passion sported a yellow blouse, brown, butter soft leather jacket, matching Chanel brown leather ankle boots and skin tight leopard print stretch pants accentuating her shapely figure and long legs. Most of her clothes were borrowed from Mercedes. But it didn't matter. Whatever Passion wore, she looked good in it. It could be anything, a borrowed negligee, a cast away outfit deemed no longer trendy, a tired pair of old jeans, it found new life when Passion put it on. Standing on the corner, Passion seemed sprung from the cover of some glossy glamour magazine, a pinup model brought to life.

Strolling beside her was Desire, dressed in Skinny jeans and leather knee high boots. A tight brown top pressed was pressed against her breasts. Her blond hair was pulled back in a ponytail.

Just a little further up the street, Mercedes was wearing a True Religion denim jacket over a provocative mustard colored Dolce Gabana mini dress with spiked dark brown patent leather red bottom pumps. Her hair was streaked blond to match the color of her nails and outfit.

Mercedes always made it a point to stand away from the other working girls. She was of the opinion that tricks were most likely to approach if they saw her by herself than in the company of other girls. For the most part, she was right. She had a regular clientele, and they liked to be discreet, even on the street. If they saw her with other girls they were less inclined to approach her.

Mercedes attracted johns like bees to honey but always left them wanting, if not frustrated. She was hardly the most obliging prostitute. Mercedes always demanded her money upfront and wouldn't hesitate to walk away if a client tried to bargain down from her set price. She saw it as an insult to give herself for anything less than what she asked for. But once she was paid, she simply went through the motions of pleasing her clients, leaving many unsatisfied and feeling played. "Hurry up," was her favorite command to eager tricks. Mercedes was always more concerned with johns messing up her expensive clothes or sullying her high glamour girl looks, than worrying about providing cheap thrills or fulfilling anyone's tawdry sexual fantasies. If anything, Mercedes looked down on any man who had to pay for sex.

While they all stood on the corner, Desire took advantage of the quite night to start up a conversation.

"Passion you know that you are too good to be out here with us," Desire started in. "You're better than this. I saw how you helped that bitch Renee, with filling out that application for food stamps. I see you always writin' shit in that diary of yours. I used to think you were a cop. I don't know where you came from but you not from the skreets. I know that much. I could see you doing something better, like being a nurse or something. Or even a model. Can't you?" Desire said.

"I like what I do, D. I'm making money and having fun, too," Passion responded. Passion was tired of the older women like Desire telling her how she didn't really belong with them, that somehow she was better than this. She knew that many of the women had come from far less than she and that they had little else. She didn't want to feel better than them in anyway. Besides, she was addicted to the street life.

"I know, Passion, but after a while this gets old, Desire continued. "You make a lot of money some nights and other nights you come away with nothin'. And then we gotta give what we ain't got to Lavender. I been doing this for more than 10 years and I'm tired of it. I don't want to be a call girl like Mercedes. I'm ready to get out of this business but I don't know what else to do. I feel trapped here. I mean what else can I do?" Desire said.

Passion felt pressed now, trying to respond to her friend and still spy for potential customers. "Desire, you can do whatever you want. You just don't have to do this. You can stop anytime you want," she said, not really knowing what Desire could do. Desire was not very well-read, illiterate, in fact, and tricks were known to cheat her out of money because she couldn't count. But she was a white woman and she could get over on that. Besides, she wasn't unattractive and still had nice legs for a woman her age.

"I'm sure you could do something," Passion said with not much conviction in her voice. "Why don't you go back to school or something if you feel that serious about it?"

"I thought about that," Desire said. "But I don't really have time. Plus, I have to feed my kids. Between this and public assistance, I'm just getting by. Being a single woman with three kids ain't easy. I would like to do something other than this. This is old. I'm tired of getting fucked in cars."

Just then, a white, late model BMW pulled up to the women. Passion and Desire weren't sure who the man wanted because the windows were tinted, or if he wanted them both. Desire had her share of threesomes with other girls but never with Passion. She wondered if this would be the first time.

A black man in his late twenties, with short cropped hair, clean-shaven except for a goatee, drove up to the women. He wore a sleeve of tattoos on his right arm. He rolled down the tinted windows on the passenger side.

"Hey, ladies, wanna a ride?" he said, his eyes fiery red and glazed over. His name was Stefon Grey and patronizing prostitutes was his favorite hobby, that and smoking weed.

The man gazed at the two women, his eyes falling hard on Passion. He recognized a good looking prostitute when he saw one. He wanted her. He beckoned for Passion to come to him, staring right at her with bloodshot, lustful eyes.

Passion saw his desire for her. But before she could step forward to gauge his intentions, to question him as to whether he was a pimp or a cop and see if there were anyone else in the car, Desire quickly stepped into the street, reached for the car door and jumped into the BMW and closed the door behind her. "See you later, girl" Desire deadpanned.

The high-as-a-kite trick was feeling too good to make a fuss about Desire getting in his car instead of Passion. Besides, he was horny. He simply winked at Passion and pulled off leaving Passion standing there. He would come back for her another time, he thought.

It was four in the morning and the streets were absurdly quite. It had been hours now since Desire had got into the BMW. Passion had declined several solicitations from dates because they either wanted too much for too little money or they just looked creepy, but the real reason was because she was concerned about Desire. She didn't feel comfortable with that man she went with. She wanted to make sure that Desire came back all right. She wouldn't leave until she came back.

Meanwhile, Mercedes had been picked up several times during the night. She was earning her money. Her latest date was with a white man in a Red Dodge pickup truck. When Mercedes finally returned, Passion told her what had happened with Desire and shared her own concerns about her safety. Mercedes simply shrugged it off as Desire's old ass still trying to stay in the game and admonished Passion for not being more upset with Desire for stealing her money.

"Don't you worry your pretty little head about that crazy ass bitch," Mercedes said. "If anything, Lavender always has our back. You should knock that bitch out for stealing yah trick," she said as she started spying for a trick.

Passion couldn't find it in her heart to be mad at Desire. Desire was her friend, her close buddy on these streets. She had her back before. But she knew that she had to make some money tonight because Lavender would be ready to beat her ass, whether she lived with him or not, but she couldn't stop worrying about Desire. She tried to focus on finding a trick and making money before the night was out.

A silver, late model Cadillac Escalade suddenly pulled up not too far from where Passion was standing on the corner. It sat there long enough for Passion to finally notice. Passion recognized the Escalade sitting parked under an overhanging tree, its engine purring softly, beckoning to her. Passion relaxed and a smile quickly defined her angelic face. It was the handsome, well dressed, middle-aged man she had been with more than a few nights ago. The man she had come to know as Roger.

"Well, hello stranger," Passion said still smiling. She leaned into the SUV, looking to make sure there was no one else inside the car, as was her habit.

"How ya doing, sweetness," the pastor returned. "Are you going to get your pretty self in or are you going to stand there and make conversation until the police come by?"

Passion smiled even more and went around to the passenger side and climbed into the SUV.

"I know a good place where we could be real comfortable, a nice hotel just off the highway," the man said and proceeded to drive the SUV onto the highway.

▲

"C'mon, hurry and take off your pants. The police already know about this spot," Desire said as she was bent over on all fours, naked from the bottom down, on the reclined front seat of the BMW. Her lily white ass cheeks exposed to her young customer.

Desire wasn't a very limber woman but she was very adept at having sex in tight places. She chalked it up to the tricks of the trade that a woman working the streets needed to be ready to have sex in the most unusual and unlikeliest of places. So when the young man with the blood red eyes demanded to have sex in the front seat of his BMW while they sat parked under the highway underpass, she knew what to do.

"Shut up, bitch, I'm trying to get my pants down. Stop fucking rushing me! Matter o' fact, you got to get me ready, again. Come on, you made me go down," Stefon said, referring to his flaccidness.

"Look, you only givin' me, $35--and you haven't even given me that yet--and you want sex and a blow? I don't like this; I'm worth more than this," Desire said while turning back around, sitting down and started performing on the man, vigorously taking him in her mouth. Desire remembered not so long ago when she was able to double what this young trick was offering her, command a certain price on the streets because she was the hottest chick in town. But she was younger then, and her body was firmer and tighter. That was before she started having babies.

"Come on now," Desire said, as she saw Stefon had recovered his erection. She got back in the doggy style position ready for him.

Stefon rolled his True Religion Jeans down below his knees, exposing his heady erection, and getting on his knees, awkwardly positioned himself behind Desire. He groaned, somewhat annoyed by the effort but excited nevertheless as he stared at Desire's pasty White, butterfly-tattooed behind.

With one hand on Desire's ass and the other gripping himself, he thrusted forward to enter her.

"Lower," Desire said, before quickly grabbing him and properly guiding him into her vagina. The young man moaned in pleasure. He started pushing slowly before proceeding more aggressively, stroking Desire faster and faster, quickly establishing a rhythm.

Desire had much bigger than him. But he was wide and he filled her up. His strokes were strong and forceful. She wanted this to be over as soon as possible so she could cop some cocaine from her pimp.

"Damn, what you said your name was again," Stefon managed while thrusting faster and faster, striving to go deeper into Desire.

"Desire," she said, still thinking about how little money this trick was paying her.

"Oh, shit, I'm coming," the young man, shouted excitedly. "Shit!" He started to thrust faster and more forcefully. "Shit, shit!" He kept saying. Then finally he groaned and exhaled loudly. "Oh that shit was good."

Then he slapped Desire's bottom so hard as to leave a red hand print. Desire quickly turned around now and started to pull up her pants before feeling warm wetness coming down her leg.

"Where's the condom?" Desire said, anxiously looking around for it in her seat and then on the young trick.

"Oh, I had to take that shit off. I don't like how it makes me feel," he said.

"Nigga, that's extra! What the fuck?" Desire fumed.

"Bitch, I ain't giving you no money. You know you enjoyed that shit, anyway!" he interjected.

"What?" Desire said, incredulously. "You owe me my money and extra! You betta give me my fuckin' money, nigga!" Desire shouted. "You can't just bust off in me!"

Without warning, Stefon pulled back his hand, closed his fist and punched Desire so hard in the face he caused a tooth to fly out of her mouth. Desire quickly put her hands to her face, warm blood filling her mouth. Her head was spinning as she struggled to avoid blacking out.

"Now shut the fuck up about that extra money shit, White bitch," Stefon shouted, starting the car up and driving out of the secluded spot as he headed back onto the highway. "I don't pay for pussy, bitch!" he said. "If you didn't know, now you know."

Silently, Desire reached inside her purse and quickly texted a code on her smartphone. She then put it back in her purse before the young man could notice. She sat back quietly, boiling with anger.

Stefon had driven the car no more than a mile toward the highway before he had to slam on the brakes. A late model black Dodge Charger with sliver trim on the grill, 24 inch spoilers, dark tinted windows and out-of-state vanity license plates that read "PIMP" suddenly blocked his path.

"What the fuck? Where did he come from?" Stefon shouted. "Hey, move your shit!"

The car sat there for what seemed like an eternity, before a tall, lean Black man outfitted in oversized bomber coat, Gucci denim jeans and custom-made lavender Timberland boots stepped out the car. He was holding a Glock pistol by his side, its shiny steel glistening in the darkness. He was Lavender the pimp. Two other men with thick gold chains dangling from their necks, slowly came out either side of the car, one large, the other small and slender, both wearing hoodies; one with high top sneakers; the other wearing black timberland boots.

"Yo, my nigga, get the fuck out the car!" the pimp said in a calm, deep voice standing on the driver's side of Stefon's car.

Stefon Grey froze, his eyes fixated at the pistol at the man's side. If he was confused before, he knew exactly what was happening now. This was the white prostitute's pimp. She had called him somehow when he wasn't paying attention. His high was completely gone, chased away by the adrenaline pumping through his veins. He was afraid for his life.

"I said get the fuck out of the car now!" Lavender said, pointing the gun sideways right at the young man, "Or, I'm going to blow your mothafucking brains out!"

At that, Stefon quickly came out of the car stumbling. He could barely feel his legs under him as he was scared to death. Fear gripped his heart. He stood to the side of his car facing the pimp with the gun, holding his hands timidly in air.

"Listen, I, I ..." he stammered.

"Shut the fuck up!" Lavender yelled. "Yo D, you all right? Come out here!"

Desire came out the car staggering. She was still holding her mouth from the pain. She was crying and spitting blood, even as it stained her mouth and hands.

"This motherfucka hit me and wouldn't give me my money," she said, crying from the tremendous pain.

"Yo, it was an accident, I..." the man tried to explain.

"I said, shut the fuck up," Lavender interrupted him. "Yo, give her all your fucking money, all of it!" Lavender demanded. "Everythin' out your motherfucking pockets!

Stefon reached inside his wallet quickly and pulled out four hundred dollars in small bills. He gave it nervously to Desire, with an awkward smile on his face. He also gave her a few crumpled up bills that was in his front pockets. He was trembling all over.

"See, I was going to give it to her, man" he said nervously. "I was just going to drive her back..."

"Yo, D, get in the car." Lavender directed. Desire got in Lavender's car after taking the money. She hadn't gotten this much from a date in some years. But she knew that the Lavender was going to take the extra anyway.

"Yo, you like beating up on my bitches?" Lavender said with the most angry, twisted look on his face, staring down the young man even as he moved closer to him.

"No…I didn't mean…I was going to, to drive her back then p-pay…" Before he could finish his sentence, Stefon felt cold hard metal smash across his mouth. And then again on the side of his face. Sharp pain went through his body. He dropped to one knee in excruciating pain. Stefon gathered himself. He rose up unsteadily and bravely swing back wildly at the pimp with a closed fist.

Lavender easily countered the errant punch and hit him again across the face this time with his fist, which felt as hard as the pistol, dropping Stefon where he stood.

Lavender then commenced to pistol whipping him, mercilessly raining blows on the hapless young man.

"Don't you ever fuck with my bitches, again, you understand, motherfucka?" he screamed, as he continued to pummel Stefon with blows, bloodying his head, face, and blue Polo shirt and True Religion jeans. The enraged pimp continued to beat him, callously pounding him into an unconscious, bloody pulp.

CHAPTER 7

Roger looked pleasingly on Passion's naked, curvaceous body as she moved about the modest hotel room fishing for her makeup in her Michael Kors clutch. He delighted in admiring her smooth, flawless complexion and hour glass figure. Passion's perky breasts and round behind brought pleasure to his eyes.

He fixated on the Betty Boop cartoon tattoo on Passion's left thigh and the lavender colored tattooed scribbling on the side of her long neck. She was a child of the world sent by Satan to tempt men like him, the man thought to himself. He felt helpless to overcome her seductive power.

"Why are you looking at me like that?" Passion said, trying to find her lipstick in her Coach clutch, feeling the man's eyes all over her. "You like me, don't you?" she said,

"My child, you are a beautiful creature of God. I can't help but admire you as fine as you are. You don't need tattoos to make you look any better. That's the Devil's paint, y'know," he said.

"What?" Passion turned around confusedly. She had found her Mahogany lipstick and was applying it generously to her succulent lips. "What are you talking about? What's un-holy?" she said. "These are my tattoos. You don't like them? Everybody else does."

"You're old school anyway, Daddy-O. What do you know? You want some tattoos? You not too old. How old are you? I know where you could get some," she said, feeling she was trying to help him out.

The man laughed. "No, thank, you, my dear. How old are you, my dear?"

"Twenty two," she said, all innocently, lying about her age. Ever since she started working the streets, Passion had been trained to always say she was 22, even when she was 17 and even now when she was really 18.

The man thought that she could be his own daughter. The smile on his face became more serious. He felt sorry for the young girl. He knew she had a story. He knew that she was probably some runaway, some wayward girl who Satan had led astray. A feeling of shame quickly passed through him.

"What happened? You ran away from home?" the man asked.

"Look, Mister Roger, we have a cool relationship so far, don't fuck it up asking me no dumb ass questions that's none of your business," Passion responded angrily in an outburst. She was very uncomfortable with sharing her personal life with tricks. She hated when people brought up her past. She hated even more when they were right. She wondered if her father was still looking for her.

"Well, my dear, I'm sorry, by no means did I mean to offend you," the man said a smile returning to his face. "So beautiful...was it drugs that brought you here?"

"I don't know what the fuck you talking about, Mister but I know what I'm doing and I am nobody's fool," Passion said feeling angry and a little uneasy now. She didn't know what the man was talking about and his religious talk really confused her. What this had to do with God and Satan, she thought to herself. And why is he bringing up her parents. She wondered if he was a detective sent by her father to look for her. She liked this older man a lot but he had never talked like this before. She wanted to know where this was going. She instinctively started looking for her cell phone in case she needed to call her pimp.

"So are we done or you want to go again, 'cause I'm ready to be out." she said to her client, remembering she had her cell phone in her bag. And a switchblade, if needed.

The man became instantly aroused. He had an insatiable desire for Passion. He wanted more.

"Come here, my little temptress," he said with a big smile on his face. "Come to me, my dear." He removed the thick bed sheets from his naked body revealing his fully aroused manhood.

"You know this is going to cost you double," Passion said, smiling playfully.

Chapter 8

Lavender's large, black, calloused hand knocked lightly on the metal apartment door. He waited patiently until the door slowly creaked open. A woman with small beady eyes, pressed deep into her dark, wrinkled face, peered out from the darkness of her apartment. A broad smile creased her face when she saw the large pimp clad in a True Religion denim outfit over a white hoody with the words Swag Doesn't Come Easy in bold letters, standing outside her door.

"Just one minute. I'll go get her," the woman said instantly in a sinister voice. She closed the door behind her, leaving the towering pimp standing in the cavernous hallway of the seedy Brooklyn housing project.

A few minutes passed before the wrinkled woman returned and opening the door wide this time, gently pushed a shapely teenage Puerto Rican girl out into the hallway. The teenager looked older than her actual age of 15. Her face was youthful and pretty but hardened from years of parental neglect and a life in the streets. Her body was fully developed with pronounced hips and ass. She wore oversized gold hoop earrings, and a brown North Face fleece jacket, and tight, faded blue jeans. Worn, retro Air Jordan sneakers were tied loosely on her feet.

The girl looked up at Lavender the Pimp with a blank, glazed look in her eyes. Her eyes fixated on the pimp's expensive oversized timepiece and gaudy diamond earrings.

"Now, now this is the man from the agency, Peaches," the elderly woman lied. "He's gonna take you to your new foster home. I told you that if you keep running away, like you do, they would take you from here, from me. I hate to see you go but they don't think I can manage you. I'm sorry but this is the way it has to be. Now you go to him, now," the woman said.

Peaches barely understood what the woman said because she was drunk. Her foster mother secretly allowed the teenagers in her home to drink alcohol, even encouraged them in the habit of getting wasted.

Peaches moved unsteadily toward the man she believed to be from the social services agency, too drunk to question why he was picking her up in the wee hours of the night.

"Her name is Lauren but we call her Peaches, sir. She's a really sweet girl just a little confused. Likes to drink, a lot" Ms. Jacobs laughed an evil laugh. "Take care of her, won't you? Find her a good home," the foster mother said, slyly, playing the game she and Lavender have been playing for the past few years. Ms. Jacobs had long supplied Lavender with girls in exchange for drugs and money.

"C'mon along—Peaches," Lavender said, matter-of-factly in his deep throated voice, doing a half-hearted job at being reassuring. "You're with me now; I'll take care of you, "he said with a charming smile that put the girl at ease.

"And thank you, Ms. Jacobs. Here is the package." Lavender handed the foster mother a large bulky manila envelope.

Ms. Jacobs' beady eyes suddenly grew large as she grasped the envelope, eagerly taking it from the pimp and putting it behind her back, as if she didn't want anyone to see it.

"Ok, bye, now, Peaches, and you take care. I hope I see you grow into a nice young woman and finish your schooling, ya hear?" she said. "Thank you, mister. I have to see to my other foster kids now," she said, abruptly slamming the door shut.

Lavender escorted the girl known as Peaches down the maze-like hallway, to the pissy-smelling elevator and finally to his car parked outside the towering housing project. He was more than eager to initiate Peaches into his stable. He already had a plan for her.

Once inside her dark apartment, Ms. Jacobs quickly bolted to her bedroom and unsealed the large envelope under her night light. Reaching inside the envelope, she took out a brick of crisp hundred dollar bills and small plastic bags filled with white powder. A big smile glided across Ms. Jacob's face, exposing her rotting teeth. Then, lest she forget, the duplicitous foster mother quickly picked up the phone on her mahogany nightstand to report Peaches had run away again.

PART 2

CHAPTER 1

Jameer planned to announce his new outreach at the monthly Deacons' Meeting scheduled every first of the month. The meetings were where new proposals by the deacons were put forth and old business reviewed, among other things. The Pastor Emerson would be there.

Jameer couldn't wait to let the pastor and his fellow deacons know of his desire to spearhead an outreach ministry to the prostitutes in the community. He was encouraged after speaking it over with his mentor that it was a worthwhile endeavor. He had prayed on it the past few weeks ever since he had met that woman in the food pantry and he was deeply convinced that God spoke to him and was guiding him. He could barely contain his enthusiasm.

The Deacon's Meetings usually took place in the large conference room on the second floor of the church just above the sanctuary. It was a spacious office space, with a large, round glass table in the middle of the room. Executive business chairs were placed all around the table. A large, black leather sofa stood against the wall. The room had little decoration except for a large crucifix on one wall and on the opposite wall, a series of framed portraits of all the church pastors from the very first to the present one, Pastor Emerson; a huge pot with an enormous snake plant stood in the corner.

The meeting was scheduled for 6:30pm. By 6:15pm, most of the deacons started to fill the room, with the younger deacons arriving in first and most of the older deacons arriving later. Jameer was there before anyone else, seated promptly at the glass table in a collared shirt and dress slacks and shoes. A notebook and Bible were placed before him on the table.

All the church deacons arrived one by one. There was Deacon Aaron Drummond, a bail bondsman by trade and well known in the community for helping young black males in trouble with the law; he was also chairman of the deacons; Deacon Jo Bolden, probably the most pious of all the deacons and the oldest too, at 69; he was a retired boxing instructor; Deacon Stan 'The Man' Wilson, was a gifted pianist and choir leader; Deacon Timothy Anderson, a former ex-convict who turned his life around; Deacons Richard and Missy Meadows, the brother and sister deacons; Deacon Buddy Woodson, who was also the building custodian; Deacon Margaret Simmons, a nurse, who made it her personal mission to be a voice for the female parishioners; Deacon Greg Nolan, the church youth leader who turned away from a life of drugs with the help of the pastor and his wife; Deacon Jason Bruer, church treasurer and the only attorney in the church and the youngest deacon at 35. He was also Jameer's mentor.

The pastor was the last one to appear wearing a Hershey brown suit with a crisp white shirt, brown lace ups and a gold tie. As expected, the meeting wouldn't begin without him and started the moment he sat down at the table.

"Ok, good evening everyone; I am calling this meeting to order," bellowed Deacon Drummond.

"The opening prayer will be offered by Deacon Jo."

Deacon Jo stood and delivered the Lord's Prayer in a soft but steady voice as was his custom, his head bowed the entire time.

"Amen," the pastor said.

Deacon Drummond, in a loud voice, reviewed the previous minutes from the August meeting. The minutes were promptly approved by all the members. Then Deacon Drummond passed around contact information sheets for all the church deacons with their names, addresses and phone numbers. Each deacon looked over the information and initialed by their name, if the information was correct and updated it if it wasn't, as they had been accustomed to do.

Then it was time for the new business. "The first order of business is the upcoming Deacon's Retreat. It's scheduled for next month and we still have some member's sitting on the fence. We need to know how many people are actually going. I have several rooms booked so far but the hotel wants a final head count so that they know what rooms to reserve. Listen, guys, I know it's a little expensive but it's the Marriott. This isn't some hole in the wall," Deacon Drummond said.

"We all don't have deep pockets like you and Jason, Aaron," Deacon Greg interjected. "I already put my name down as going but I need some time to get some money together."

"This wouldn't be the first time, my brother. You always need time to put something together. How about putting some of that money you spend on those expensive suits to other things," Deacon Aaron returned, drawing some laughter and snickers from the deacons. It was well known that Deacon Greg had a fondness for expensive clothes. He made a good salary as a Manhattan doorman but it seemed like the majority of it went toward his attire.

"Look, before this goes any further, the Deacon's Retreat is very important and we need a final roster and payments by the end of the week, understood," Deacon Drummond said. "The next order of business is Wednesday night services. Deacon Meadors you have a report?" Deacon Drummond said.

Deacon Missy Meadors rose to her feet and reported: "The Wednesday night prayer services have been well received and attended. We have so many people from the community, young and old, coming in to fellowship. It makes me so proud to see how much the community feels the need for prayer," she said with a wide smile on her face.

"Amen," the pastor said, prompting others at the table to also respond with their own, "Amens."

"On that note, I want you deacons of the church to continue and engage lay members of the church and even nonmembers in helping to put an emphasis on the church's mission to promote healing and wholeness in the community," the pastor said. "Remember you are my liaisons to the church, helping the lay members to get more involved in the church."

Jameer was anxious to speak right now. He felt that this was his cue to make known his new outreach. But Deacon Drummond went on.

"We have a motion to discuss the Benevolence Fund. Deacon Jason report, since this is your baby."

"Deacon Jason sat upright as he gave his report, "Ok, it was noted that members of our church, including children, are in a vulnerable situation with regard to minimal or no healthcare insurance coverage. The possibility of increasing and expanding the benevolence fund to provide support to such members was discussed. Greg and Margaret and I were appointed to further look into this. We can increase the benevolent fund but we would be asking a little more from our members. I know many are already complaining that we are asking for more money for the building fund and money for the food pantry other church projects, but I think this is important. Many have expressed a need for health insurance. We can do it," he said matter-of-factly.

"So all in favor of passing another offering plate around...," the pastor said half-jokingly.

"At least once a month, we could do it, once a month and let the congregation know that this is why we are doing it," Deacon Jason said.

"Don't forget the building fund," put in Deacon Jo.

"And the gym fund; that gym needs rehab to the hardwood floor," added Deacon Stan. "Our boys enjoy playing basketball in the church than in the streets where they could be shot at any minute."

"All in favor of increasing the benevolence fund say, 'Aye', Deacon said, putting it to a vote.

"All the deacons except for Deacon Buddy and Deacon Stan responded with hearty "Ayes!

"Let it be noted that we have two nay votes for the benevolence fund," Deacon Drummond said. "The ayes have it. Now any other business before we conclude our meeting?" Drummond said, anxious to get home to watch the basketball game.

Jameer stood up, shaking and nervous. He was anxious but ready to speak.

"Brother Jameer Creston, you have our attention and the floor, "Deacon Drummond said, somewhat annoyed. He knew Jameer was always ready to show everyone how hard he was working to become a deacon. He was also wary of Jameer, for as he saw it, trying to outshine the others members in his quest for deaconhood.

"As, as y'all know, I-I have been running the food pantry for some time now," Jameer began slowly, humbly. He always stuttered when he was nervous, a habit reminiscent of his childhood when he struggled with a speech impediment. "And, and it has been my baby and I am glad to say that it has been successful. I would like to thank you all for your support with helping make the food pantry a success, especially Deacon Drummond and my mentor Deacon Jay.

"But I have been called to another ministry. So I'm stepping down as head of the food pantry. Deacon Jo has agreed to take my place and will be running the food pantry from this day forward," Jameer said.

"You did a great job, my brother. It won't be the same without you. Thank you." Deacon Stan said. "But what are you gonna do now?"

"It's been my pleasure, y'all. And thanks. But, I- I w-would like to now volunteer to start, to start an outreach ministry to-to the p-prostitutes in the community," Jameer said nervously.

"What?" Deacons Stan and Greg said in unison. Jameer suddenly had everyone's full attention.

"Did I hear you right? You want to preach to prostitutes? Hookers?" said Deacon Stan. "What the hell for?"

"Wow, I'm excited about that; it's something we definitely need in this community," applauded Deacon Margaret.

"That sounds like a heavy undertaking, Brother Jameer," put in Deacon Buddy. "You sure you ready for that? Do you know what it entails?"

"More, like a waste of time," said Deacon Stan. "You can't help those nasty women."

"Well, how about that!" stated "Deacon Missy. "You will definitely be doing God's work there."

Deacon Drummond voiced his skepticism. "Brother Jameer, this might be over your head. Do you know how long prostitution has been around here? There has been prostitution for as long as I can remember. And I can remember a long time," said the head deacon. "I grew up in this neighborhood.

Even the police can't stop it. I even heard how they allow it at certain times. Do you think you can tackle this? Are you trying to impress us? I mean you are doing a good job and I can see you becoming a deacon any time soon. But this… You don't have to do this."

"He has a point, Jameer, a street ministry? C'mon now. Keep in mind that you are not only dealing with prostitutes but their pimps, too. I don't mean to discourage you my brother but…I don't know about this one. Sounds too dangerous." said Deacon Richards. "Did you talk this over with the pastor?"

Everyone looked at the pastor but he remained silent.

"And what about that nasty strip club over there on the boulevard, Fool's something," put in Deacon Stan. "And all those hot sheet hotels where they do their business?"

"You mean, Fool's Paradise," stated Deacon Richards, all too knowingly. "Fool's Paradise is the name of that strip club."

"Yeah, that's it! Fool's Paradise!" Deacon Stan said excited that someone knew what he was talking about. "Yeah, you gonna shut that place down, too. You know all kinds of things goin' on in there, prostitution and drug dealing," he said.

Jameer expected the reaction he was getting from around the table, doubt and skepticism. He felt strongly about this though. He could still see Passion's face in his mind's eye.

"Listen, I know that this is a very tough thing, to preach to prostitutes and that it's not going to be easy; but a few weeks ago at closing time, one of those women came into the food pantry. She was so young; I felt like she could be helped. And, I know that there are more young women like her who need to hear about salvation. I know that I probably won't save everyone, but if I could just save one…" Jameer said sincerely, full of honest belief.

"So that's what this is all about. You got a thing for that girl who walked in the pantry," joked Deacon Bruer. Some of the men chuckled.

"Jameer, that is so beautiful, I for one, believe this ministry is long over-due," said Deacon Margaret. "And it's worthwhile. You have my support."

"Me, too" said Buddy. "When I come home from work late in the early morning, that's all I see, young girls, walking around half naked in the streets, shaking they ass. They need someone to minister to them but I ain't the one. I will support you, though."

"I didn't know that there was a prostitution ministry," said Deacon Bruer. "Good for you, boy! But how are you going to get them to come to church, boy?"

"The Bible tells us that we are called to be lights in a dark world and to be salt of the earth," said Deacon Margaret.

"Now just hold on," said the pastor, rising to his feet now. Everyone held their breath to hear what he had to say. Beads of sweat could be seen forming on the head of the pastor.

"Our brother Jameer has come before us willing to embark on an honest and heart-filled endeavor. He deserves our support. I am proud that he has volunteered to take on this most challenging assignment but I want to know if he really understands how challenging a street ministry is. Do you have a plan? How will you protect yourself?"

"I don't understand, pastor, protect myself?" Jameer said puzzled. "You mean if I have a gun? I been in the streets. Y'all know, I know how to handle myself." Jameer said. He had expected more support and praise especially from the pastor.

"I been doing my homework and I know that I need help, people who are willing to work late nights, willing to reach out and talk to these women late nights. We might be in danger from pimps, if that's what you're talking about, but I am willing to talk to them too," Jameer said.

"Brother Jameer," the pastor said, smiling. "I feel your good heart and you are full of good intentions. But I have worked a prostitution ministry, myself, and it is the most challenging ministry anyone could undertake. I don't mean to discourage you, my brother, but I want you to know that ministering to prostitutes and their pimps involve a great deal. And I don't know if you are ready for this, quite frankly."

"Listen to the pastor, Brother Jameer," Deacon Drummond said, hoping it would bring Jameer to his senses.

"Why don't you start a homeless outreach for the homeless in our community, brother?" said Deacon Aaron. "Help get them off the street. That's safer and more worthwhile."

"Let me explain," the pastor went on. "A prostitution ministry means going into the dark, dangerous world of drugs and violence. It means entering into the Enemy's camp, the Kingdom of Darkness," the pastor said. "Now if anyone could do this job I would pick you and Aaron because of your background. But understand my brother most of the women who prostitute are already lost to Satan. They are creatures of lust and sin. If they are to be saved, it is in those first few months when they first enter into that life, when there is still hope. But after that, count them as soldiers in the Devil's Army. I myself did it for one year before my wife died but then I became overwhelmed."

"Let him know, pastor," Deacon Drummond chimed in.

The pastor went on. "These lost women become trapped in that lifestyle trapped by the pimp and the drugs and in doing the work of the Devil. For every one hundred of those lost woman you approach, you might reach two; you will probably save none.

"To minister to these women, you have to be out there with them in the wee hours of the night when Satan walks the Earth, losing sleep, fighting temptation as well because they are good at their craft. And then if you do happen to get the attention of a few, then you have their pimp willing to do whatever he needs to keep his flock. This ministry is not for the faint of heart. Are you ready for all of that, my good brother?" the pastor finished.

All the deacons now turned to Jameer, expecting him to throw in the towel and give up his so-called new calling.

Jameer paused before responding.

"I-I think I understand the dangers, pastor. I am aware of the dangers, working late at night. I can imagine it will be hard. B-but I'm willing to do whatever it takes. I'm asking for volunteers to help me with this. If you could help me, sir. I know that we are talking working late at night, and losing sleep sometimes but I believe in this ministry. I also think it's much needed and overdue. Prostitution has been on these streets much too long and if the police can't clean it up then maybe we the church can make a difference. I owe so many people for saving me when I was lost. I just feel that I need to reach out and do the same for someone else," Jameer said, the image of Passion still in his mind's eye.

"I will help you," Deacon Margaret, offered, inspired by Jameer's words and his spirit. "I'm tired of coming home late and men stopping me asking me to give them a blow job, thinking I'm a damn prostitute," she said, hardly blushing.

"I will help you, too, Jameer but I'll answer phones or whatever; I ain't going out no midnight," put in Deacon Richards.

"Count me in, too, my boy," said Deacon Buddy. "I'm proud of you."

The pastor raised his hand to speak. "I believe the steps of our dear boy Jameer have been ordered by the Lord. Listen here, Jameer, my boy, I am going to help guide you in this challenging ministry," he said, taking the pulse of the assembled deacons and hearing them wanting to support this ministry. "It is a good thing what you want to do. Jesus intentionally ministered to prostitutes. He spoke to them with gentleness and compassion, knowing the greater the transgression, the greater the transformation. That being said. You and I are going to sit down and I will share with you what worked and what didn't work in my experience with ministering to prostitutes. I am going to help you turn this community around and get some of those fallen women off the streets," said the pastor all magnanimously.

Jameer kept his composure but he was bursting with delight that everyone including the pastor was willing to help him.

"Ok," said Deacon Drummond, looking to close the meeting. "All in favor of the outreach ministry to prostitutes in the community to be spearheaded by Brother Jameer say, "Aye,"

The majority of deacons voiced their approval with a chorus of 'Ayes',

"All against, say 'Nay', Drummond continued.

Deacons Timothy Drummond and Stan voiced their disapprovals. And Jason abstained from casting a vote.

"All right so we will come back in two months for updates on this outreach ministry headed by our deacon-hopeful Jameer. This meeting is adjourned," Drummond said. "Pastor, will you pray us out?"

"Surely," the pastor intoned. Then they all bowed their heads.

Chapter 2

In the little more than two days which had passed since she was given over to Lavender, Peaches quickly realized there was no way he was with social services. For one, she'd never heard of any social services case workers with a name like "Lavender." She'd also never heard of any case worker who earned enough money to buy all the expensive clothes and jewelry she'd seen during her short time at Lavender's Bronx apartment. Not to mention all the expensive things he'd bought for her, everything from new Air Jordans sneakers, a smartphone, the elaborate floral tattoo on her arm, to a brand new Gucci bag.

Peaches cherished the Gucci handbag above everything else. It was the first "high-end", luxury item she'd ever owned. For days after receiving the generous gift, Peaches would leave the handbag to sit on the night stand in her room so that it was the first thing she saw in the morning and the last thing she saw before falling asleep; its gold inter-locking letters which formed the clasp, shimmering in the artificial light made by the small television she always left on when she slept. She was still afraid to sleep in any room alone in the dark. She often wondered as she drifted off to sleep what Lavender would say if she actually worked up enough courage to ask who he really was and what he really did for a living.

Peaches no longer cared about the answer to either of these questions. Lavender was kind to her. He hadn't even mentioned her returning to school, which she hated, which was good. Lavender was "Big time." He commanded respect on the street and everybody knew him. She also decided even though she was only fifteen and he was so much older, that just maybe, Lavender had feelings for her. The word "Love" scared her when she thought of the prospect of Lavender caring for her. But, then she thought, "What else could it be? He's so funny and nice." "And, why else would he do so much for me without asking for anything in return?" she wondered. She pushed aside any questions and decided she had found a home.

Chapter 3

Passion spent the whole day sleeping, tired from the night before. She woke up later in the evening to accompany Desire to the Emergency Room at the hospital. She roused Desire and her three children from beds and called a cab right away which arrived in less than fifteen minutes, parking right outside their apartment building. Desire and Passion quickly got in the cab and proceeded to the hospital, leaving the children with the prostitute/babysitter Star who was still nodding on the heroin she used to start her morning. Star had also worked the night before and came over to Desire's apartment to wind down and watch Desire's kids, as Lavender told her to so Desire could go to the hospital and get treated for her broken jaw.

When Passion first saw Desire's face, swollen lip and jaw all black and blue, a shudder went through her whole body. She had feared the worst when Desire jumped into that young man's car. Passion never liked getting in cars with very, very young men. Her experience on the streets had taught her that they were either undercover police officers looking to make a bust or crazy-in- the-head boys looking for a good time at someone else's expense—usually the prostitute's. She learned that young men picking up prostitutes often demanded the most and offered very little in exchange and, that they were the most likely to beat a bitch down for no good reason.

Passion preferred older, middle-aged tricks like the one she had been seeing for the past few months, Roger. She believed older men were more thoughtful, kind and considerate. And more, generous. So far, Passion had few incidents in the few years she has been working the streets by simply following her own rules, number one of which was avoiding young tricks.

"Lavender really showed that punk ass, what was up?" Desire said, as she got dressed, trying to hold back the blood still filling her mouth, then spitting it out. "He thought he could fuck with me and get away with it," she said, still angry.

"Lavender always comes through for us; I give him that," Desire continued.

Passion had mixed feelings about Lavender, the pimp she has been working for the past year. When he was protecting his girls, he was the best, she thought to herself, no one was better; but when he was beating a girl's ass, no one was worse. She still remembered the beating he gave her when she found out she would be working for him and tried to run away. She remembered nursing broken ribs for weeks.

"You should've seen that punk crying for Lavender to stop pistol-whippin' him. I wish Lavender would've kept beatin' the shit out of him, beat him to death. He left that punk right there to stew in his own blood." a cruel smile moved across Desire's face. Then her emotions changed.

"Look at my face, girl. Look at my mouth! How am I goin' to make money like this? And I have an appointment at the welfare center tomorrow. Fuck! They are going to ask a lot of fuckin' questions." Desire started crying now and dropped her head into her hands. She felt sorry for herself.

"I can't keep livin' like this," she said. "I need to do somethin' else with my life."

Passion held Desire in her arms, lending her a shoulder to cry one. She felt Desire's pain. She tried to comfort her.

"It'll be all right, D. Just wait in a few days you will be just like new. As a matter of fact, we will be back out there come next week Friday. You should be pretty healed by then," said Passion.

"Ok, but you better be with me," said Desire, feeling better having Passion with her. She loved Passion like a younger sister. In the short time that she has known her, they bonded pretty quickly. Desire appreciated how Passion didn't look down on her like the other girls, how she didn't see her as a washed up ho. Even though she secretly envied Passion's youthful body and looks, she wished that there was a way she could show her how much she cared for and appreciated her.

Once they arrived at the Emergency Room entrance at Bronx Lebanon Hospital, they went to the triage window.

"How can I help you?" The medical assistant said behind the glass window.

"I was robbed," Desire said.

⟁

One night, while sharing a blunt in Lavender's apartment, Mercedes pulled Peaches aside to say Lavender needed to talk to her.

"Hey, girl, get up. The boss man needs to talk to ya," Mercedes said.

Peaches went in the bedroom to find Lavender sitting on his king sized bed, alone in the dark, smoking weed and drinking heavily from a bottle of brown liquor labeled Hennessy. Only the small warm glow from the bulb of a cheap plug-in lamp designed to look like a candle which sat on the distressed end table in front of him, illuminated his face. His expression appeared genuinely forlorn, the look of a man who was desperate.

Peaches moved tentatively to sit beside Lavender on the bed curious as to what he needed to talk to her about. Lavender offered her straight liquor which she accepted. Its soft but bitter taste flowed over her tongue. She continued to savor the taste. Lavender spoke straight from the hip.

"Look, girl, its time you started bringing in some money. This shit here ain't cheap and it sure as hell ain't free," he said. He explained that he had a lifestyle to maintain and men to whom he owed money, money he spent on her.

Lavender offered her the joint as a way to relax her mind.

"Here, don't let it stress you," he said, his calloused hand holding the perfectly rolled joint. "But at the same time, I need you to step your hustle game up, big time and I don't take no for an answer, you understand?" he said, ominously.

Peaches was already high from sharing a blunt with Mercedes, and when Lavender offered her the stuff he was smoking, she took more than a few drags before her mind started racing and her head felt like it would explode. Lavender didn't tell Peaches that what she'd actually smoked was weed laced with cocaine. Between the chronic and the Hennessy, Peaches found it increasingly hard to concentrate. She was dizzy and a little nauseous. During this time Lavender spoke of his childhood and, his time in prison. He explained that he wanted to help girls like her whom he thought were "special," but that people didn't understand.

"I want to see you shine, Ma, that's all this is, really" he said, as trails of smoke escaped his mouth.

Peaches could hardly focus on all the words that Lavender said only the thought that she owed him so much. It was at this point Lavender asked her a personal question. "I know you ain't no virgin, right?" he said, a sinister grin on his face. "When was your first time?"

Peaches spoke but, to her mind it felt as if her voice were that of a third person, a narrator off in the distance telling her story. She explained that a young man named Daquan, her foster mother's son, who frequented the foster home had been her first. Ms. Jacobs often left her son to watch the other girls while she would run errands. He was less of a "Big Brother" around the place and more of a defacto care guardian.

DaQuan was African-American with a dark complexion, athletic build and, natural hazel-green eyes. He was learning disabled, a special education student like Peaches but very street smart. He spent all his disability money on fancy bling and clothes. Peaches remembered being attracted to him right away and being very flattered at the attention he showered upon her, and the gold jewelry he bought her. He was the one who bestowed on her the nick name "Peaches" because of her golden brown, Latina complexion. She seemed to feel an immediate connection with him and in as much as could be achieved discreetly, they were inseparable. DaQuan was 20 and she was 14. She idolized him. He turned her on to alcohol and weed. It was during one of their daytime drinking sessions for which Peaches would cut school that she and DaQuan had sex for the first time. The sex was rough, almost sadistic. Although it was painful, Peaches found that she couldn't get enough. She was surprised at how much she wanted it. She had never thought much about sex before but, DaQuan seemed to know things about Peaches that she didn't know about herself. There was an experienced, no she thought vaguely, intuitive way in which he seemed to handle and guide her. Over the next few months, Peaches and DaQuan would share many intimate moments. Peaches believed Ms. Jacobs knew about it but didn't care. And then, Daquan was gone. He never came around again. There had not been anyone since.

She felt her pulse quicken and her breath become slightly shallow when Lavender leaned forward to kiss her on the forehead. Her head reeled back as though buffeted by a force beyond the impact of his gentle kiss. She was like a sapling tree engulfed in a storm produced only by the strength of his will.

She raised her face to meet his lips with hers as he kissed her passionately. The taste of the alcohol as he probed her mouth with his tongue and the effects of the Chronic made the experience seem surreal. His bloodshot eyes framed by his dark raccoon-like face were illuminated by the table lamp. In her drug and alcohol intoxicated state, it appeared almost as though the light not so much as danced off the reflection of his intense staring eyes, but rather emanated from a light within like a Halloween's Jack-o-lantern. He cupped one of her breasts with a large hand, squeezing as she reclined back on the unbelievable sofa but firm bed. Arching her back, she closed her eyes in submission to his lustful intentions. Slowly and with a well-practiced dexterity, Lavender slid his hand down her body, undoing her belt and sliding a hand into her designer jeans palming her crotch.

"Yeah, Baby girl, dat's it. All you gotta do is just give them what you wanna give me right now. It'll be alright. Just make that money for me, aight!" he kept whispering in her ear until she nodded her head, saying "Ok, ok, I will, I will."

CHAPTER 4

Jameer knocked urgently on the pastor's door. It was Tuesday morning, about one month after the Deacon's Meeting. Jameer had found it increasingly difficult to meet with the pastor and talk about organizing the outreach. Jameer was lost. He didn't know where to start. As a result when he had to give updates on the ministry to the other deacons and lay members interested in signing up, Jameer often had nothing to say. He attempted to speak to the pastor again, hungry for guidance and direction.

It was noon time when he found his office in the rectory; he knocked gently.

"Come in," the pastor's voice could be heard from behind the door. Jameer turned the door knob and walked into the pastor's office. The stark whiteness of the pastor's office always intimidated him. The sunlight that flooded the office from the large gothic windows made the whole office glow. Only the window panes and the pastor's silhouetted frame, softened the extreme brightness of the office. The office was very structured and orderly. One side had bookcases filled from top to bottom with rows and rows of religious books. A large oak desk with the latest desktop computer with a slender flat screen monitor occupied another side of the office space. The pastor sat behind the desk, his back to the window and the light so he could face whoever entered his study; his all too familiar cologne hung in the room like a dead weight.

When the pastor looked up from his computer desk and saw Jameer, he immediately stood up, as if he was caught doing something wrong.

"Hello, Jameer, how are you? How can I help you?" he said, an awkward smile distorting his face.

"Good morning, pastor. I was wondering if we could discuss the ministry how..." he started.

"Jameer, my boy, I would love to, but right now I have a meeting to go to. Let's reschedule this for this time about next week, ok, son?" he interrupted him.

"Yes, yes, pastor that would be fine," Jameer said hardly hiding his disappointment.

"Now don't get to feeling all sad and everything, my boy," the pastor said, reading Jameer's downcast face. "We are going to help you with this new ministry. It's just that am I so busy right now. I have so much on my plate with all these meetings and the churches convention coming up. But I am going to make sure this church cleans up the streets in the neighborhood. Ok? I am very proud of you, son," the pastor said as he gathered his leather brown satchel, stuffing some seemingly important papers in it and preparing to leave. "You're doing a good thing for the community, yes sir. Let me ask, you son," the pastor paused now to question John. "Do you have a team together for this ministry? I know you not going out there by yourself. Do you have that, son?"

"No, pastor, I wasn't sure..." Jameer stammered.

A smile formed on the pastor's face. "Well, you need to get one, son, yes indeed. You will need a group of men and women to go out into the streets with you. You and your team will be like David going out to slay the Goliath of sin that are those women and their pimps. So come back to me when you have that and we will talk, ok?" The pastor started to make his way out the door, stuffing books into a leather satchel.

"Yes, pastor," he said, feeling a little more enthused. "But, sir, that's just it---I don't really know who to ask."

The pastor paused. He put his satchel down. It was his habit and custom to provide guidance to those in need. He couldn't ignore Jameer's pleas.

"There is a woman in our congregation, Mrs. Judy or Judith Hernandez…
she is well-trained in working with women in the sex industry," the pastor
said. "I would start with her and use her wealth of knowledge on the subject. I believe she also has personal experience on the subject. She is a living
example of the power of faith to change lives. Ok, my boy. Now I have an
important meeting to go to. Good luck."

The pastor stepped out his office, leaving Jameer behind to plan his next
course of action.

Jameer took the pastor's advice and sought out Mrs. Judith Hernandez. She
was a 42-years-old, married woman of three, a former prostitute and heroin
addict and now a prominent church member. She cleaned herself up in order to get her children back from social services. Now working as a Family
Advocate in the Bronx family court, she would be the only one actually
trained to work with prostitutes. Jameer realized he needed Mrs. Hernandez
as part of his street team more than anyone if this ministry was going to be
even remotely effective. Finding her contact information in the church da-
tabase, Jameer left several messages for her on her cellphone and email. He
was ecstatic when she finally returned his phone call and said she could be
counted in.

With Mrs. Hernandez in his camp as the anchor to the outreach, Jameer
knew others would follow. And they did. Deacons Timothy Anderson and
Jason Bruer signed up for the outreach as did Deacons Greg Nolan and,
Margaret Simmons. Lay members Michelle Jefferson and May Alston also
came aboard responding to flyers Jameer posted in the church bulletin. They
were women who lived in the neighborhood and had for years believed that
the church should be at the forefront of any crusade to rid the community of
the nuisance of prostitution but found their pleas falling on deaf ears. They
were delighted to hear that Jameer finally took up the challenge.

Jameer organized a meeting at his apartment in the evening, inviting
all those interested in joining the outreach to strategize a plan of action.
Jameer still lived in the modest five story apartment building where he was

raised by his adopted mother. The two bedroom apartment was small, with a step down living room, and hardwood floors. The kitchen was surprisingly large. The apartment was modestly furnished, with a large brown old fashioned sofa and loveseat which was the centerpiece of the living room. Colorful drapes his Godmother Mabel hung long before she died adorned the windows. Jameer decorated the apartment with African and afro-centric themed artwork, the kind you see for sale on busy street corners by unlicensed street vendors. Numerous pictures of Jameer and his Godmother peered out from an antique oak wall cabinet. A Samsung, 40 inch smartTV flat screen TV was mounted on a bookcase filled with huge Bibles and religious literature. The whole apartment was a curious mixture of the old fashioned and the new.

Most of the invited guests arrived early and sat in the living room on the sofa. Everyone exchanged handshakes, hellos and smiles. A pitcher of chilled fruit punch, a dish full of donuts and chips served as refreshments. Jameer started it off.

"All right, let's get this started," Jameer said as he stood in the middle of the floor. "First, let me thank all of you again for coming out to help me with this ministry," he said. "Ain't no way, I can do this by myself."

"Deacon Jason, I'm surprised to see you here. You didn't show an interest in this ministry at the meeting," said Deacon Simmons.

"Let's just say that I have reconsidered," Deacon Jason Bruer said, looking down as if he were hiding some hidden motive.

Everyone in the room was glad to have Deacon Bruer on the team. He was an attorney. He was educated; he knew the laws, and he was known to bring his considerable knowledge to any project he was involved in. His very presence emboldened the group.

"So we need to have a plan of how we going to get out there with this ministry. We are going to be the street team, actually going out there to speak with the women. What are your thoughts?"

"What exactly did the pastor say about this? I didn't get the feeling he was too much in support of it during the deacon's meeting last month," Deacon Simmons put in.

"No, he was just concerned for our safety, that's all; I didn't get the feeling he wasn't for it," Jameer said annoyed, feeling that the question was distracting.

"Maybe he doesn't feel it's a ministry we could handle," Deacon Timothy mouthed.

"He gave me his blessings. Trust me, he's all for this. He asked me to do what we are doing now, get a team together of men and women who are willing to go out at night to minister to these women. How many here can do that?" Jameer asked.

"I mean, we are all here for that purpose, to go out at night but what are we supposed to say to these women? These are hookers and prostitutes, many been in and out of jail, come from broken homes," said Deacon Anderson. "What are we gonna say to them that they haven't heard already?"

"A lot of them are hooked on drugs too, don't forget that," put in Mrs. Hernandez. "But it's more than that. It's also a behavior addiction. When I was out there in the streets, I was just as addicted to the score and the chase, and feeling wanted, as I was to the drugs," she confessed.

No one responded to her comment. The silence was deafening.

"Let's make them come to church, and have the pastor talk to them," said Mike Jefferson, a married father of two girls, finally breaking the silence.

"I like that idea," said Ms. Alston, secretly concerned about going out at night. Scenes of some ruthless pimp, robbing and beating her up for trying to proselytize to his prostitutes played out on the stage of her mind.

"The pastor really should be here to direct us in this; those women have real medical issues caused by drug addiction, STDs, and it's going to take a lot to get them off the streets, He should be here." said Deacon Simmons, a nurse at the local hospital. She wasn't comfortable with the young, aspiring deacon leading such a potentially dangerous undertaking.

Jameer asserted himself. "Well, we all have to agree that these women who work the streets don't know God 'cause if they did they wouldn't be doing what they doing."

"So how do we get them the Word? Maybe they don't care." Deacon Anderson asked. "How do we get them to listen?"

"I know they have pimps who won't take kindly to our trying to stop their girls from making money; I'm not trying to get shot," Deacon Anderson said.

"Me neither," said Deacon Simmons, sounding like she hadn't given much thought to the danger but thankful someone brought it up. She started to have second thoughts about joining the ministry.

"Look, we have to meet the women on the streets where they work and make plain to them what it says in the Bible, let them know that salvation is not impossible," Jameer said with urgency in his voice. "Mrs. Hernandez will be leading our group while we are out there as she has the most experience and is best trained in dealing with this community."

Mrs. Hernandez nodded her head in agreement.

"Sounds good, I'm all in," said Michelle Jefferson. "I wouldn't mind going out there."

"Are there specific verses in the Bible we have to show them?" asked Deacon Simmons.

"The pastor told me that we will know what to say when we go out there, that the spirit will lead us," said Jameer, embarrassed for not having something more definitive to say. "But I don't think it would hurt to read from specific passages we think could help with our message."

"Well, look, when are we going to go out and get this thing under way? Are we going to need police officers to accompany us?" said Deacon Jason. "I'm ready."

Jameer responded quickly to that question. "While we are out there, some of us will be lookouts for pimps and just watching the groups back. But we all need to keep our eyes open. I have already made contact with the local precincts, given them my name and informed them that we would be reaching out to prostitutes in the community to help get them off the streets. So when they see us out there talking to them they won't arrest us too, y'know," he said, happy he did have a definitive answer to a question.

"Very good, Brother," said Deacon Jason, "That's thinking ahead. Also, a lot of these prostitutes might be minors and we should alert child services or the police."

"Ok, so who is going to go out there, first?" asked Ms. Jefferson.

"The first group will be myself and Deacon Simmons, Mrs. Hernandez and Deacon Timothy," said Jameer reading from a notepad. "It's important that we always have a group of men and women," he said. "We will start on the corner of Prospect Street where most of the prostitutes hang out."

"I will prepare some care packages for the women, too," said, Mrs. Hernandez. "It will have things that they need while they are out in the street, you know, condoms, toiletries, makeup. Just to show them that we really care about them," she said.

"I'm excited," said Ms. Alston, who had been nursing second thoughts the whole time. "I been wanting to give those women a piece of my mind for the longest; let them know how they have destroyed our neighborhood," she said.

"No," Jameer said. "We don't want to make these women feel bad or scare them away. We want to bring them into the church."

"That's right," said Deacon Simmons. "I believe for our ministry to work, we have to get them on our side by showing we forgive them but that there is another way that they don't have to do that."

"Yes, yes remember these girls are mostly young, runaways, hooked on drugs and sell their bodies to support their habit and make their pimp happy. They are victims as well. Trust me, I know, what I'm talking about," remarked, Mrs. Hernandez, again alluding to her own past.

Ms. Alston shifted uncomfortably in her seat. "Well, all right, I will hold my tongue then." The group laughed as one.

"Good idea," Jameer said, proudly. "So let's agree that the first team will meet right here at eleven tonight."

⚔

Passion and Desire walked out of the hospital emergency room arm in arm. It was after midnight by the time Desire was released. Desire figured she and Passion could turn tricks before they went home. Desire had her mouth and jaw wired by the doctor and was feeling somewhat better about herself, especially with Passion at her side. Her feelings for Passion grew more and more and she counted her as a true friend. Still Desire felt she needed to get high. But she needed money for that.

"I feel like something to eat, maybe a pizza," said Passion, as they walked down the Grand Concourse.

"I'm not really hungry," said Desire. "Let's see if we could find some tricks. I'm broke. Plus, it's a weeknight."

"Desire, you just got beat up. You don't look so good, either. You want to work tonight?" Passion said incredulously.

"I'm all right. I know a nice street we could pick up some tricks. Besides, these horny motherfuckers don't really care how you look. They just wanna bust a nut. Anyway, I'm feeling good. Let's walk down there," Desire said. She was addicted to the life and the streets.

"All right, D. But I'm just watching. I'm not doing anything." Passion said. Passion and Desire walked in the direction of Prospect Street and found the streets dark and quiet. They stood on the corner for more than an hour. They walked up and down and back and forth several times. Several johns would cruise by, slowing down, hoping to get Passion's attention but Passion ignored them all, not wanting to leave Desire. Finally, she turned to Desire after a few hours.

"It's no real action out here tonight, D. Let's go home. We can take the bus home. I have a metrocard." Passion said.

"Ok, "Desire relented, seeing as how it was a really slow night. They walked toward the bus stop. Passion started taking selfies with her smartphones.

Jameer and his outreach team took to the streets, this their first night out. They were all visibly nervous and uncomfortable. Many were not accustomed to walking the streets this late at night, especially in "the Zone." Everyone knew what they had to do. Jameer and Mrs. Hernandez would engage the women on the streets. One would pray for them. Deacon Simmons and Mrs. Alston would keep their eyes out for signs of danger.

"I'm excited about this," said Mrs. Hernandez. "I been meaning to do this myself, on my own but I never thought I would," Mrs. Hernandez said, as the group of three men tried to keep pace with her. Just then, they spotted two women walking down the deserted streets. They appeared to be street-walkers. It was Desire and Passion.

Jameer looked up and couldn't believe that it was the young woman he had met in the food pantry. She was just as attractive, as he remembered. He was excited and nervous all at the same time.

"Look, I see some women in need of prayer," said Mrs. Hernandez, spying the women and knowing their business. She was eager to help get women off the streets. "This is our chance."

Following Mrs. Hernandez lead, the group of two men and two women deliberately stepped to Passion and Desire, politely engaging them.

"Excuse me, ladies. Good evening," Mrs. Hernandez said with an honest smile. "Can we speak with you?"

"Who the fuck are you?" Desire said, already upset she wasn't able to make money tonight. Passion immediately recognized Jameer by his lean body and caramel complexion. She smiled curiously.

"Hey, it's the man from the food pantry," she said.

"Jameer, do you know this young woman?" Deacon Simmons said. "She seems to know you."

Jameer trained his eyes on Passion. She was dressed a little more casually with tight jeans, a tight cream colored sweater and black knee high boots. He still couldn't get over how attractive she was.

"Oh, hey, hey! Hi!" Jameer said. He looked somewhat uncomfortable, not wanting his church family to think that he consorted with these types of women. He quickly moved to explain the situation.

"Yes, she came into the food pantry...you were in the food pantry, weren't you?" Jameer said, blushing. "How are you? Good to see you. Is this the friend you were talking about, that you had to help?"

'Yes, this is my friend, Desire," Passion said, beaming.

"Is she all right?" Mrs. Hernandez said, noticing Desire's face and swollen jaw.

"I'm fine missus, I'm good." Desire said, feeling somewhat offended.

"It's all right," said Jameer. He realized this was his chance to engage these women to speak to them about changing their lifestyles, about bringing

God in their life. It was obvious that the woman was assaulted and probably in the course of doing what she does for a living. He saw this as an opportunity to practice to convince them to turn away from a life in the streets. He seized the moment.

"I never did get your name," he said to Passion, stepping forward and out from the rest of the group.

Passion remembered how he wanted to know her name but she wouldn't tell him. She liked his face and manner. She was flattered that he pressed her to know her name.

"Oh, yeah, I never did give it to you," she said. "Passion, you can call me, Passion. What you doing out here so late? You looking for some fun?" she said with a naughty smile.

"Well, actually our church could always use more members and our Lord and Savior did charge us to spread the Word. Would you like to know more about the Good Word, you and your friend, here" Jameer said.

Desire saw what was going on and didn't like it. She hated church people and felt like they were all hypocrites. She remembered how as a child they would look down on her and her mother because she was a single mother doing what she had to do to put food on the table. She saw Passion flirting with the young man and felt disgusted. She wanted to get away from the scene.

"Oh, no, they Jehovah's Witnesses! Passion, let's go, these people are all hypocrites, waving their Bible and telling us how we need to change when they are the ones who are dirty," she said.

"We are all sinners in the eyes of the Lord," Jameer responded, feeling Desire's contempt for them. He had heard it all before, how people viewed the church and those who went to church as hypocrites. He didn't want to argue with them, but let them know that he was no better than them except that he had accepted God as his Lord and Savior.

"Listen, ladies, we are no better than anybody out here. We are not judging anyone but we have found our salvation in the Lord God. We want you to know our joy and to share it with you, that's all," he said humbly.

Passion remembered going to church with her family as a little girl; she stopped going when her parents divorced.

"Just wait, Desire, let me hear him out," Passion said. "So what does the Lord have to offer us?"

"He offers hope and salvation to the lost, "Jameer said, stepping closer to Passion. "He offers comfort to those who need comforting and hope to the hopeless and joy to those who mourn. You just have to accept him," Jameer said. "He can help you turn away from the life that you are leading."

"Listen there is nothing wrong with my life," Desire shouted. "I'm making money!! Probably more than you, Oww!" Desire felt a sharp pain in her jaw from shouting.

"Desire, please," Passion said, trying to calm her friend down so that she could hear more about what the man has to say. "And what if we don't accept Him? What then?"

"My sister, it's your choice but I believe that you won't pass up an opportunity to know about his joy and salvation. Look, it says here in Matthew...." and then Jameer took out his white leather bound King James Bible and tried to show Passion a verse to prove his point.

Passion saw the Bible and was intrigued. It reminded her of her father and how he would read it to her at night. She felt like messing with Jameer. She deftly grabbed the divine book out of Jameer's hands.

"Let me see this big book that you got here. How does it end?" Passion said, playfully. She opened the leather bound Bible and flipped through its gilded pages to the back of the Book, the very last chapters; Passion looked down and read the random verse she opened to. As she read, her smile changed to a frown and her face became deathly serious. She looked like she just saw a ghost. She quickly gave the Bible back to Jameer, almost shoving it back to him. She turned to Desire.

"Come on, Desire, let's go. Let's get out of here. I got better things to do than to listen to these people. Let's go," she said, putting her arm under Desire's armpit and quickly walking away toward the nearest train station, almost pulling Desire with her. Passion left Jameer and his group standing there perplexed.

"What happened to her, Jameer?" Ms. Hernandez said as she and the other church members huddled around him under the pool of light made by the street lamp.

"Do you know what she read?" Deacon Simmons.

"I'm shocked that she could read anything" said Ms. Alston. "They were prostitutes, right?"

Jameer had managed to keep the Bible opened to the page that Passion had read from. He saw the passage that she had read and thought it ironic. He read it to the other members.

"Check this out," he said. "She had read from the Book of Revelations," Jameer said slowly. "'...And the unbelievers, the corrupt, the murderers, the whoremongers, and idolaters, and all liars, shall have their part in the lake which burns with fire and brimstone which is the second death.'

⚜

Peaches couldn't recall the ride she took with Lavender as he drove her to the Ambassador Hotel on 37th St. between 9th and 10th Avenues in mid-town Manhattan later that night. All she remembered was the rainbow of colors of the street lights at night, the changing hues of neon lights and traffic signals as they danced and floated passing beyond the windows of Lavender's black Charger. She could never recall if they spoke during this ride or if she simply retreated alone into a private world of her own. She remembered only being drunk.

Her only tangible memory was of being in the bathroom of the hotel room 317, getting ready as Lavender spoke to two middle-aged white men outside the bathroom door in the swanky hotel room. She recalled Lavender's demeanor being free and easy, not at all like that of a man in danger. Their interaction seemed business-like but very amicable as they praised Lavender on his street savvy.

"I like the senoritas. See Tommy." said one white man to the other, "This is a business man."

"Yeah, he's a smart one." The one called Tommy agreed patronizingly. Then he said, turning to Lavender "What about you throw a "free one" our way for two guy's on the job?" the man said.

"You know the rules, boys. Ain't nuthin' free in this world." said Lavender, light-heartedly but, in earnest. "Besides, I pay you guys not to fuck with me, right?" added Lavender, still relaxed and upbeat.

"Yeah, yeah." said, the first of the white men, dismissively. "You good. Hey, where is she?"

Peaches, still in the bathroom heard the sound of money changing hands followed by the sound of the door to the hotel room closing behind Lavender as he left. It was Peaches turn to enter the room and give the men what they wanted. She quickly took a swig of liquor from a metal flask Lavender had given her. She walked in the smoke filled luxury suite. She was wearing nothing but panties and a bra and a see-through negligee. The light, billowy material caressed her supple, curvy body. The two men turned to look at her as one with sex in their eyes. Their sweaty hands reached up to grope the girl in her intimate places. Peaches felt sick, pushing back the urge to vomit. Then she gave into their desires.

Peaches would spend the next few days holed up in the hotel, playing host to a steady stream of strange johns seeking to use her body and indulge their sexual desires. Although, Lavender kept her numb with drugs and as much alcohol as she craved, Peaches felt herself die a thousand little deaths as she had loveless sex with a parade of johns.

⚔

The man who called himself Roger drove almost unconsciously to Prospect Street in the dawn hours. It was such a distressing habit that he felt like he could find his way to the area blindfolded. He knew every turn and corner, every block, every one way street on Prospect Street. He didn't know if this was a source of pride or shame. He didn't know if he were addicted to sex or to Passion. He didn't want to dwell on it too much. He wanted to get what he came for and leave; almost like a quick fix.

As he turned the corner leading to the notorious tracks, he looked anxiously for the prostitutes, hoping to find Passion. It was daylight. They weren't hard to find. He drove down one of the most frequented blocks, a one way street where prostitutes would stand discreetly in between the parked cars lining the street. He drove slowly so that he could get a good look, of the women on the street.

Once he reached the middle of the block he could see the young working girls. He became excited all at once. A nervous energy took hold of his body. He passed one brown skinned woman, wearing a white mini, exposing her white underwear. He kept moving. He saw another young Hispanic woman in a short trench coat and stilettos. She was very attractive and inviting in her own way. She reminded him of Passion. The man paused. His car slowed. He became even more excited and anxious. He was interested in this one, but he was looking for Passion. Where was she, he wondered. Probably with someone else, he surmised. He didn't have time to wait. He stopped his car just ahead of the Hispanic prostitute. She quickly walked toward the passenger side of his car as he knew she would.

"Are you a cop or a pimp?" she asked, her lips covered in glowing lipstick.

"Naw, I'm cool, suga. Get in," the man said. The young prostitute smiled and walked to the passenger side and opened the car door and climbed up the Escalade and sat in the seat. Her trench coat opened to reveal her scarlet lingerie.

"What could I do for you, cutie?" she asked smiling wickedly. "Nice cologne," she said, smelling it.

"I'm going to tell you in a minute. We gotta be quick, though. I'm in a hurry," the man said.

"Ok, Papi, just turn here and park in that spot. This is a quite block," she said.

The young Hispanic prostitute directed the horny man to park on a residential block lined with attached houses. But just as they pulled into the spot an elderly man walking his dog walked past the car and noticed the prostitute in the car with the man as it was daylight. He kept walking.

"I hope he didn't see us, the man said nervously. He had very rarely considered that he might ever get caught but then he realized how embarrassing and devastating it would be for him. It would be scandalous.

"We'll my name is Remy. What's yours, Papi?" the young prostitute said, getting comfortable in the car and putting her seat back.

"You don't need to know my name, suga," the man said, still thinking about getting caught with the woman in his car, wishing they had time to go to a hotel.

"No problem, Papi. What chu want? Head? Lay?"

Just then, the man looked in his rear view mirror and saw a police patrol car slowly coming up the block. He panicked.

"Oh, shit! It's the police!" he said, definitely flustered now.

The prostitute looked at the side mirror and also saw the police car approaching. She didn't panic. She knew what to do.

"Papi, Papi don't move! Stop moving! Just relax and lay your head down. Stop moving!" she said calmly but assertively. She put her hand on the man's thigh to calm him.

The john observed the prostitutes body language and demeanor and listened to her. She obviously knew what to do. He put his trust in her completely. The thought of being caught, of being arrested for soliciting a prostitute, him of all people—he couldn't imagine the fallout. His heart started beating faster and faster. He felt like he was going to pass out right then and there.

The police patrol car drove slowly past the Escalade. The officers in the car did not look into the SUV and did not see the man and the prostitute sitting quietly. In a moment the police were gone.

The man's heart stopped racing. He felt like his life had just passed before him. For the first time in a long while he feared that his private life was about to be exposed and made public. He was light headed.

"You all right Papi?" the prostitute known as Remy said, trying to calm the pastor.

"Yeah, I'm fine," he said.

"You ready now?" she said.

The man thought whether he could still do this after the close call he just had. He realized that everything he had worked hard for would've been lost in a moment. He wanted to kick her out of his car and drive away. He thought that's what he would do. But he looked at her supple body, half exposed breasts and long tan legs and the nervous energy returned. He couldn't overcome his lust.

"Yeah, let's do this so I can go on ahead," he said.

CHAPTER 5

It was late Saturday night and Lavender stood outside the South Bronx police station noticeably irritated. He hated bailing his women out of jail. Money was hard to come by. He was of the opinion that he had taught his women enough about the police and the streets not to get caught or arrested. Still, there was always one or two who just were too dumb to learn. It bothered him even more because he had friends at this precinct, dirty cops who would look out for him and his girls as long he provided them with special services and paid his "taxes." But these same police officers always warned him that they still had to do their jobs and if his girls were found at the wrong place, at the wrong time, they would get locked up. No matter, he would just take it out of her earnings.

"I'm so sorry Lavender," said Desire, who came running out of the police precinct, eager to hug her pimp and thank him for posting her $700 bail. "Thank you so much. I hate being in fucking jail. That's one place my fat ass doesn't belong."

Desire looked even paler in the night sky, under a full moon, her white skin making her look like a ghost with a head full of blonde hair.

"Not as much as I hate bailing out ur dumb ass!" Lavender returned. "I shoulda left your fat ass in there," Lavender said as he started walking with Desire hanging on his arm. "How the fuck you gonna get picked up for giving a blowjob on the street. You don't let those muthafucking tricks tell you where to give 'em head. You too old for that. You should be schoolin' the new hoes on how to handle their muthafucking customers, not gettin schooled. You were smoking that shit weren't you? Wait till I get you back to the crib," he said.

"I'm sorry, Lavender. Please don't be mad. I will get you your money back. I swear," she said. "It was a dark corner. I knew it was a bad idea but I didn't think anyone would see us. He gave me a lot of money too. See," Desire said trying to show him two twenty dollar bills.

Lavender snatched the money out of Desire's hands. "Bitch, this ain't shit. Come the fuck on!" he growled as they went to his car. Desire knew that once Lavender got her back to his apartment he was going to beat her. That was how he got down.

"How are my babies? Did you get Star or one of the girls to watch them?" Desire asked, trying to quell his rage.

"Yeah, bitch," Lavender said.

"Oh, thank you, Lavender. I swear I will repay you," she said.

Lavender reached his black Dodge Charger and after getting in started the engine. Desire jumped in the car, riding shotgun as they headed to Lavender's apartment. Desire reminisced about the days of being Lavender's bottom bitch. She still held out hope that Lavender would give her that job back.

An intimidating presence due to his size, Lavender stood about 6 feet four inches tall with a lean physique made for a boxer. Lavender had strong, prominent features marred by untreated facial eczema that created a raccoon-like effect about his face. He had bug eyes that bulged when he was angry and a penetrating gaze that bore deeply into your soul. Still, his poised surface calm and demeanor never betrayed his true emotions, carefully crafted over the years to hide his boiling inner nature. Sleeves of tattoos made all of gang symbols, arcane signs and the names of past and present prostitutes embraced his sinewy arms, hands and chest reaching to his neck. He wore a massive gold rope chain and an oversized white gold, diamond encrusted timepiece at all times.

Lavender had a tangible magnetism, an abundance of street swagger that made pimping a natural fit for him. Raised in the South Bronx housing projects, Lavender was one of four children born crack addicted to a crack addicted single mother. Lavender's real name was Rom-el Smith; he later took the street name, Lavender because his only memory of his father was of him wearing a lavender suit and fedora.

Lavender was naturally strong and skillful in the use of his hands and gained a reputation for his fierce scrappiness. He was well-respected and feared by his peers and maybe with the proper guidance, he might have been a professional boxer. But Lavender started getting in trouble with the law early. He was a juvenile offender at the age of 15, arrested for selling drugs for the older drug dealers on the block. By the age of 18, he was incarcerated for armed robbery and felony assault.

While serving time upstate in Hudson Correctional Facility, Lavender was schooled to the prostitution game by an old timer, a convict doing hard time who impressed him with tales of the pimping business and how he could still make money while the prostitutes themselves bore the majority of the risk of getting locked up.

"Bitches could be sold over and over again, my man, and still turn a profit. You can't do that with nothin' else, nothin' else,' he explained.

The old timer bragged about the number of women he used to pimp and the money he made; the fancy clothes he used to wear and cars he used to drive. "I was livin' large," boasted the old timer.

The old timer confessed that the only mistake he made was prostituting minors across state lines and got busted by the feds. "I got too big for my goddamn britches," he lamented.

Lavender left the correctional facility after serving a five year bid and immediately went about plying his new trade on the streets. He canvassed group homes in the Tri-State area, luring girls into the sex trade or bribing their foster parents to traffic them in exchange for money and drugs. Lavender always sought the most troubled teenage girls, those with drug problems, behavior problems and those without direction; he would offer them food and shelter, take them to his apartment, get them drunk and high on drugs and then rape them. He would then convince them they had to pay him back for the food and board he provided them by working for him or suffer a serious beat down.

Lavender employed recruiters, young thugs desperate to get into the pimping game, to infiltrate youth homeless shelters and malls to lure young girls into the sex trade.

Lavender quickly rose in the pimp game. He had some of the finest prostitutes working for him, many of them recruited from down south and states like Connecticut, Maine, Pennsylvania and Rhode Island. If a rival pimp wasn't on top of his game, Lavender would take his girls too. He would also loan money and cars to other low level pimps and if they couldn't pay him back he would have them hand over their best money-making girls.

Lavender lived about a mile away from Prospect Street in a tenement building just above a bodega store that also doubled as a trap house, trafficking in illegal drugs. Everyone in the neighborhood knew that Lavender was a big time pimp. The older adults in the community feared and hated Lavender as a symbol of all that was wrong with the neighborhood; young boys admired him.

Lavender's apartment was on the top floor in the back of the building. The only window view was of a brick wall; no sunlight could enter the apartment. His two and a half bedroom apartment was large but dirty and filthy just like the building itself, the result of years of neglect from the absentee landlord. Garbage often spilled out on the floor. A menacing black pitbull dog roamed freely. A musky odor persisted from the constant drug use. The apartment was extremely messy, only the pimp's staggering collection of Timberland boots that he often used to beat down his women, and numerous Jordan sneakers were neatly stacked in boxes in the closets.

Lavender's master bedroom was where he "auditioned" new recruits to his stable; he ravished young girls in his King sized bed, told them what their sex game was worth on the streets. At any given time a young woman could be found languishing in Lavender's bed, passed out on drugs or raped by the unscrupulous pimp.

Lavender drove up to his building, easily parking in the space unofficially reserved for him in the front of the building by local residents fearful of him. He stepped out the car and walked with Desire trailing behind him.

Once they made their way inside his apartment, they heard moaning, grunting and steady flesh slapping coming from one of the bedrooms.

"Sounds like someone is gettin' it on," Desire quipped.

Lavender went to the source of the sound, peeped in and saw his 18-years-old prostitute Star, her real name Shaneeka Hudson, completely naked except for an oversized white tee, servicing two White plainclothes detective. The dark-skinned prostitute was self-absorbed in shooting selfies on her Galaxy smartphone as one of the detectives, his pants at his ankles, was taking her from behind, doggystyle. The other detective stood by patiently, his pants also at his ankles, riveted by the sex scene, furiously stroking his erection, anxiously awaiting his turn. Star and the detectives looked up at Lavender as they saw him looking in on them smiled, then went back to enjoying each other.

Star was a very petite but shapely young woman from Oklahoma City. She had straight black, shoulder-length hair, high cheek bones and a straight nose courtesy of her mixed black and Cherokee Native American Indian heritage. She had worked seedy strip clubs and lounges in order to pay for college but got addicted to the heroin that was regularly sold inside the clubs. She was kicked out of her home after her grandmother caught her stealing money to support her drug habit.

Lavender and Mercedes picked Star up off the street in Oklahoma City, luring her with the promise of an endless supply of dope if she turned tricks for them at a local hot sheet motel in New York City. They gave her a pricey smartphone and put her to work. The only thing Star loved more than heroin was her smartphone and posting raunchy pictures of herself on Facebook, Twitter and Instagram.

Lavender often allowed corrupted detectives to sex his prostitutes in his apartment more times than he cared to remember. He had mixed feelings about the whole thing. He couldn't shake the feeling that the corrupt officers, in addition to getting the VIP treatment, were also privy to the intimate details of his operation, seeing the whole layout of his pad. In the event they eventually had to collar him or take him down, they knew where to find him. Fortunately, he had another apartment or hideout in case something did go down.

Lavender paid "taxes" weekly to the dirty cops, to allow him to conduct business without fear of arrest. Other hustlers in his neighborhood did everything they could to avoid police muscling in on their business. But, Lavender figured as long as the police never threatened his profit margin better to pay it and not lose any time on the street. Besides, an added benefit was that the local cops would "pull his coat," warn him about any rivals on the street planning to move against him. As a result, Lavender's pimp game flourished while competitors often had theirs interrupted by arrest and prison time. Lavender still wondered if he wasn't playing himself.

Lavender smiled to himself before closing the door to let the detectives finish their business. He then went directly to his master bedroom peering in on Desire's three children, Diamond, Marquis and Tiffany and a 20-years-old prostitute named Rave. They were all sleeping under the covers in his bed except for his son Marquis who was watching the classic rap movie, "Belly" in an endless loop on Lavender's 55' inch flat screen TV.

"What's up, son? You good?" he murmured to his son.

Grim-faced, Lavender went for his stash of cocaine hidden in a small safe behind a picture of Allen Iverson. After opening the safe, he grabbed a large plastic bag filled with the drug. He then closed the small safe door, replaced the framed poster, and went to sit at a round marble table in the living room. He unrolled the white plastic bag and started cutting the cocaine before snorting it with a tightly rolled 50 dollar bill. Lavender long had a cocaine habit and struggled daily not to let it consume him despite his excesses.

"Can I get some too, baby," Desire said sitting on the dirty couch, watching him with a gaze. "I swear I will get your money back. You know I always do," she added.

"Bitch, you costin' me too much money as is. I don't even know why I keep yo ass around," Lavender said, but knowing full well Desire was his baby mother and Marquis was his son and he couldn't hide his feelings for them.

Without warning, Lavender backhanded Desire hard across the face with his left hand, sending her backwards and over the couch. Desire slowly got back on her feet only to have her pimp grab her by her hair.

"Bitch, you betta work extra hard to get back that money I spent gettin' your white ass outta jail. You hear me? I don't care that you're my baby mama," he shouted, half lying.

"I-I will work hard, Lavender baby, I swear I will. I will get your money back, baby. Please, you're hurting me," she said, crying from the pain.

Lavender looked at Desire, almost enjoying the pain he was causing her. He then let her go. After all, she was his baby mama, he thought to himself.

"Now go back out tonight and don't stop working until you made back my money; work that ass off. You understand me?" he said.

"I will, baby, I will," she said, wiping the tears. She hated getting beat by Lavender, but she had long learned to accept it. She felt he was getting soft on her, though letting her get off with just a bitch slap. She had experienced worse when she first started working for him.

Desire sat down next to Lavender by the table. She stared at the dope on the table. He was making lines out of his stash of cocaine.

"Can I have some?" Desire said, almost shyly.

"You want some? You know what you gotta do, bitch!" Lavender said.

"I promise you boo, I will make back the money. I promise, ok," she said.

Just then, the two plainclothes detectives in the back room walked through the living room on their way to the front door.

"Lavender, we out. Thanks, man" one of the men said, paying no attention to the dope on the table.

"Just remember, your girls can work the streets until five in the morning, after that, if we see them, we locking their asses up."

"Aight, Al. Hit me up, later," Lavender said and started snorting the cocaine. Desire joined Lavender at the table. They both started doing white lines together.

"Hey, leave some for me," shouted Star, as she came bouncing out of the bedroom, still wearing only a white tee. She joined Lavender and Desire at the table. She was holding her smartphone in her hand. She started rolling up a 20 dollar bill, ready to put the dope up her nose. After taking her first few hits, Star began taking selfies on her smartphone. Lavender said nothing but turned to Desire.

"D, you betta get my money or you gonna be one dead ho," Lavender whispered in all seriousness.

"All right, baby." Desire said. "Alright."

Star started playing "CoCo" by O.T. Genasis on her smartphone while snapping countless selfies of herself getting high.

Chapter 6

Ever since Passion read that passage in the Bible, she was never quite the same. She had learned to look at prostitution as a hustle and nothing more, a business. She wouldn't even call herself a prostitute. She rationalized that she was providing a service, like someone in the store selling clothes or food. She was simply selling sex for money, that's how her old boyfriend CJ put it; and that's what Lavender always said. She didn't see it as anything more; no one was being hurt or victimized, she had reasoned. She had even heard how what she was doing was even legal in other places in the country and around the world. She never really understood why she had to avoid the police or why the police would look to lock anyone up for what she had to do to survive. Or, arrest anyone who would pay her for her service and time.

But now there was that passage in the Bible that called into question what she was doing, that it was against God, and that she would burn in Hell for it. Passion always believed in a Spiritual being who was somehow responsible for the world, who would right wrongs and punish the wicked. Her father never tired of telling her that. She was very bothered to know that God was against her hustle. She thought maybe she read it wrong. Maybe there was more to it. She was unsure. She didn't want to think about it anymore. She had to make money to survive. She didn't know anything else. Ever since she left high school, this was all she knew. She took another gulp of the Patron liquor she was sharing with Mercedes in her stylish co-op. She was feeling nice now. She put everything else out of mind to focus on what she had to do. She was ready to go back to work.

Mercedes was busy on her high speed MacBook Air laptop and talking on her smartphone, trying to set up a date for one of the girls. She hung up now, eager to share with Passion.

"Yo, check this, out P! This dude wants me to set him up with a girl who's too wasted to know he's having sex with her. He calls himself having a rape fantasy," Mercedes said, looking at internet messages on the Lonely Hearts website she set up for the business. "That's some crazy ass shit, ain't it?"

"Don't respond to him, Mercedes." Passion said. "He sounds like a fucking serial killer. And definitely don't set him up with me."

"Yeah, but he is offering a shit load of money for the experience…hmm. I wonder. Anyway, I got some other clients to hook up with girls. I will work on that other crazy ass later. Come on, it's about that time. Let's go girl, you ready," Mercedes said, looking at the oversized clock on her wall. It was well after midnight. Mercedes allowed Passion to stay for a night or two, only because Desire was locked up. After Desire was arrested Passion didn't feel like being alone in Desire's apartment, especially after reading that she was going to burn in hell. Passion had mixed feelings about Mercedes. She never felt like she could completely trust her but still, it was Mercedes who gave her her first red bottoms when she started working for Lavender, so she couldn't be that bad, she surmised.

"Did Lavender get Desire out of jail yet?" Passion asked Mercedes.

"I believe he did," Mercedes said. "He told me that he was going down there to the precinct this morning."

'This is like her third arrest in a month. She's my girl, but she's too sloppy and open with her shit," Passion said.

"I don't know why Lavender keeps that washed up, ratchet ho around," Mercedes said. "If you ask me that two dollar ho costs more than she's making for him."

"Maybe he's trying to help her out because she has those kids," Passion responded, agreeing with Mercedes.

"Those kids or his kid?" Mercedes said sarcastically.

"What?" Passion said, naively.

"One of those kids belongs to Lavender," Mercedes said. "You didn't know? She didn't tell you?"

"No," Passion said, incredulously. "I thought they were all trick babies."

"Desire got pregnant soon after she started working for Lavender; that's why he made her his bottom bitch. But she wasn't good at it, trust me when I tell you. No one listened to her or respected her," Mercedes said. "Marquis is Lavender's son. He's the baby daddy."

"You mean, little Marquis?" Passion said still surprised but now understanding why Desire favored him above her other children.

"How do you know for sure?" Passion retorted.

"I told you, Lavender told me. He tells me everything. Why do you think, he's always having one of his girls babysit those bad ass kids?" Mercedes said. "He knows better than to ask me to do that, shit. Anyway, let's go, it's about that time," Mercedes said checking her iPhone. It was about one in the morning, Saturday night. They had finished the bottle of Patron and finished sharing a blunt. They were both feeling nice and ready to work.

"How did you get in this business, M?" Passion asked, hoping to get Mercedes to rationalize what they were doing as not a wholly bad thing, "You're smart. You go to college. Why do this?"

"Who me?" Mercedes said. "I'm trying to get paid. When I was little, I caught my aunt and uncle gettin' it on one night. The next morning, he gave her money to take me shopping. So one day, I told him I would suck his dick if he gave me money. He gave me twenty dollars."

"Damn, how old were you?" Passion asked.

"I think I was 12-13. I turned my first trick on my aunt's perverted ass boyfriend," she laughed. "He made me promise not to tell anyone. I neva told nobody. But I think my aunt found out cuz she called the police on him. As I got older, ah, dated men who could be my "suga daddy" and take care of me and buy me nice things. I'm about the money, always was, always will be. Now, ah, get a thrill having girls like you, taking y'all to a hotel with a trick and knowing when you come out, you're going to hand over $500 to me,"

Mercedes said, all smug and sure of herself. "You can't make this money doing a regular job. That's the mentality that got me into this game. That's the mentality you need to have. When Lavender met me, me, already had two gals working for me. I'm not workin' for no pimp. We workin' together. C'mon, let's get out of here."

Mercedes and Passion left out the stylish co-op building and headed in the direction of Prospect Street. They could see the full moon lighting up the night sky. Mercedes hailed a cab that stopped immediately for them. In a moment they were on their way.

"Hey, it's a full moon tonight," it's going to be on and popping tonight," Mercedes laughed. "Money makin' time."

Chapter 7

Jameer stood on the corner of Prospect Street with deacons Alvin and Margaret beside him waiting for the others in their group to arrive. The cool air was blowing lustily against their ears. It was past one o' clock in the morning.

Jameer and his group of three deacons and two lay people had established their routine. They would go out every night, five days a week, from midnight to four in the morning, approaching the prostitutes in the community in the The Zone. Armed only with their Bibles and prayers, they would do their best to preach the gospel to the prostitutes, warn them of the dangers of the sex trade and try and convince them to turn away from that life. So far they were finding little success.

"Hey, man, this is our fourth week at this and I don't see us converting anyone or turning any of these women around," Deacon Alvin said. He believed in the mission but saw how daunting a task it was ministering to prostitutes. He had serious doubts about the ministry.

"We are making some headway, guys. You gotta remember that this is all these women know. They don't know anything else. Remember, this is how many of them support themselves. I never said that it would be easy, but if we could turn one around, we are doing a lot," Jameer said.

"Listening to you Jameer, I would believe anything," Deacon Alvin said.

Just then two more of their members came walking up the street. It was Mrs. Hernandez and Ms. Denise Simmons. The women brought along the care packages for the prostitutes, bags filled with toiletries, make-up, feminine products, and food gift cards, small Bibles, clean syringes and condoms.

"Hey guys, everybody well rested? We got a long night ahead of us," Mrs. Hernandez said.

"Let's do it," said Jameer.

Once they all gathered together on the street, they started walking down Prospect Street and into the foreboding darkness. After twenty minutes of walking they approached a young woman on the stroll. It was Peaches. Her hair was dyed blond. Peaches was popular on the strip because she was new and pretty and very young. The streets loved fresh new meat.

Peaches wore a designer denim waistcoat, loose fitting burgundy blouse, two hundred dollars tight designer blue jeans, and black sling back Prada pumps. Her streaked hair reached down to her back. Heavy make-up was applied liberally to her face in an unflattering manner. A tan Gucci bag hung over her shoulder. She was chewing hard on mint flavored gum to hide the smell of heavy alcohol on her breath. Peaches was drunk. She noticed the group approach her and tried to ignore them. She pretended to be talking into her smartphone. Jameer was the first to approach to her.

"Hello, Miss. How are you? It's really cold out here tonight. Are you waiting for someone?"

"Are you the police? If not, fuck off!" Peaches said rudely, trying to walk away.

"No, we are not the police but we know what you are doing out here and we are trying to help you. What's your name?" Jameer said in a soft voice.

"My name is Peaches, and unless you are buying, gets the fuck out of my face. I don't need your fucking help," she shot back.

"Ok, Peaches, my name is Jameer; it's kinda chilly out here. Do you want to go to a diner or someplace warm and get some hot chocolate or something to eat?" he said, feeling he wasn't reaching her.

"Mister, I don't need any hot chocolate or any help. I'm working, and you are fucking up my hustle. Do you fucking mind? "Peaches said.

"Listen, Peaches we want to help you. You don't have to do this. We want to help you find another life. Is anyone making you do this? Your pimp?"

he asked, feeling her resistance but refusing to give up just the same. While Jameer was talking to her, other members of the group were keeping the lookout for pimps who might be lurking around.

Ignoring him, Peaches started walking away unsteadily in her high heels, failing to hide her drunkenness. Jameer noticed her eyes were glazed over. He realized she was intoxicated.

"Peaches, if you ever change your mind and decide that you don't want to do this anymore, here is my card. I am a member of Grace Baptist Church, and we are reaching out to women like yourself trying to help you choose a different lifestyle. You can call me anytime. This is not the way. Believe me. Here take this gift bag. We really do care about you but you have to want something better for yourself, just as we want something better for you," Jameer said. He handed the young prostitute the gift bag. Peaches refused his card and the gift bag and walked away. "Can we pray for you?" he asked.

"No," Peaches said. "Please get away," Peaches said as she continued walking away, feeling like they were making her lose prospective clients. "I'm trying to work; I'm praying that you leave me the fuck alone. How about that?"

"God bless you, Peaches," the group said in unison.

"Please be safe, girl. You're such a beautiful girl," Mrs. Hernandez said, hoping the young woman who could be her daughter, heard her. "My God, she looks like a teenager," Mrs. Hernandez said to Jameer. "We should call the police. I'm calling the police," Mrs. Hernandez said, pulling out her smartphone. "That poor child can't be more than 16," she surmised correctly.

"C'mon let's go," Jameer said. "The police don't come out here until its early morning. I think they allow these girls to work out here. I mean they drive by and don't do nothing," he said, shaking his head.

"I'm calling them anyway," Mrs. Hernandez said as she dialed 911. She reported underage prostitutes on the streets and gave them the location.

After Jameer and his ministry group moved on down Prospect Street, Peaches came back to stand on her designated corner. Pretty soon a man in a flashy, late model red Maserati stopped by the curb. Peaches quickly got in the car and they drove off. A few minutes later the police arrived looking for underage prostitutes.

More than a few blocks away, Passion and Mercedes stood on the corner. Mercedes' black spandex tights accentuated her hips and ass. She wore black Jimmy Choo platform pumps to match. Her hair was dyed blond to go with her lipstick and nail polish.

Passion came out in a white leopard print stretch pants and a red blouse. She also wore red platform pumps. A Coach bag hung over her shoulder. Passion was tipsy more than anything. She was hoping to meet the big, handsome man who called himself Roger, her favorite client. She looked closely at every Escalade that passed by hoping it was him. She also checked her cell phone, hoping to catch his text. Every so often her thoughts would drift to Desire, wondering if she was still in jail or if Lavender got her out.

Just then, Lavender's black Dodger Charger drove up to the curb. Desire was riding shotgun. Her three children were sitting in the back seat, looking about wide-eyed.

Passion found it more than a little funny to see Lavender pull up with Desire and her kids. He looked every bit the family man taking his wife to work, only work was the stroll.

"Bye mommy," Desire's eldest daughter Diamond shouted through the back seat.

"Bye, mommy," joined in little Marquis.

"Bye, my little darlings," yelled back Desire. Desire got out of the drive's side. She was obviously high on the coke she and Lavender snorted just hours ago. She was giddy and feeling supremely confident. She thought that she could make back the money she owed her pimp. She stepped onto the curb, joining Mercedes and Desire on the stroll.

"Yo, M, hold it down. I got to go pick up some girls up north, Maine," Lavender said proudly to Mercedes before peeling off in his Charger. He just nodded to Desire and Passion.

Mercedes understood that Lavender was depending on her to manage his girls until he came back. Lavender had prostitutes up and down the east coast. Mercedes quickly walked away from the two women to stake out her own territory. She did it, partly because that was her practice and partly because she wasn't fond of being around Desire.

Desire took quick note of Mercedes' behavior and just as quickly ignored it. She hated Mercedes. She simply turned her attention to Passion.

"Hey, girl how you been?" she said, giving Passion a hug.

Passion returned the hug and was really happy to see Desire.

"Girl, you know I was so worried about you being up in that jail? Are you all right?" Passion said.

"I'm fine, P," Desire said, still reveling in her high. "Y'know, Lavender won't let them keep his best piece of ass locked up for too long when I could be out here making him money," Desire said, giving Passion a high five. Passion laughed. She was happy to see Desire and really enjoyed her friendship. She really cared about Desire.

"You been sniffing, I see," Passion said, noticing Desire's hyped up attitude and glazed over eyes.

"Yeah, me and Lavender," Desire said, proudly. "Now I have to get back on my grind, make some money out here!" Desire almost seemed to shout. She was ready and eager and supremely confident in herself now, even though it was a Saturday night and there was much younger competition out on the streets. She waved to passing cars and ran at some if she thought they slowed down for her.

Passion had seen Desire like this only once before, when she was also high on coke. She didn't like to see her like this even though it was kind of funny. She thought it made Desire even more reckless and not use her better judgment when it came to picking customers.

"Hey, sweety, looking for a good time," Desire shouted to a passing car.

"Desire stop, you don't want to get picked up by the police," Passion said.

An old, dusty blue Ford Explorer pulled up to Desire. Inside was an ugly, middle-aged Hispanic man.

"Hola caliente mama! Venaquí!" he shouted to Desire.

Desire looked at the man and the car and was repulsed. She knew she needed to make money and couldn't afford to be picky but she was turned off by the man. He was the type of customer she would go with on a slow night, or just before she was ready to turn it in. She wasn't feeling him right now. She ignored him.

"No alejarse. Conseguíloque usted quiere.¡Venga aquí!" the man said, desperate for the White prostitute. He tried following her in his soiled and muddy pick-up truck but she was ignoring him.

"Sucia puta!" the man said before finally turning up the block.

Desire was high and feeling herself. She felt she could get better than that man as she walked back to the corner.

A White, late model BMW pulled up to the corner where the girls stood. Desire saw her chance.

She quickly ran to the car then stopped. She immediately recognized the car as the same one when she had to call Lavender for help. She started to turn around and head back to the corner with Passion.

"Hey, shawty, what's popping tonight?" a young African American man shouted at Desire from the driver's side of the car. It wasn't the same guy who had picked her up before. It was a different guy; he appeared older and was light complected with thick lips, wearing a fresh Yankee cap.

Desire turned back around and slowly walked up to the car, still suspicious. As she approached the car, Desire immediately looked to see who was driving. It was another young man who appeared to be Hispanic. He had a bushy mustache and wore shades. Desire tried to look into the back of the car but the windows were too tinted.

"What's up, fellas, you looking for a good time?" Desire said, feeling more comfortable.

"Yeah, baby, c'mon let's ride," the man with the thick lips said, a huge smile on his face making his lips look bigger.

Passion also saw the BMW and ran quickly to tell Desire to let them go. She remembered what Desire had told her what happened; she remembered how her face looked.

"Desire, don't fuck with those young boys. They're trouble," Passion whispered to Desire in her ear when she reached her. "C'mon there are other tricks out here. It's Saturday night. Remember that was the same car as the other night.

"Hey, baby, we just got paid! We lookin' for some fun," the Hispanic man shouted his head and shoulders sticking out the car window, now.

Desire saw the eagerness and smile on the young man's face and found herself unable to resist. They were both cute, she thought. She knew that that looked like the same car as the other night but Lavender took care of that guy, left him for dead. She thought that it was just a coincidence that they had the same car. Besides she thought to herself, she needed to make money for Lavender, to pay him back for bailing her out. They might want a threesome and pay her more. She was supremely confident in herself now and feeling incredibly sexy. She smiled back at the two men.

"Look girl, I got this. If any trouble, I got my cell phone, just charged it, too," she whispered to Passion. "I got to pay Lavender back or I'm dead, feel me."

"Desire, I don't think…" Passion tried to say.

Before Passion could finish her thought, Desire ran to the car and the man got out the passenger side to let Desire ride shotgun. He sat in the back. When he opened the door, Passion, saw another man in the back seat sitting behind the driver, then the door closed. The car drove off headed south toward the Sheridan Expressway.

Passion quickly retrieved her cell phone out of her bag and texted Lavender what happened to Desire and her fears. Lavender never responded to his girls' texts but they knew he received it and would act if he thought there was trouble.

Once settled in the car, Desire immediately felt uneasy, like a mouse so eager for the cheese, realizing too late that he had suddenly stepped into a mouse trap. The hair on the back of her neck stood on end. Something wasn't right. She noticed that there was an extra person in the car that she hadn't seen before. But before she could make him out, the man with the thick lips who was sitting directly behind her reached over and put her in a neck lock, almost lifting her up off the seat. She gasped, unable to breathe.

"Get her bag!" one of the passengers in the back seat said. He reached to the front seat and grabbed Desire's Fendi bag with such force that he broke Desire's nail, causing her to bleed from the cuticle. He then rifled through the bag until he found her lavender cell phone, and promptly threw it out the car window. Then he threw her bag with all its contents also out the car window.

"Now, Bitch, now, what?" the young man said. Desire managed to turn her head to see the man who grabbed her bag with her cell. It was the same young man she had to call Lavender about for refusing to pay her extra. His eyes were completely bloodshot from the pistol-whipping Lavender gave him and his face was still swollen and black and blue on one side.

Desire's heart started racing as she could hardly breathe as the choke hold made breathing impossible. She saw her life race before her eyes and thought about her children.

"We gonna do this all over again," said Stefon Grey, revenge in his eyes and a devilish grin on his face. "And this time ain't nobody gonna save your white ass!"

⅄

As Passion stood on Prospect Street, spying for a trick, she was approached by Jameer's outreach ministry group. She recognized Jameer immediately, his kind and honest face appealed to her as did his sturdy frame. The others in his group weren't quite as familiar. She couldn't believe that they were out this late in the night. She couldn't help thinking about their safety. It was way past three in the morning. They all looked like easy targets to be rolled on for their money.

"Hello, there Ms. Passion, how are you, my dear," Jameer said, a smile framing his face. "The next bus isn't until 4," he said, jokingly.

"I guess I will have to wait then," Passion responded in kind, playing innocent.

"Well, we both know that you aren't waiting for the bus. It's good to see you again, by the way. What are you doing out here?" Jameer said, his smile turning serious.

"I'm working so please, this is not the time," Passion retorted.

"If not now, when?" said Deacon Mitchell.

Jameer looked at the deacon and smiled.

"Passion, we are out here trying to talk to you and girls like you about choosing a different life, a different path; one that doesn't include standing on the street, trying to get picked up, risking your life," Jameer said.

Passion responded sarcastically. "Listen, you kind of crowding me here and you messing with my money."

"Listen, here, take this, it's for you," Mrs. Hernandez said, stepping forward and handing Passion the gift bag filled with make-up and food gift cards. "We don't want you out here. You can turn this around; I was out here too, doing what you're doing, but I was able to find God and now I'm married and I have back my children. I'm living proof that it's possible to change. It's not too late for you. You are so young. Let us help you. Is it housing you need? Food? Are you on drugs? Are you running from an abusive home? Let us help you, my dear child," Mrs. Hernandez said, her words soaked with honest emotion.

Passion heard the sincerity in the woman's words and saw the honesty in her eyes. She also saw the same in Jameer's face, all their faces, in fact. She wanted to walk away as she spied cars slowing, trying to get her attention, propositioning her, but somehow she felt compelled to listen to this street ministry. The Bible verse she read was still in her head. She accepted the care package.

"Let us pray for you our dear but lost sister," Jameer said. His group slowly started to form a semi-circle around Passion and started to pray following Jameer's lead.

"Oh Heavenly Father, please shine your light on the lost souls out here and bless and protect our sister Passion so that she may find her way to You and away from this path of death and destruction that she has been following. In Your name we pray, Amen."

Passion was taken aback. She believed this bible group really cared about her. She didn't know how to respond. She wanted to cry.

"Passion here, take this Bible and inside is my card, our church and contact information. If you feel like you want a different life, call me, come to our church and we will help you," Jameer said.

Passion took Jameer's small Bible and removed his card with his phone number and the address to the church, looking at it intensely as if she were committing it to memory.

"Ok, ok, Passion, please go home. Remember, it's not too late," implored Mrs. Hernandez. The group left Passion out there and continued on looking for more prostitutes to minister to.

"Take care of yourself, Passion, please," said Jameer.

Passion kept looking back at the group as they walked away. She knew that she couldn't go home but felt strange, like her life was about to change. She didn't know why or in what way.

Just then, an escalade pulled up to the curb a few feet from where Passion was standing. Passion recognized the car as belonging to the man she had come to know as Roger. Passion smiled a big smile which lit up her cherub-like face. She quickly climbed up the SUV but not before putting away the gift bag and miniature Bible in her Coach bag.

⋏

The blood red Maserati was parked conspicuously on a deserted side street in the black of night. Inside the sports car, Peaches was finding it extremely difficult to make the sandy-haired, thirtysomething trick get off. Even after several minutes of constant fellatio, the john managed only a soft erection.

"C'mon baby, what's wrong?" Peaches said softly, eager to finish with this trick. "C'mon, relax, baby."

Unbeknown to Peaches, the glassy-eyed john was stoned on crack cocaine and ecstasy drugs. He was sweating profusely and growing more and more paranoid even as he sat there stoic, his pants below his knees and his dick in

Peaches' soft grip. The john was preoccupied by drug-induced thoughts that Peaches was somehow setting him up to be robbed by her pimp.

Peaches continued performing on him, amazed at how ineffective she was. She was ready to leave and be done with it, take her money and go. She was used to johns getting excited simply by the sight of her. She wasn't used to having to work so hard. Still she resolved to keep trying.

Peaches wasn't paying attention to the man's erratic behavior focused instead on doing what she had been taught to do. Had she been more experienced in the game, she would've known that the man was high on hard drugs.

"C'mon," the man said, looking out the car windows, into the dark, desolate side street they were parked on, seized by an uncontrollable, drug-induced panic that an attack was imminent. His eyes darted wildly.

"C'mon," he said again, even more loudly, impatience in his voice. He became fearful and frustrated, feeling that at any minute Peaches and her pimp would pounce on him, rob him, take his car and leave him for dead.

Peaches just kept on sucking the man's flaccid dick, her head bobbing up and down in his lap, trying to get the man to come, oblivious to what he was saying or how he was acting.

The man suddenly imagined he saw a shadowy figure lurking by his car. He freaked. "Fuck this, shit!" he said. He quickly reached into the glove compartment of his car and grabbed a 9mm with a silver plated pistol grip. Pulling Peaches' head back by her hair, he quickly shoved the gun in her mouth before she could react.

"Here, bitch! Suck on this!" the crazed man said. He squeezed the trigger and the gun exploded in Peaches' mouth, causing her head to recoil back violently. He then shoved Peaches' body out of the car and onto the cold pavement. The man was so panic-stricken; he drove off without bothering to take back the money he had given her.

Peaches lay face down on the street, her body twitching violently and sporadically in an ever-expanding pool of blood.

⋏

Lavender read Passion's text on his iPhone 6s as he drove on the Interstate 95 corridor north.

Desire got in the car with some crazy tricks. She is in danger.

He hoped that Desire wouldn't make the same mistake twice. He was tired of her already. Anyway, he hadn't heard from Desire herself since then. He resolved he would find out what happened on his way back to New York City from Maine.

Lavender had long made it routine to pick up Michelle Brown and Yolanda Workman, two teenage prostitutes from Kittery, Maine, every Friday night. They were known on the streets as Cat and Sunshine, respectively. He would bring them to New York City to work some of the newer hotels the city had put up by Yankee Stadium. Both Michelle and Yolanda were single mothers who had their children removed by child services. They worked minimum wage full time jobs during the day to show that they were committed to getting their children back. They prostituted at night to support their drug addiction and make their pimp money. Lavender met both women while running drugs through their neighborhood. Michelle, the younger of the two women became his girlfriend and got Yolanda, her best friend, to prostitute for Lavender in exchange for more drugs. Pretty soon, Lavender had them both working for him.

"Oh, baby, I don't feel so good. I think I'm having your baby," Michelle said as she rode shotgun in Lavender's car. Michelle was already two months pregnant, but she was afraid to tell him, as he might make her have another abortion. She felt like this was the right time. She long noticed her breasts had started to swell.

Lavender became very angry upon hearing the news. "What the fuck do you mean, you think you pregnant. You still gotta work. That ain't goin' stop you from workin.' You betta get rid of it, if you are. I already got enough kids, I don't need another right now. Anyway, you got to work," he said. "We ain't got time for this right now."

"Oh baby, I know, I know. I worked pregnant before remember with my first one. Let me keep this one, please. I want to have your baby," Michelle begged.

"Bitch, I said no!" Lavender barked. "Take your ass to the clinic in the morning."

"Lavender!" Yolanda shouted, the police are behind us."

"What the fuck?" Lavender said as he looked at the side mirror and noticed police vehicles behind him, their lights shining brightly like Christmas lights in the dark of night.

Two police vehicles rode up behind Lavender's car, their lights flashing. Lavender became nervous. His license was clean and he had been going the speed limit. He couldn't understand why he was being pulled over. He pulled the car over to the shoulder just the same.

Two police officers walked to either side of Lavender's car. Then two other state troopers in the second car pulled over, their guns drawn.

"Please step out of the car! And put your hands on the roof of the car!" the officer commanded from the police horn.

Lavender was pissed. He and the girls got out of the car and did as they were told.

"What's up, officers?" Lavender said angrily. "I was doing the speed limit; what's this about?"

"We gonna let you know in a minute, sir. Please come out the car, slowly and keep your hands out your pockets," the officer said in an authoritative manner.

The first police officer came behind Lavender and patted him down, removing Lavender's gun and identification and a gold plated money clip, full of hundred dollar bills. The other officers then frisked the female prostitutes, after having them also step out the car. The officers lifted the women's' EBT cards and freshly rolled marijuana joints.

"Mr. Smith, we been watching you for months now, "the officer said. These two women are known prostitutes. It's illegal to transport prostitutes across state lines," the officer stated. He then began reading Lavender his Miranda rights.

Lavender rolled his eyes. He was going to jail again.

Chapter 8

Early Sunday morning, an elderly woman was walking her Shitzu dog in the brisk morning air. She passed two voluptuous prostitutes, provocatively dressed coming from Prospect Street, retiring for the night. The aged woman spied a wildly burning dumpster in the area of the local elementary school. The woman watched the flames lick the sky for several minutes before she reached for her cell phone and dutifully reported the fire. She hated the neighborhood she grew up in, and counted the blaze the result of another wild Saturday night in a neighborhood she so desperately wished she could leave. The fire soon attracted a small crowd of community residents, blithely curious as to what was the cause. Everyone covered their noses from the pungent smell coming from the dumpster.

Three local fire engines finally arrived on the scene and trained their fire hoses on the blaze. Several police cars and paramedics stood fast on the scene. After several minutes the fire was finally extinguished, black and grey smoke billowed steadily from the dumpster. Police then began cordoning off the area around the dumpster with yellow tape, declaring the area a crime scene.

The same elderly woman who had reported the fire hours ago, bravely approached one of the police officers on the scene, a slim African-American officer with a light complexion.

"Excuse me, sir, what happened here? What caused the fire?" the aged woman said softly, curiosity getting the best of her.

"A burned body, ma'am! A female's body was found in the dumpster. Somebody set her on fire. Now step back!" The officer said sternly.

"Oh my" the elderly woman uttered in amazement. "Oh my, I have to get out of this neighborhood," she said.

⚓

Passion woke up to hard knocking on the apartment door. It was late Monday afternoon and Desire's three children were already up making a mess in the already messy kitchen. They were hungry and going through the refrigerator with a vengeance. Passion got up from the couch and went to answer the door. She was exhausted from working the night before. She looked in the bedroom to see if Desire had returned home but there was no sign of her. She wondered if Desire was still working or went to stay with Lavender. Passion found some clothes, a blue robe, to cover up her naked body as she walked to the door.

"Who is it?" Passion asked without opening the door.

"Children's services!" a mature woman's voice shouted back from behind the door.

Passion froze.

There was a time when Passion was fearful of children's services. When she ran away from the group home she was always thinking they would eventually find her and return her to her father. But ever since she turned 18, her boyfriend CJ told her that they couldn't do anything to her anymore as she was considered an adult. Still, it gave her pause.

Passion confidently opened the door and was surprised to see two tall female police officers, one black, the other white standing behind a petite, sun tanned white woman.

"Hello, can I help you," Passion said, an ominous feeling closing about her heart.

"Yes, my name is Ms. Webber, I am with child protective services and I am here to see the children of Mrs. Cassidy, Yvonne Cassidy. I believe they live here with her," the social worker said.

Yvonne Cassidy was Desire's real name before she started working the streets. Passion found that out the first time Mercedes had to bail Desire out of jail.

"Yes, her children are here. What's the problem?" Passion said, hardly as confident as she pretended to be.

Child services were regular visitors to Desire's home. There was always someone making reports about Desire not being a good mother. How she was a prostitute; how she was always having different men frequent the home; how her children were not safe in her care. Desire had had her children removed twice before only to have them returned to her on the condition she stop prostituting, complete her drug program and stop leaving the children home alone. Passion thought that this was about that again.

"Can we come inside?" the social worker said. "We need to see the children."

"Oh, why sure," Passion said, ready to go through the motions of proving the children were well cared for. Desire had coached her children to say that they were never ever left alone.

The woman and the police officers entered the apartment, looking around cautiously, searching for any signs of danger. They immediately took note of the untidy apartment but focused on finding the children. Desire's three children were all in the kitchen eating Captain Crunch cereal out of the box. Spilled milk and sugar was on the table and the floor.

The street savvy social worker sized Passion up in an instant. She couldn't help but admire how attractive she was. She lamented how such beauty was wasted on such a pathetic young woman who was obviously either a drug addict, a prostitute or both.

"Are you babysitting for Mrs. Cassidy?" Ms. Webber said, wondering what role, if any Passion played in the home.

"Ah, uhm yes, yes, I am," Passion said getting annoyed, nervous and wishing Desire was here. "What is this all about? Des—I mean, Ms. Cassidy is going to be home soon and she's…"

"Ms…what is your name?" the social worker said, cutting her off. "I have never seen you here before."

"I'm not giving you my name," Passion returned, getting feisty. "What the fuck is this about?" she demanded.

The social worker stooped, gave Passion a stern stare and took her aside into the living room so as not to talk in front of the children. A police officer stood by the children. The other followed the two women.

Once alone, the social worker spoke frankly. "Well, listen-Ms?

"Passion. My name is Passion."

" Well, Ms. Passion, Ms., Mrs. Cassidy won't be returning home. Her body was found burned in a dumpster early this morning; it seems she was murdered," the social worker said matter-of-factly.

The social worker's words hit Passion like a brick. Passion stood dumbfounded. She thought she had heard wrong. She started to feel light-headed and seemed about to fall back.

"Ms., I think you need to sit down," the officer said, quickly moving dirty clothes off of a nearby chair in the living room and having Passion sit down.

"Her body was found where?" Passion said, softly, her head spinning, trying to get a grip. "What did you say happened to her?"

"They found her body on Prospect Street in a dumpster. Someone had set her on fire. They are treating it as a homicide," the female officer said. "Now are you the babysitter? Do you know someone who could of done that to her? A boyfriend? Did she have a pimp? Was she prostituting again? Do you know if she had any family?"

Passion didn't hear the rest. She just sat stunned, trying to process what she was being told. Desire was found burned to death. She had been murdered. Desire was dead.

"I-I don't-don't know. No, no, she didn't have family up here. She's from the south-South Carolina," Passion spoke softly as if in a trance.

The social worker jumped in. "Well, Ms...Are you able to care for Ms. Cassidy's children?"

"I—I, me? What? No, no, I'm not their mother, just the babysitter," Passion said, in complete shock, but knowing that she was hardly in a position to care for three children.

"Well, I am going to have to take Mrs. Cassidy's children in protective custody until a resource for the children can be found. If you know of anyone who is willing to care for these children, please let me know. Here is my card with my phone number and cell number. Now please help me put clothes on these children so that I can take them downtown. There is a van waiting for us outside," Ms. Webber said in an authoritative tone.

"Of course, of course," Passion said, shaking. Passion got up as if in a trance and slowly helped the social worker with putting clothes on Desire's children. She offered no resistance to the social worker. She moved about as if she was sleepwalking. She simply did what she was being asked to do. In no short time, Passion had packed some clothes for the children, their asthma pumps, made tearful goodbyes to the children and soon the children, the police and social worker were all gone, leaving Passion sitting on the chair still in shock.

Chapter 9

Passion was sitting on the couch in Jameer's living room, tears streaming down her face. She was wearing berry-colored stretch skinny Jeans and a black halter top. Her white gold necklace and matching gold bracelet reflected the light in the apartment, causing it to dance on the ceiling. On the floor beside her was a large, thousand dollars Louis Vuitton bag filled with all her belongings. Passion stole the bag from Desire's apartment. The designer bag belonged to Desire who stole it from another prostitute who got it from Mercedes.

Jameer sat across from her, still stunned that she was in his apartment. He could see that Passion was visibly upset and shaken. He wanted to call the pastor to come to his house immediately as he didn't know if he was ready or qualified to counsel this young prostitute. He wasn't a trained counselor, like the pastor or even Mrs. Hernandez. Still, he recognized that she came to him; that she was comfortable with him and she was in need of comfort, and so he resolved to try his best.

"Here take this," he said, handing Passion a box of Marcal tissues that he had nearby on the coffee table. "Tell, tell me again what happened, Passion, and try and speak slowly," he said, softly.

Passion tried to compose herself. She made liberal use of the tissues to dry her tears and wipe her nose. She spoke carefully.

"My, my friend, Desire, she was killed…murdered, I mean. I tried to warn her. This trick she had went out with before, a crazy date came back to get her. He and his friends killed her. I-I know they did. Her, her body was found in the dumpster; she was burned to death. The-the police came to my house and social worker. They took her kids," Passion said, and then started sobbing again. Her mind kept thinking about the Bible passage she read, about burning to death for not believing in the Lord.

'I'm so sorry to hear that, Passion, so sorry, Jameer said. He had grown up in the streets and saw firsthand how prostitutes were often raped and beaten by their customers and their pimps. He knew the life that Passion was living would lead to death and destruction, a deadend. He recognized this was a wakeup call for her. "Did you go to the police?"

"No, no. I-I can't. How could they do that to her?" Passion said, "She was the nicest, sweetest person. "Why did this have to happen? She was a mother with three children," she said, searching for some kind of explanation.

"Passion, it's a terrible, terrible thing that has happened to your friend. I am so, so sorry for your loss," Jameer said leaning forward and placing his hand on Passion's shoulder. "But, Passion, why did you come here? How did you know where to find me or where I lived? Tell me, how I can help you," he said.

Passion didn't really know the answer to that question. She knew that she needed someplace to stay, first and foremost. She was homeless again.

"You, you gave me your card in this Bible and said call you for anything." Passion finally responded. "I went to that big church; the address on your card. I-I followed you home from that big church. I-I didn't feel like talking to you in that big ol' church. I want you to help me. I don't want to die, I don't want to burn!" The Bible verse was fresh in her head.

"Are you sure no one followed you here?" Jameer asked nervously, getting up and carefully peering out the windows. Jameer had pulled the shades down on all the windows when Passion arrived. He feared her pimp may have followed her to his apartment. Satisfied she wasn't followed he turned back to her.

"Passion, I want to help you. I think you came here because you are afraid and don't want what happened to your friend, to happen to you. Am I right?"

he said. "But that's what's going to happen if you don't walk away from that life. Do you understand? "

Passion continued sobbing, the image of her friend burning to death kept playing in her mind. She sat on the couch with her head down. Her eyes were trained on the hardwood floor as if the answers were hidden there.

"Passion, tell me, what is your real name, or is that your real name?" he asked.

"Yes, I mean, no, no, my real name is Dominique, but my pimp told me to never tell no one that," she said, still frightened and confused.

"Why? Is someone looking for you?" Where are your parents?" Jameer asked, softly, his voice almost a whisper.

Passion trusted Jameer, even liked him. But she still wasn't sure she could confide in him. All of a sudden she became guarded, falling back into the tangle of lies she had been trained to tell.

"My, my father…my mother and father abandoned me a long time ago, gave me up for adoption" Passion said. "I ran away from an abusive home," she continued to lie.

"Where is your mother?" Jameer asked, confused.

"I don't know," Passion lied.

Jameer was from the streets so he knew when someone was trying to play him. He knew Passion wasn't being completely honest with him. He briefly reflected on the many lies he used to tell about his family before he told the truth, afraid that someone would actually help him and afraid that they wouldn't.

"Look, Dominique, if you want me to help you, you have to be straight up with me and tell me the truth. Please," he pleaded with her softly.

Passion paused. She reflected on her life and where she's been. She didn't see the point in lying but couldn't help it; she had been doing it so long. She sat silently on the couch.

"Where are you from," Jameer asked again, framing the words delicately. "Where did you grow up? You from New York?"

Passion lifted her head to speak more clearly.

" I, I used to live in Connecticut—Danbury, Connecticut. But my parents divorced and I went to live with my mom in Stamford. But things didn't work out there; I had to leave, I was on my own. Then, then I started working the streets in New York," Passion explained.

The pastor said that he would encounter women like this in his outreach, Jameer thought to himself. "Ok, I'm so sorry. You musta been through a lot. But, don't you want to go home?" Jameer asked.

Passion shrugged her shoulders. "I'm not really ready yet," she said, secretly terrified of what her father would do if she did decide to go home.

"Can I stay here with you? I'm afraid that the same people who killed Desire will come for me," Passion said.

"You want me to help hide you from the people who killed your friend or do you want me to help you get out of this life?" Jameer asked.

"I don't know," Passion said, too sad and fearful to think.

Jameer thought carefully about what to do. He had a prostitute asking him to let her stay with him, but did she really want that or something more because she could find a place to stay anywhere or go into a woman's shelter. Would he wake up and find all his stuff stolen. He suspected she wanted more. He was confused but he couldn't see himself turning her away. He wanted to know her story but understood it would be some time before she was ready to talk. His heart went out to her. But isn't this what his outreach is all about? Jameer resolve to put his trust in God.

"Ok, ok, Dominique, You can stay here until we decide what to do. I will give you my room and I will sleep in the other bedroom. But you have to understand. I am going to also help you find a way out from the life you've chosen for yourself. That means no one coming to my apartment; no drugs and you have to be willing to attend church with me. You have to also clean up. Deal?" he said, not sure if she would be willing to accept those conditions and not sure he was doing the right thing having a prostitute living with him. A part of him wanted her to stay and say yes.

Passion thought about it, wondering if she were doing the right thing. She really believed the people who killed Desire might come after her. But she also needed somewhere to stay. Staying with Lavender wasn't an option anymore. She found Jameer nice and his place clean and spacious. No one would find her here. Not even Lavender.

"Ok, we have a deal," Passion finally said.

CHAPTER 10

Jameer masterfully poured the pancake batter into the frying pan, watching it form a perfect circle. He lowered the flame under the frying pain, just a bit, seeing as how the pancake batter was heating up too quickly. The batter needed to cook thoroughly, he was taught by his adopted mother. When the bottom was golden brown, Jameer didn't hesitate to flip it over for the other side to cook before tossing it on top of the other pancakes resting on a plate on the counter. His adopted mother would've been proud.

Jameer was in deep thought. He wrestled with telling his pastor that he had a prostitute staying with him but even after three weeks, he couldn't bring himself to do it. He didn't exactly know why either. He liked to think that he was preparing her to meet the pastor and didn't want to scare her off. He also liked to believe he was protecting her from her pimp who was probably out looking for her and from whoever killed her friend. He knew there was another reason that was closer to the truth.

Jameer finished stacking four golden brown, banana pancakes on a plate, now ready to serve. Pouring hot coffee in a cup, he put the plates on a tray and headed toward the bedroom, where Dominique was fast asleep.

In the bedroom, Passion's smartphone threatened to fall off the nightstand as its incessant vibrating marched it closer to the edge. Passion slept soundlessly, ignoring the phone calls and text messages she knew were coming from Mercedes or Lavender.

For the past few weeks, she was basking in the comfort of Jameer's queen-sized tempur Pedic bed and the soft oversized cobalt blue comforter. She welcomed this break from going out on the stroll, night after night. Without the benefit of coffee, red bulls, Mollys, ecstasy, cocaine and other natural and unnatural stimulants beating back the sleep and keeping her up through the night, Passion's body was finally able to go through a normal sleep cycle. This was a much needed break, a vacation of sorts, from the streets, Passion thought to herself. Still the fear of facing Lavender's wrath for running off remained ever-present in her mind. The thought of him finding her was real. The last girl who ran away caught a vicious beat down from Lavender that had her in the hospital for weeks.

"Dominique, I have some breakfast for you," said Jameer, standing on the bedroom threshold, holding a tray in one hand and holding the door open with another. "I thought you might be hungry. Its 7 o'clock and I have to go to work. Let me put this on the nightstand for you," he said. Jameer put the tray of food which consisted of the pancakes, a side of scrambled eggs and over cooked sausage, with a cup of coffee on the nightstand near her incessantly vibrating smartphone.

"Hey, good morning," Passion breathed lazily as she roused herself from sleep. The sight of the food on the tray, reminded her that she was hungry. She pulled the comforter over her bare chest.

"All right Dom, I'm headed out. See you when I get back; if you gotta leave, please call me," Jameer said as he headed out the door, hoping that everything would be in his apartment when he came back.

Passion barely said goodbye before feasting on the breakfast. Once finished, she fell back to sleep.

Hours later, Passion sat up in her bed. She looked around the bedroom. She wondered how long she could stay here. She didn't know if she could get used to this. It was too much to get used to. She went back to sleep.

"Hey, wake up! Wake up!" Jameer said as he gently prodded Passion from her slumber. "Its 5:45pm. You been sleeping all day?" Jameer said, surprised to see that nothing appeared missing in his apartment. Even more surprised to see Passion still here.

"Oh, damn. I been sleeping all day." Passion said. "Gotta get up. Sorry."

So it was, day after day, Jameer would come home to find Passion fast asleep in his bed, getting up only to eat the breakfast he made for her and to wash her clothes. He couldn't help but check to make sure nothing was missing or stolen. He didn't really know this woman who he allowed to stay with him, other than she used to work the streets. He wondered if he were doing the right thing.

Then one day, Jameer came home to find Passion sitting, lotus-style in the living room, writing in her diary. She was wearing one of Jameer's robes over light blue spandex pants and one of his white t-shirts.

The smell of cooked food tickled his nose.

"How is it going? Dominique? What you been up to?" Jameer said, pleasantly surprised to know she had taken the time to cook.

"Nothing, just chillin'," Passion casually returned. "There's some baked chicken in the oven and white rice on the stove," she said just as casually. "How was your work or job? Or whatever you do?" she said, eyeing Jameer's Local One union shirt.

Jameer walked into the kitchen and looked in the oven and saw a tray of chicken wings, sautéed with onions.

"Wash your hands!" Passion shouted.

"It was crazy; we're rewiring this office space so they could install more computers," Jameer said, remembering how cantankerous and demanding the office managers are. He looked at the food Passion had prepared. "You didn't have to cook. But, it looks good. I'm hungry, too. Are you going to join me?" Jameer said as he went into the bathroom to wash his hands, eager to get back and taste her cooking.

"Sure, cool," Passion said, putting her diary away. She quickly got up and going in the small kitchen, setting the table with plates for dinner.

Jameer watched as Dominique deftly set the table with forks and knives in their rightful place. She set a bowl of salad in the middle of the table and poured glasses of water for the both of them. Jameer marveled at her skill and knew that she came from something better than how she turned out. He was dying to hear her story again. Since she arrived, she hasn't spoken about her past and he hadn't pressed her about it.

"When did you learn how to cook, didn't know you knew how to throw-down," Jameer said, as he sat down at the table across from Passion. "Who taught you?" he said, looking for some way to get to know about her past.

"I was bored. Nothing to do and I knew you would be hungry when you came home. My mother taught me how to cook," Passion said. "We used to cook for each other."

Passion sat down across from Jameer. He couldn't help but marvel at Passion's natural beauty, her hair wrapped in a simple head wrap and no makeup.

"What's wrong?" Passion said, often unaware of how her beauty affected men.

"Nothing. Nothing. So what happened to your mother, Dominique?" Jameer ventured, as he watched Passion prepare his plate. Passion served him first then made a plate for herself and prepared to eat.

Passion paused before beginning. Once she took her seat, she started talking. "The police raided her house and she and her boyfriend were locked up for selling drugs, "she said matter of factly.

"I'm sorry. I'm really sorry. Is that why you got into working the streets, to support yourself?" Jameer asked, probing carefully not wanting her to shut down by asking too many questions.

Passion sighed but was glad to recount her past. It felt good being able to talk about it. It reminded her how she used to talk to the law guardian about the pain of her parent's divorce so many years ago.

"No, I don't know. Maybe. In high school. I fell into the wrong crowd, I guess, because I just wanted to fit in. I grew up an only child in a big house. My father was a sheriff and my mother was an investment banker. I was pretty spoiled. I went to private schools.

"Oh wow! That's cool," Jameer said, with a mouthful of food.

"When my mother and father divorced, I was devastated. I mean it really hurt me. It was the worst day of my life. I wanted to die. It was the worst day of my life. My father got custody of me but I wrote the judge when I was 12 asking to be with my mother. When I went to live with my mom, she took me out of private school and put me in a public high school so she could use the extra money to support her drug habit. I used to watch her do cocaine in the morning at breakfast.

"A lot of the kids I started hanging out with in high school taught me how to hold my liquor down, smoking weed and doing other stuff."

"What 'other stuff?' Jameer asked, digging into the chicken Dominique cooked, amazed at how easily it slid off the bone, savoring its taste.

Passion remained silent. Jameer didn't press her.

"I just started messing up in school and everything. I was failing everything. My mother didn't really care. I wanted her to care.

"She was always too busy working and doing drugs and being with David, her drug dealing boyfriend. She didn't care about me," she said, casually, a tear coming down her face.

"After I caught my mother sniffing coke in the bathroom, she didn't bother to hide it from me anymore. She said that she wasn't a drug addict but that she needed the boost it gave her to help her deal with the pressures of being a black woman working in the white man's corporate world. Then I met Clarence, CJ," she said.

"Who is Clarence?" Jameer asked, thinking that was her pimp.

"He was my boyfriend, in my sophomore year of high school. Everybody called him CJ. He was very popular. He liked me. When I was with him, I felt like I was on top of the world," Passion said, smiling in remembrance of that time, not so long ago.

"He was the coolest guy in school. Everybody was jealous of me. We started hanging out, cutting class and everything. He was buying me new clothes, taking me out to dinner in nice restaurants, making appointments for me to get my hair done, treating me to manicures, anything I wanted. I swear I was in love. He was my first; he took my virginity. I was drunk, I think, so I don't really remember too much, only that it was painful. I was fifteen. I didn't care because I was in love, you know."

"He was older," Jameer inquired, somewhat fatherly.

"Yeah, he was. He had dropped out of school a while ago and was a hustler. I swear I loved CJ. He was my world," Passion's demeanor and voice was more serious, more reflective.

"Then when the police raided my mother's apartment and she got arrested, her and her boyfriend, David, they put me in foster care until they could reach my father to come and get me. But I didn't want to leave CJ. I knew my father wouldn't approve of him. I texted CJ where I was, what foster home they had put me in and he came and got me. I left that place with him," she said. "We lived out of hotels and stayed with friends and family after that."

"What about your father?" Jameer asked.

"I wrote him a letter, told him that I was all right. I heard he was looking for me. It was just me and CJ, staying with his mother and then his aunt. They all liked me. It wasn't a problem.

"But after a while, the money I saved that my mother gave me ran out and we had no money to buy CJ the clothes he wanted. CJ couldn't find a job cause he had a record....I was thinking he was my boyfriend, thinking he loved me," she paused. "Then one day, he punched me in the face so hard, as hard as he could. And he said, 'you're gonna make my money.' I did it because I loved him, I guess."

"He started having you make money for him?" Jameer asked.

"No, I mean, yeah, I guess, He used to get me high and began bringing me to the homes of his friends, made me have sex with them. I gave him the money. I couldn't do it unless I was drunk or high but after a while, I just did it because that's what Clarence wanted. I got used to it.

"Then he made me work the streets, to go after older men in expensive cars because they would pay more money to be with me," she went on, reflecting back, her voice almost a monotone.

"How did that make you feel, turning tricks like that? How old were you," Jameer said, fascinated by her story, wanting to hold her and squeeze the pain out of her.

"I had just turned 16 or 17 when I started doing all that," Passion said. "I didn't care, though. I just wanted to be with CJ. He always made me laugh. Whatever he wanted me to do, I did it, basically," she said regretfully.

Jameer listened to Passion with rapt interest, relating back to his own troubled past.

"I feel for you," Jameer said. "I'm so sorry you had to go through that," he said empathizing with her plight. "And what you are still going through."

Passion smiled.

"So you're boyfriend, Clarence or CJ, is that who's making you go out and sell yourself? Is he your pimp?" Jameer asked.

"No, no, not anymore," Passion said softly.

'Not anymore?" Jameer said, perplexed.

"No, not anymore," Passion said, exhausted. "CJ started owing the pimp I have now a lot of money, money he used to buy drugs with so we could get high; so the only way he could pay him back was to give me to him; he told me I had to go with him and work off the money he owed. He said that it would only be for a little while and then he would come back for me. He is the one who brought me here to New York City. Then after a few weeks, CJ called and broke it off with me, saying that he couldn't have another pimp's girl for a girlfriend. I never saw CJ again after that. He broke my heart," Passion said, letting the tears flow down her face unchecked.

"I'm so sorry, Dominique," Jameer said, holding her hand gently across the table.

"It's all right. No, really. I heard Clarence was caught trying to hold up a gas station or something," Passion said with a careless, painful laugh, wiping her face of tears.

"Oh wow...What's his name?" Jameer asked,

"Who's name?" Passion asked, getting up to clear the table.

"The pimp you're with now—what's his name?" he said.

Passion paused. "I can't tell you his name," she said, putting the plates in the kitchen sink and then wiping the table with a damp rag.

"Are you protecting him?" Jameer said confused.

Passion paused again. "No, I just can't tell you his name, that's all." she returned. "I can't."

Jameer was taken aback that after sharing everything else, she wouldn't give up the name of her pimp. Jameer looked at Passion's neck and the elaborate lavender-colored tattoo, trying to decipher the tattoo graffiti but failing miserably. He decided not to press the issue.

"Did he give you that chain and bracelet? It looks expensive," Jameer asked, knowing that Passion couldn't afford it doing legal work.

Passion looked down at the white gold chain on her neck. She touched it softly as if it were something precious.

"Yeah, it was a gift," she said, remembering the time Lavender gave it to her when she started working for him. No one had ever given her something so expensive, not even CJ. "He gave it to me for my birthday," Passion said, "after he beat my ass for trying to run away."

"Oh my God! What about your father?" Jameer asked.

Passion paused. "What about him. He might be looking for me, I guess," she said. "I don't think so. It's been a long time. I haven't seen him since I was fourteen. He probably thinks I'm dead," Passion said, knowing that that wasn't true.

"But didn't you say that he was coming to get you when they put you in foster care? Don't you want to see him again?" Jameer asked, confused why this girl was working the streets.

"I don't know; I never thought about it," she said. "I don't want to talk about this anymore. I'm tired. Now you know everything about me. I'm goin' to bed. I need some rest." Passion retired to the bedroom. Jameer went to finish cleaning up the kitchen.

Over the next few days, Jameer and Passion grew closer. Jameer would prepare breakfast before going off to work in the morning. Passion would prepare something to eat when he came home in the evenings or they would order Chinese takeout. They would sit and talk about their lives over dinner and share their hopes and dreams. Jameer couldn't remember ever being so eager to get home from work. It was inconceivable to him that he might be falling in love again. But he was.

At night, with Jameer's gentle urging Passion got into the habit of studying the Bible. They read the Scriptures together on the mahogany coffee table in the living, from his gilded Bible.

"Jesus, asked them if any were without sin, they should throw the first stone at her," Jameer read out loud from his Bible. "When none of the men would throw the stone to condemn her, the Christ forgave the prostitute of her sins, and told her to go and sin no more.'

"I remember this story when my father used to take me to Sunday school," Passion said. "I never could understand why the men wanted to throw stones at the woman."

"Because they thought they were better than her. They were self-righteous. But the Bible says, 'For all have sinned and fallen short of the glory of God," Jameer explained.

"But I haven't hurt anyone," Passion said. "How have I sinned?"

"We must honor our bodies, Dom. You allow men to use your body, to take advantage of you; you are being used by your pimp to make money. We must respect our own bodies in holiness and honor; for every other sin we commit, like stealing and killing is outside the body but having sex for money is a sin against our own body," Jameer tried to explain.

"Those who continue to sin and not acknowledge God as their Lord and Savior would die from fire in the second death," he said. "But the Bible offers hope. Look read here," Jameer said, flipping the Book to the Scripture and handing it to Passion.

She took it and read, haltingly, "For God so loved the world that he gave his only begotten Son, that whoever believes in Him shall not perish but have eternal life."

Passion wrestled with what Jameer was telling her. She thought about Desire and felt sad, believing that she died without ever knowing God. She felt like she didn't want that to happen to her.

"How, how can I get to Heaven and not burn," Passion asked like a little girl asking for directions to the candy store.

Jameer smiled, glad that she wanted to go to Heaven, that she wanted to be saved. "In order to make it to heaven, Dominique, you gotta turn away from your sins and accept Jesus Christ as your personal Saviour," Jameer said. "If we confess our sins, the Bible says that he is faithful and just to forgive us our sins and to cleanse us from all unrighteousness," said Jameer, having committed that passage to memory.

"Oh, is that what you did?" Passion asked, playfully.

"I'm still doing it," he said. "I do it every day."

Passion smiled and snuggled up to Jameer, placing her head on his shoulder, letting a smile form on her face. She put the Bible down.

"You make me feel safe, Jameer," she said, also locking her arm under his.

"That's enough for tonight, Dom," he said trying to hide his feelings for her. "Let's shut it down, Good night, D. I see you in the morning, alright?"

"Ok," Passion said, and they turned in for the night.

Jameer felt like he was really making a difference in Dominique's life by keeping her off the streets and teaching her about the Bible. He would still go out at night with the outreach ministry but he didn't tell anyone either that he was sheltering a prostitute. But at the right time he told himself he would. Being there for Dominique was more important now.

For Passion, it had been a long time since she had received such treatment and attention from a man without having to provide sexual services in return. She deeply appreciated it. She wondered if it was real.

"Do you have a girlfriend?" Passion asked Jameer as she sat in the living room the next night playing with her hair. "All I see you do is go to work and go to church and talk about God. Don't you have a girlfriend? You too cute not to have somebody."

Jameer smiled. "I am devoted to following the Lord."

"Well, I hope the Lord is devoted to keeping you satisfied," Passion said. Passion suddenly had a thought

"I want to go out with you and your group," Passion said,

"You mean the outreach group? Are you sure, Dom? It's pretty intense." Jameer said, surprised by her request. "Are you ready for that? I thought you were afraid and hiding from your pimp and the people you killed your friend."

"I want to," she begged. "Please. I feel I have to. I want to be like you. I never met anyone like you before."

Passion was grateful to Jameer for his kindness and generosity. She wanted to show him how much she appreciated what he had done for her and what she learned. "Besides, I know a lot of the girls working the streets. They will listen to me," she said.

"Ok, ok!" Jameer smiled. "If you really want to."

It was a late, bitter cold, Thursday night, when Jameer and Passion joined the street ministry. Mrs. Hernandez and the other group members were standing on the corner waiting for them when they saw the two of them approaching. They were encouraged to see Passion joining them. It made them believe their work was not in vain. "Nice to meet you," Mrs. Hernandez said to Passion, her words a cloud of moisture in the cold air. "You make our work that much meaningful." Mrs. Hernandez had so many questions but decided this wasn't the time. "Let's get going shall we?" she said.

In no time, the group ventured out in the winter night before they encountered Renee, a well-known crack addicted prostitute on the tracks. She was Passion's old friend.

"Hi, Renee!" Passion said, her warm breath forming a cloud in the cold air. She gave her friend her a hug. "Hey, you lookin' good. How are you? Here you go, Renee," Passion said, handing a care package to the rail thin prostitute she used to work with. 'I know you going to need those wipes," Passion said jokingly.

"Where you been, girl? Haven't seen you in a long time," the prostitute inquired. "People been lookin' for yo ass. You aight! You wit another pimp."

"I been taking a break," Passion said. "But no, truth is, I'm not doing this no more. Listen to these people, Renee, there is a better way, a better life than this," Passion said. "And I know it's hard but I wouldn't want to see what happened to our friend Desire, happen to you."

"What? Girl, I hear you and I'm happy for you but this is the only life I know," the 32-years-old prostitute said, her butt cheeks and thighs exposed in the cold night. "I been doing this since I was 16 years old, that's half my life. I thank you though for this, and I'm glad for you, if all of that is true, but I got to get my hustle on before my man beats my ass."

"But let us pray for you, Renee," interjected Mrs. Hernandez. "Is that all right?"

Renee was taken aback by the unusual request. She didn't even know these people. Still she didn't see no harm in it.

"Ok but make it quick, cuz my ole man is watchin' and your praying ain't goin' to put no money in my pockets," Renee said.

The group said a short prayer for the drug addicted prostitute before they allowed her to move on. Passion felt dejected, sad that she couldn't convince her friend to listen to her.

"C'mon Dominique," Jameer said, "We have to keep trying until we find one who will listen, but you being out here means a lot."

"I know, I know but I'm afraid for them, they are my friends. I love them." Passion said, tears coming down her face.

The outreach group walked with Passion through the "Zone" corridor, ministering to the prostitutes working the streets. Many of the prostitutes came up to Passion when they saw her, to give her a hug and a smile, happy to see she was alive and well, but then walked away when they saw and heard her message and how she was trying to get them off the streets. Passion couldn't help feeling torn, wanting to go back to the life she left behind and with her friends on the streets, and the money she was making but then she thought about what happened to Desire and knew she had made the right decision.

⚓

That night, Passion was tossing and turning, caught in the throes of a terrible nightmare. She soon let out a gut wrenching scream that could be heard throughout the small apartment. Jameer woke up in the middle of the night, roused by her scream. He ran to be by Passion's side. Busting into the bedroom, shirtless, he could see Passion wrestling in bed with herself, as if fighting off an invisible assailant. He tried to comfort her.

"Dominique, Dominique, wake up! Wake up!" Jameer said trying to wake her from her nightmare.

"Dominique, you're having a nightmare," he said, clutching her. Passion woke up suddenly in Jameer's arms. She was sweating profusely. Her clothes were damp. She was in a fearful and confused state. She was caught in rapid breaths. She couldn't stop shaking.

"Help me, help me!" she said before finally opening her eyes and calming down.

"It's alright. It's alright, Dominique," Jameer said, as he held her tightly in his arms. Passion's eyes were darting wildly as she tried to adjust to waking up from her nightmare. She was still disoriented as to time and place but, she finally came to her senses. She found Jameer staring in her eyes. His concerned, kind face calming her down.

"You musta been having some kind of dream," Jameer said.

"I-I had a dream...I was burning," Passion said, between deep breaths. "I had a dream that those guys who killed Desire had come back for me. They forced me in their car and wanted to burn me up, set me on fire," Dominique said, frightened and still dripping wet with perspiration. "They were pouring gasoline on me, all over me," she said, tears coming down her face, and trembling.

"It's gonna be alright, Dominique," Jameer said in an effort to reassure her. He held her close to him in his muscular arms. "It's going to be all right; it was just a dream. No one is gonna hurt you," he said. "No one is gonna hurt you,"

"Please, hold me and don't let me go," Passion said, as she buried her head Jameer's barrel chest.

"I won't," Jameer said. "I won't." Jameer gently held Passion in his arms; it was something he had unconsciously wanted to do from the moment he laid eyes on her.

Then without warning, Passion grabbed Jameer's face and started kissing him uncontrollably, peppering him with moist kisses. Jameer was taken aback and pulled away.

"Oh, I'm sorry..." Passion said. "I didn't mean..."

But before she could finish, Jameer held Passion's face, studied her, and said, "It's all right. I mean, I..." He kissed her gently on the lips, at first slowly, then more purposely, deliberately. Passion hesitated at first and then returned his advances, welcomed it and locked lips with Jameer in kind. Wrapping their arms around each other, Passion and Jameer surrendered to their longing.

Jameer hadn't been with a woman ever since he started working in the community and with the church, having made up his mind to dedicate himself to serving the church and becoming a deacon. He didn't want the distraction a relationship would cause. But from the first moment he saw Passion, there in the food pantry, he was attracted to her, sensing in her a kindred spirit. He wanted her and not in an empty, sexual way but in a real way, completely, body and soul. As he caressed and embraced Passion now, Jameer savored every moment of what he was so afraid to express. He was a dam of pent up sexual energy finally finding release. He felt his desire for her busting through the wall of poise and reserve he had built up for so long, flooding Passion with all his emotional longing. He was overcome with desire for her.

He ravenously traced Passion's neck with his tongue, planting hundreds of soft kisses all over her, like a kid teasingly relishing his favorite dessert. He cupped her breasts softly, enjoying their supple firmness. Moving down Passion's body, touching and petting every curve, arch and bend, from head to toe, and ever so tenderly.

Their hands met separating into each other's fingers, meshing together into a closed fist.

For Passion, making love to a man was a welcome almost forgotten experience from the endless series of empty, detached sexual encounters, she had grown accustomed to over the years. She had long learned to separate her feelings and emotions when having sex with clients and johns, usually with the help of drugs and alcohol she got from her pimp or Mercedes. Now, with this man, Passion was free to make love without reservation, without pretense, letting her emotions flow unchecked. She felt his desire for her and basked in it.

Jameer slowly stripped Passion of her clothes. She just as quickly removed his pajama pants. Their clothes found the floor, coming to rest into a careless pile. In their nakedness, they continued to probe each other's mouth with their tongues, pouring themselves into each other with an unquenchable craving. They continued tonguing each other down as Passion slowly positioned her body on the bed, ready for him. Jameer climbed on top of her, ready to claim his prize. He caressed the soft flesh of her thighs. Passion then jerked from him penetrating her, feeling him inside her, spreading her wide. Jameer continued to kiss Passion, and gently teased her nipples to full hardness. Jameer pleasured Passion with long, strong deep strokes. With her legs wrapped tight around him tightly, they were in the throes of ecstasy.

"Ooooh, don't stop! Please don't stop." Passion purred. Enjoying his raw power. Then Passion rolled over, positioning herself on top.

Now straddling Jameer, Passion was riding his manhood. Moaning with pleasure and desire, she buried her nails greedily into his chest, tossing her head back in frenzied delight, relishing him impaling her with his desire, with careful measured strokes, repeatedly, forcefully with a rhythmic, lustful zeal. Passion's body was a sensual instrument and he manipulated it masterfully. Their bodies were joined in a single rhythm. They continued making love, bringing each other to climax again and again. Jameer suddenly screamed loud, caught in a convulsion of pleasure. He was fully spent. Passion's fell forward her sweat drenched arms and body into his. Their sweat soaked bodies were tangled in a love embrace. Their faces were flushed. They fell asleep in each other's sweaty embrace, finally exhausted by their love making.

Chapter 11

Summer in the city brought a flood of new and former prostitutes out on the streets. Casual street walkers, women who didn't normally make a living out of selling their bodies but suddenly desperate to make ends meet, came out in an effort to hustle up money.

Lavender's women dressed provocatively in keeping with the warm weather. Wearing camisoles and fishnet stockings, thongs and daisy dukes and miniskirts, the women lured many more men into quickie sexual encounters, even men who would never think to patronize a prostitute, but found the temptation too much to resist.

The outreach ministry found their hands full trying to engage the dozens of prostitutes who lined the streets. But they were more than up for the challenge, spurred by a desire to spread the Word. Mrs. Hernandez dutifully led the outreach ministry this night to preach to the prostitutes. With Mrs. Hernandez were Deacons Jerome Williams and Deacon Margaret Smith, some carrying Bibles, others, care packages.

Two new church members to the group were Mrs. Sharon Walters and Derrick Strong. Mrs. Walters was a single mother of three who helped her own teenage daughter overcome drug addiction. She felt she could help reach some of the young women who are also supporting a habit by selling their bodies.

Mr. Strong was an engaging man in his early thirties. He was well known for being involved in every church activity and function, from teaching

Sunday school to organizing cake sales to raising money for the senior members. So it was when Brother Strong heard about the street ministry, he knew he had to be a part of it. Brother Strong craved excitement, above all else, wherever he could find it, and in his mind, what could be more exciting than a street ministry. He really didn't know what to expect but couldn't imagine passing up the experience reaching out to prostitutes.

Mrs. Hernandez had reservations about allowing Brother Strong to join the outreach ministry. She knew all about Strong's activities in the church but always thought his motives weren't pure, that they didn't come from a genuine place. Still, she couldn't see turning him down when he volunteered to go out with the group. After all, he was a man and they needed all the help they could get walking these dangerous streets at night.

Darkness painted the night black as the group walked the streets together at about two o' clock in the morning. Among the working women was Mercedes who stood out from the other prostitutes, sporting gold colored platform pumps with red bottoms heels, gold, hip- hugging hot pants, putting her ample butt cheeks on display. She also wore a black transparent top, showing off much cleavage and breasts.

"Man, the women are working tonight," said Strong, his eyes wide as saucers, gawking at all the enticing, partially nude women displaying themselves shamelessly in the street. He had never seen anything like this before. Strong's wife always had him in the house by 10pm, unless he was working late, which wasn't often. He was a carpenter by trade.

"The summer always brings out the most prostitutes. I remember when I was out here. I usually made the most money during the summer," said Mrs. Hernandez reflecting on her sordid past.

"What made you turn away from this life," asked Mrs. Walters, herself a member of the church choir and school teacher.

"Seeing my daughter growing up without me because I was too strung out on drugs made me decide to turn my life around. That and the church," Mrs. Hernandez replied, matter-of-factly.

"She looks like a model," blurted out Brother Strong staring unabashedly at Mercedes in the distance, her full bosom and partial nudity arousing him.

Mr. Strong was quietly happy that he made the decision to join the street ministry, hoping it would provide him with the excitement he craved. He wasn't disappointed.

"It's a shame that she is so beautiful and selling herself, selling her body out here on the street," remarked Ms. Hernandez. "Maybe we can reach her. Let's try, anyway," she said.

Following Mrs. Hernandez lead, the group approached the buxom Mercedes, their first prostitute of the night.

"Hi, there can we talk to you?" said Mrs. Hernandez politely. My name is Judy and we are with Grace Baptist church. What's your name?"

Mercedes looked with disdain on the group. She had heard about the outreach ministry, simple church folk, going out at night and trying to talk street prostitutes into giving up their lifestyle and turning to God. She found it amusing. She remembered how much she hated when her aunt used to drag her to church by her aunt but found church people to be the biggest hypocrites. She remembered how often her aunt's church-going boyfriend went to church then come to her room late in the night looking for fun. She reflected how much money she made off of him.

"My name is Mercedes. But listen, I'm working. What the fuck do you want? My time is money," Mercedes shot back her voice dripping with attitude.

"We just want to give you this," Mrs. Hernandez said, holding out a care package for Mercedes. "You probably were out here a long time. It's just some things you might use, toiletries, you know, things. Condoms. Clean syringes. Do you have a pimp? Is he making you do this? Are you supporting a drug habit?" Mrs. Hernandez politely asked.

"Listen, bitch, this is none of your business. I'm working, ok. I'm trying to pay for my college tuition, if you really want to know. I probably make more in one night than you make in a month. Please step off. Get away from me," Mercedes said, dismissively, refusing to accept the care package as well and turning her back on the group.

Mrs. Hernandez wouldn't back down though. "Ms., I don't doubt that you make a lot of money. I used to do what you're doing. If you want to know. But this isn't the way you want to live. You are a beautiful, beautiful woman.

You're body and beauty is a gift from God. This isn't what it was intended for," Mrs. Hernandez pleaded. "I mean, you don't have to live like this. We want to help you make a change for the better."

Mercedes looked Mrs. Hernandez up and down contemptuously. She wanted to curse her out but didn't think she was worth her time. Instead, she scrutinized the other people in the group, especially the men. She noticed how Brother Strong, in particular, was, ogling her body. She instinctively knew when she had a catch. In an effort to prove Mrs. Hernandez and the group the hypocrites that she believed them to be, Mercedes moved closer to Brother Strong, full of crafty intent.

"Tell me, handsome, what you think my body was intended for?" she asked the young man, a devilish smirk on her face.

"It's-its f-for…" Brother Strong started to stammering, finding himself all excited by Mercedes and embarrassed by the attention she was suddenly giving him, in front of the group.

"Do you like that, mister?" She asked all seductively. "I like you; you're not as stuffy as your friends, let's go someplace where you could tell me what my body is intended for."

Mrs. Hernandez quickly jumped to stand between them.

"Don't try and mess with the members of my group, young lady. We are not here for that. We are trying to save you. Move away from him!" Mrs. Hernandez demanded, suddenly losing her composure.

"Ok, whateva," Mercedes said, stopping and casually walking away from Brother Srong. She didn't have time for this. She continued walking down the block.

However, Bother Strong couldn't let the fashionable prostitute go. Lust had taken a hold of him. He was excited. He was weak. He couldn't resist Mercedes' subtle charms. He was shaking, hungry with desire. He tried to think of his wife but couldn't keep his eyes off of Mercedes exposed body. She had seduced him with her smooth talk and her curves.

"I-I'm just going-going to talk to her, ok?" he said to the group to their astonishment. "I'm going to just talk to her," he said, following after Mercedes as she kept walking away. "Maybe she just needs to just talk one on one, not having all of us up in her face. Y'know--I-I will be back," Mr. Strong said, all in a pathetic tone of voice.

"Hey, hey, hold up," Brother Strong shouted to Mercedes, who was more than a few feet away.

Mercedes turned back to see the strapping man calling for her. She smiled a wicked smile. She knew what he wanted but kept walking, slowing only to allow him to catch her.

"C'mon handsome, I have my own place. There's no pimp there. You betta have money on you too, otherwise, you can't touch this," she said laughing wickedly.

Mercedes and Brother Strong walked away together leaving the outreach group, standing on the corner dumbfounded. They soon disappeared in the darkness.

"I can't believe it. Aren't we going to stop him?" asked Mrs. Walters. He's after that prostitute."

"Brother Strong has to make that choice for himself. I hope that he will just talk to her and nothing else. He's a grown man. What more can I say? We have other prostitutes to try and reach," Mrs. Hernandez said. "Come let's go."

The outreach ministry group continued on down the dark street, one less member.

⋏

Mercedes brought Brother Strong to the crash pad all the prostitutes used for johns who didn't have their own car or weren't driving. The crash pad was a vacant studio apartment located in an old three story building not too far from the "the zone," 1385 Prospect Street apartment 1B. Lavender had long made a deal with the building super to allow his girls to make use of the vacant apartment to turn tricks. In return, Lavender would pay the super "rent" for use of the space and to clean it up every now and then, what with all the used condoms and drug paraphernalia his girls were known to leave behind. The building super, a Mexican man with five children and a wife, was more than happy to oblige as long as he made a little extra cash on the side to help take care of his family.

"Is this where you live?" asked Mr. Strong, as he entered the dirty, studio apartment. The floor was littered with used condoms. It was furnished with only a dirty, old couch, small stove in the corner and a sheetless queen sized mattress with box spring that looked like it was hauled off the street. A fetid odor hung in the air, the stench of illicit drugs.

At this very moment, Brother Strong wanted to turn around and go back to the group he left behind, disgusted by the dirty apartment, but he was still under Mercedes' spell and was unable to resist the lust in his veins for her.

"Yes, boo," Mercedes lied. "This is my crib. You like?" she smiled, giddy about her own deception.

"You really need to change your life, Ms. Mercedes. This is no way to live." he said, while staring blatantly down at Mercedes' cleavage and trembling with desire.

Mercedes turned around to lock the door behind them. "Oh, really, and how are you going to help me to do that?" she said. Mercedes started undressing in front of the man now, taking off her top, exposing her enlarged breasts. "C'mon big man, show me how you are going to do that," she said playfully.

Brother Derrick Strong was overcome with craving and seeing Mercedes bare breasts and piercings on her belly button and nipples and, he quickly grabbed her by the waist and put his mouth to her nipples, sucking down hard.

Mercedes basked in her seductive power. She put her hand to the man's crotch, unzipped his fly and seizing on his engorged member, stroked him effortlessly to a full erection.

"Hmmm, this isn't going to help me change, that's for sure," Mercedes said teasingly, delighted by the man's size, laughing a wicked laugh. "Where's my money, by the way?" Mercedes said suddenly, pushing the man away from her, escaping his embrace and putting her hand out.

Trembling and anxious, Mr. Strong reached inside his wallet and pulled out a wad of twenty dollar bills, three hundred dollars in all; the money he had put aside for the light bill. He had never been with a prostitute before and was eager to be initiated into the experience.

Mercedes took the money, counted it quickly and squirreled it away in her Gucci bag.

"Ok, this is enough for a blow job," she said. "Are you ready for me?" she asked as she knelt down. "C'mon, then and hurry your horny ass up!"

Chapter 12

"Tell me about this pastor at your church you want me to meet," Passion said, while brushing her hair in the mirror in the bathroom of Jameer's apartment. Passion had been living with Jameer for several months now and they were living as a couple. Jameer was sitting in the living room, pouring over his Bible. It was late at night.

Jameer was more than happy to oblige Passion in telling her about Pastor Emerson.

"Well, he's the reason I'm here and not out on the street somewhere dead or in jail, him and my godmother Mabel," he said with a smile on his face, putting his Bible down. "They helped save me. They brought me to my Lord and savior. I was a crazy, troubled kid who ended up in a group home, not listening to my mother, just angry at the world.

"The pastor and his wife used to come to my house and talk to me. I was lost and angry and needed hope, something to believe in."

"You were in a group home? In foster care?" Passion said, incredulously, totally captivated now.

"Yeah, but my Godmother finally came for me and adopted me. She's the one that brought me to church. She told me that I could do much better for myself and not let my past determine my future. The pastor started telling me that he could see a bright future for me, and everything, but that I had to see one for myself. My godmother always told me that.

"His wife, Mrs. Emerson, was a beautiful, smart woman; she held my hand and made me promise that I wouldn't end up like other kids in foster care, dead or in prison. She was a really good person. They really changed my life, the both of them. They made me want better for myself. I had never had anyone pray for me, and they did that. This is the Bible they gave me," Jameer said, showing the black, gold trimmed Bible he was reading. "I never leave the house without it. That was eight years ago. I was 16 then."

"You said that his wife was a pretty woman?" Passion said, joining Jameer on the couch, locking her arms with his. She was wearing a sleeveless tee and tight gray shorts, her legs folded into the couch.

"Yes, she was a beautiful person, inside and out," Jameer reminisced. "The pastor's wife, God bless her soul, died about four years ago in a terrible car accident. The pastor was driving and lost control of the car. He was messed up over it for a while, was on leave from the church. When he did come back he had stopped doing outreach programs, which he and his wife used to do together. When I joined the church, I took up leading the outreach ministry programs for the church."

"And so that's how you met me." Passion said with a seductive smile. "So what were you doing in the food pantry? You work there?"

"No, I went to electrician school on a grant I got while I was in foster care. The food pantry was one of the outreach programs I helped lead to help poor families in the community, or whatever." Jameer said.

Passion smiled. She had never met anyone like Jameer, someone so concerned with helping others. She admired him like no other man she had ever met. She thought how her father would like him.

"So this pastor is supposed to save me like he saved you, huh?" Passion asked, a twinkle in her eye.

"I believe he can help, if you let him. But you have to save yourself and you are doing that. He's a really good man and has worked miracles in this community. God moves through him. I really believe that," he said.

"You do, huh? Well, I can't wait to meet him then," Passion said, smiling broadly and even more seductively.

"Well, this Sunday is communion, but first we have to buy you some clothes." Jameer said, smiling back at Passion.

"Of course," Passion said, then jumped up into Jameer's arms, planting a huge wet kiss on his cheek. "Whatever you want, baby," she said coyly.

CHAPTER 13

M ercedes arrived at Lincoln Hospital's Recovery Room walking with deliberate speed. She hid her face behind black Ray Ban Wayfarer shades. Her hair was dyed blood red and she had matching red Louboutin pumps. Peaches' Gucci bag and a bunch of her clothes in a large Nordstrom's shopping bag hung from her shoulder. After obtaining her visitor's pass, Mercedes marched past the charge nurse and nurse's station and into the room where Peaches was recovering from her injury.

Mercedes found Peaches lying in her bed, staring blankly at the flat screen television mounted high on the wall. A small mound of gauze pads covered the entire left side of Peaches' face where the bullet lodged. Her mouth was stuffed with cotton pads to stem the incessant bleeding. The bandages did little to hide the enormous swelling on that side of Peaches face. An IV morphine drip was fed into Peaches left arm to numb the pain.

Peaches barely turned her face when she heard Mercedes stride into her room. She tried to construct a smile but the partial facial paralysis and the bandages conspired to distort it. She was happy to finally have a visitor.

"How you feeling, girl? I heard you gonna be all right," Mercedes said, smiling behind her designer sunglasses.

"I-I'm good," Peaches said in a soft, muffled voice, the padding in her mouth making speech extremely difficult if not painful. Peaches was wondering why Mercedes was wearing shades inside the hospital.

"I-I still have headaches, though and my face still hurts. My mouth burns," she said, tears welling up in her eyes then spilling over the side of her face.

"I'm so sorry," Mercedes said behind the designer shades. "The doctor said yesterday that you so lucky to be alive; the bullet passed through yah cheek and only caused dem nerves damage. He said that you have some paralysis on that side of your face, like a stroke, but yah should be good," Mercedes said, almost mockingly.

Peaches turned her head away, not saying anything. This seemed another misfortune to go along with the other misfortunes that was her life story, she reflected glumly. A tear came running down her face.

"Listen, grrl." Mercedes bent down and started whispering in her ear, her West Indian accent more pronounced. "I heard a social worker is on her way to take yah back to that group home yah ran away from. They got your fingerprints. They know who yah are.

"But listen, nah, I got some of your clothes and we gonna get ya outta here, nah 'fo they come. Can yah get up and put these clothes on?" Mercedes said as she pulled designer jeans and a blouse out the bag. She tossed size eight burgundy suede puma sneakers out the bag, letting them hit the floor.

Peaches stared at the clothes without moving. She wanted to know who said she ran away. She was confused and the morphine drip made her feel dreamy. She didn't want to get up.

"C'mon now, grrl, act like ya got some sense. We ain't got all day, dey coming, ya know." Mercedes demanded. "And I know you don't want to go back dere to that home, nah," Mercedes said.

Peaches was perplexed and confused; she couldn't believe what Mercedes was about to do, that she was going to sneak her out of the hospital. Still she followed her commands without resistance, fighting back the grogginess; she didn't know if she wanted to leave or could leave but the thought of going back to the foster home was more then she could bear. Reluctantly, Peaches slid sluggishly off the side of the bed and started slowly putting on her clothes, one leg and arm at a time.

"Ya, lucky one of the girls saw you lying there in the street. It could have been much worse. Yah coulda been dead. That no good trick robbed yah and just left you there to die, nah," Mercedes half lied, having taken Peaches money herself.

"I just see it as a sign that it wasn't your time to go. Don't you worry, though I done told L-man no more workin' the streets for you. We gonna put you in the club. It's safer dere. That's where you'll make your money. You just have to be more careful next time, honey. Ok? Don't you worry. I done told dem I'm your aunt so they won't stop us, but hurry now, nah!" Mercedes said, wondering why the girl was moving so slow, forgetting she was recovering from a gunshot to the mouth. Mercedes couldn't help but admire Peaches' naked body, as the girl disrobed from her hospital gown. She was still highly marketable, despite her injury, Mercedes thought to herself.

When Peaches was finally fully dressed, Mercedes quickly pulled the IV out of her arm and got ready to go. Then she forced a Yankees baseball cap on Peaches head to help cover her face.

"Ok? And look, I got ur bag and some drink to help you forget the pain," she said, taking out a bottle of Hennessy liquor from Peaches' Gucci bag. "It has your name written all over it, grrl! Now let's get out a here, and just follow me, act like nottin' going on," Mercedes said, turning on her six hundred dollar heels and exiting out the room.

Peaches followed Mercedes sheepishly, listlessly past the busy nurses, orderlies and hospital staff. Soon they were both out the hospital and out in the street. Once outside and on the corner, they stopped to hail a cab. A livery driver pulled up to the curb and they both got in. Inside the cab, Mercedes shouted her address to the driver then turned to Peaches and said: "See, just follow me and you'll be alright. Ima have yah back working in no time, but not on the streets, no. Ima get you up in that strip club. The streets are too dangerous for you."

⚔

Social Worker Ms. Webber calmly walked into the patient room just vacated by Peaches and Mercedes. After a few minutes, she walked out the room hurriedly and went up to the charge nurse at the front desk.

"Excuse me, my name is Ms. Webber and I'm the social worker assigned to the case of the young girl who was shot in the mouth and found on the street. I don't see her in her room there," Ms. Webber said as she flashed her state identification.

The African American nurse turned away from her computer and said, "I'm sorry. How can I help you?"

The girl who was shot...where is she? I'm the social worker come to see her," Ms. Webber said annoyed.

The nurse got up went to the room and after looking around, immediately returned to her desk and placed a phone call to her supervisor. She then hung up the phone and turned to Ms. Webber.

"I'm sorry but it appears somebody snuck her out of the hospital. I'm sorry; I don't know how this could've happened."

Ms. Webber sighed and said, "Well, please call the police. That girl has a history of running away."

Chapter 14

Word had spread throughout the church that Jameer had taken up with a prostitute. Someone had seen Passion coming from his apartment and had recognized her as one of the working girls in the Zone. It quickly became the talk of the church that the leader of the outreach ministry to area prostitutes had fallen prey to the very women he was trying to save. It was quite the scandal.

So it was whenever Jameer came to church, people would cast mean glances at him or look away whenever he tried to approach them. They whispered about him behind his back and, laughed at him when he thought they were laughing with him. It wasn't until a member of his outreach team, Mrs. Hernandez, finally decided to confront Jameer about the rumors and let him know what the church members were saying about him.

"Jameer, may I have a word with you," she said to him one Sunday afternoon after the service was done.

"Why sure," Jameer responded, looking cheerful and happy to have good company. He noticed Ms. Hernandez agitated look and wondered what could be bothering her.

"Let's go in here," she said, directing him to a quiet office in the nave of the church.

"What's up? By the way, we meet tonight at midnight. Don't forget. I know we haven't turned around but one or two girls but I believe we are making some progress," he said.

"Listen, Jameer, I'm going to get to the point, people in the church have been talking about you. And it's not good. Are you aware of that?" she asked.

Jameer wanted to answer, no but as he thought more about it, he had to admit to hearing whispers and seeing troubled glances cast in his direction.

"Now that you mention it, I have noticed or felt that something was going on. What's up?" he asked.

"Well, and I have so much respect for you and I like what you have been doing with the outreach and everything, but there is talk going on that you have been…living with… with that prostitute. I know it's not true…but…" Mrs. Hernandez said.

So that's it, Jameer thought to himself. People in the church know that he has been in a relationship with Passion.

"No, no, I mean, yes…" he started to say. "She is living with me, but it's not like that," he lied.

"What?" Mrs. Hernandez said, stepping back in shock.

"No, no it's not what you think. Yes, she's a prostitute or was, but we are friends now. She, she came to me 'cause she needed a place to stay and protection, protection from her pimp. I'm only helping her," he said, his heart racing, unable to control his nervous stammering, feeling like he was explaining to his mother why he broke curfew but still knowing he wasn't being completely honest, afraid to acknowledge that he was in love with her, and that they had been intimate and are in fact in a relationship.

"But Jameer, why didn't you tell us? We are out there at night with you. Why couldn't you simply tell us?" Mrs. Hernandez said, feeling sorry for her friend but disgusted in knowing he was taking advantage of a lost girl.

"I'm sorry; I know I should've told someone, especially my team, but I thought I could handle this situation, get her the help she needs. I'm sorry," he said.

"We'll, who is she? And why hide her?" Mrs. Hernandez asked, still shocked.

"Her, her name is Dominique and she is really a sweet girl; she just doesn't want to go back to her pimp. And, and she's afraid he might find her anywhere else. I want to bring her to the church but I don't want to scare her off," he said.

"You mean that girl that went out with us? But Jameer, you need to get her professional counseling, rehabilitation, like I had. She's probably addicted to drugs or ran away from home. Don't take on her burdens by yourself. Bring her to the church," she pleaded with him. "Are you sleeping with her, Jameer? I have to ask."

"No, no, I mean no." Jameer lied. "It's not like that. I mean, I'm-I'm helping her. We talk about the Bible and read passages. She aint on drugs anymore. She is a sweet person. It's not like that at all," Jameer said, defending his relationship with Passion. "She is a really sweet and good person. I am working with her. But I see you're point. You are right Mrs. Hernandez. I will bring her to the church and let her meet the pastor. But when the time is right. I don't want everybody judging her or scare her away. Ok," Jameer said.

"Bring her next Sunday, Jameer. Get her the professional help she needs and get her out of your apartment before you do something you regret. She needs real help," pleaded Mrs. Hernandez.

"I will bring her to church soon," declared Jameer.

Rave, a fair skinned, crack addicted prostitute strutted across the street in a tight miniskirt, worn-out designer pumps, and a black, shimmering halter top so tight it made her flat chest seem even flatter. It was after midnight and she was turning tricks on Prospect Street, flagging down cars in the middle of the street with one hand, holding her smartphone in the other. She was desperate to make money so that she could get high.

While standing on the corner, Mrs. Hernandez, flanked by the brother and sister deacons, approached the crack addicted prostitute.

"God bless you, my dear. May we talk to you for a few minutes?"

Rave smiled as she was a very amiable, good-natured person. She greeted the group with a smile.

"Hey, what's up? Kinda late for yall to be out here. Isnt it? How can I help you? Are yall lost or somethin?" she said in her down south accent.

"We were wondering the same thing about you, my dear." Mrs. Hernandez returned politely. "We are trying to spread the word of God's salvation to women like you who are lost in the world. Do you have a pimp who is making you do this?"

Rave's affable disposition was suddenly replaced by a confused and questioning look. "What the fuck are yall talking about? I'm good. I don't need any sal-salvation," Rave responded, struggling to pronounce the word. "I'm good. Worry about yourselves."

Rave started walking away feeling offended and disrespected. Mrs. Hernandez shouted back at the drug addicted prostitute.

"I'm sorry. I didn't mean to insult you, Mrs. Hernandez said. But there is a better way. But can you tell us where we could find Peaches? Is she out here? She's a pretty young girl with long brown hair," she said, desperation in her voice.

Rave stopped, her affable nature returning, always willing to help someone if she could. She turned back around to Mrs. Hernandez.

"Oh, Peaches. You mean the girl that got shot? You looking for Peaches? She not out here, no more. She's working in the strip club over there, Fool's Paradise."

"Oh my God. She was shot? Oh, thank you, Ms. And, God bless you," Mrs. Hernandez replied. "God bless you." Mrs. Hernandez then turned around and headed in the direction of the strip club, the deacons following behind.

⋏

The pastor called out to Jameer, seeing him about to leave the church after service.

"Jameer, can I have a word with you," the pastor's deep throated words carried across the hall.

Jameer looked down the hall and observed the pastor staring at him in all seriousness. He knew that this was going to be about Passion.

Jameer followed the large pastor to his private office. He was nervous. He had wanted to speak to the pastor alone about the ministry but not like this.

The pastor opened the door for them and having seen Jameer inside his office, closed the door behind them. The pastor took a seat behind his desk. Jameer remained standing.

"Have a seat, the pastor said, gesturing casually. "Now, tell me how is the outreach going?" he said, his face not as serious but his eyes focused.

Jameer collapsed into a hard wooden chair. "It's going well, sir. I mean, we have been going out and making some progress in reaching these girls. I mean, they haven't all listened but some have responded to us, some have even…"

"Do you have one of those women living with you, Jameer?" the pastor asked abruptly, getting right to the issues. "Word has it that you have taken up with a prostitute, one of the women you were ministering to. Is that true, son?" asked the pastor, his eyes trained on the man before him, glowering as if he were boring through to his soul him.

Jameer was afraid to answer for fear that he would be thrown out of the church. He also knew that he didn't need to hide anything, not with this man. Still, he was afraid. He decided to speak the truth.

"I-I am letting her stay with me, yes, yes just a place to lay her head, yes, pastor," Jameer managed bravely to say, holding his head high but afraid to say that he was falling in love with Passion just the same and had been intimate with her.

The pastor sat silent, visibly processing Jameer's response. He then rose to his feet. A strange smile creased his face that just as quickly melted into a frown.

"My dear boy, I warned you of the dangers of a prostitution ministry. Aside from the physical dangers of going out there and ministering to those lost women in the late night, there are the spiritual dangers. You are a man of the church, but also a young man. A young, single man. Those women, those sex workers, are soldiers in Satan's army. They are practiced in the art of temptation and seduction. They know how to appeal to the flesh, to tempt you to fall into the abyss of sin. The weapons they use are their bodies, the flesh and lust and desire…"

"But pastor, you know as well as I do that so many of those girls are innocent victims of their pimps…" Jameer started.

The pastor interrupted Jameer, his voice booming. "Whether they were drafted into Satan's army by some unscrupulous caretaker or sweet talking pimp looking to profit off of them; or whether they enlisted into the so-called oldest profession in a misguided attempt to escape poverty or run away from the rule of their parents, they are all social and spiritual pariahs looking to corrupt the souls of men and lead them from the path of righteousness, my dear boy," the pastor declared, like he speaking from the pulpit.

Jameer stared at the floor in silence. He felt ashamed. He had never heard the pastor speak so strongly unless it was a sermon. He carefully thought about what he would say. He had made love with Dominique but it wasn't as client/prostitute. They had made love. He was in love with Dominique. But he couldn't tell the pastor that. He feared he would lose his chance to become a church deacon. He felt ashamed.

"Excuse me, pastor," Jameer started again. "But I am trying to help her that's all."

The pastor smiled a big smile. "My dear boy, it's all right. I know full well, what you are up against; I told you; I was a part of a prostitution ministry shortly after my wife died. Be fearful and aware of the sins of the flesh. The wise man flees from sin. Going into the night and ministering to these soldiers of sin places you in a very vulnerable position and it appears you have succumbed to the temptation of lust," the pastor smiled. "No one should ever regard themselves as so mature in the faith that watchfulness is not needed, Jameer," he went on.

"Many true and honest believers like you and others like me who have walked in the faith for many years have fallen into temptation," the pastor said, a serious almost painful look on his face.

"No, no, I-I am helping her. We read from the Bible every night. She understands…" Jameer maintained, afraid to tell the truth, ashamed at his inability to be honest.

"You must pray, my son; pray for forgiveness and the strength to walk away from temptation as you have brought a servant of sin into your very home, if not your bed. Remove her. Take her to where she can get help but don't tempt yourself more than you already have. Remember, my boy. God will not let you be tempted beyond your ability, but with the temptation he will also provide the way of escape. Bring her to the church. I will pray for you and her."

Then the pastor adopted a more serious tone. His face became more somber. He straightened up as he spoke.

"However, as the Senior Pastor, I must also counsel you that your behavior would cause you to become immediately disqualified to hold the office of deacon. This issue must be immediately brought to the attention of the Church Leadership Board. The Board, along with myself, will convene to investigate the matter as discreetly as possible. And we will be discreet. I will prepare written documentation concerning the witnesses, accusations, and evidence and submit these to the Board. If the Board agrees with the information, including your confession, you would be immediately suspended from all duties related to the office of deacon.

The following Sunday I (along with the Church Leadership Board) will delicately, yet publicly, announce the situation to the congregation, including its final outcome of your being removed from consideration as deacon. Doing so would be in accordance with what the Scripture says in 1 Timothy 5:20, "Those who continue in sin, rebuke in the presence of all, so that the rest also will be fearful of sinning." Do you understand, my boy?" the pastor said glumly and in all seriousness.

"Yes, sir, Jameer said, his head lowered in shame.

"However, so long as you openly confess and repent of this sin, there would be no further need to continue with church discipline and the congregation will be encouraged to lovingly embrace you as a repentant man and a Christian brother still, so don't despair," the pastor said, placing his arm on Jameer's shoulder. "Just bring her to church and out of your home, ok?"

"Remember your Proverbs: 'Many are the victims she has brought down; her slain are a mighty throng'" Pay heed, my son," the pastor implored him.

Jameer thought long and hard. He was in love with Dominique but now he wondered.

"I will bring her to the church, pastor, sir; I will take her out of my home before I fall into sin, like you say," Jameer said feeling he had already.

"Come let us pray," said the pastor, as he stepped from behind his desk and joined Jameer in prayer as they knelt down. The two prayed together on their knees for a long time.

CHAPTER 15

Lavender was sentenced to 20 months in jail for trafficking prostitutes across state lines, serving 18 months for good behavior. He had been under surveillance for the past several months as he went back and forth from Maine to New York, Connecticut and Rhode Island. The two women spent five months in jail and were released. Lavender's prostitute/girlfriend, Michelle, gave birth to a healthy baby boy while incarcerated. She named the boy, Rommel jr. after Lavender, before the child was placed in protective custody.

Lavender had kept in touch with Mercedes even while in prison. He learned from her that Desire had been murdered, her body beaten and burned. Lavender wept briefly. He vowed to himself that he would avenge Desire's death upon his release.

Desire's gruesome death was still the talk on the streets, even three years later; Lavender realized his reputation was on the line. Whenever a high profile pimp like himself, loses one of his girls to some crazy johns in the streets, he has to show his other girls and other pimps that he can't let that go without some kind of swift and brutal retaliation. Otherwise, his girls would lose confidence in his ability to protect them and other pimps would try to peel off other girls from his stable. He would be considered soft. Lavender had to find the guys who murdered his baby mother at all costs and make them pay for what they did to Desire and more importantly his reputation.

Lavender also learned from Mercedes that Passion saw the men that Desire got in the car with. He was also told that Passion allowed social services to take Desire's three children, including his son, Marquis. He hated Passion even more than usual and vowed to himself that he would take care of her something terrible. He was going to beat her like she had never been beaten before and then put her back out on the streets to work off all the money she owed him and more once he found her.

⅄

Fool's Paradise was the only legitimate gentleman's club in the Zone. The expansive red brick single story building stood nestled on a dark peninsula in a desolate street area not far enough removed from the row of poorly constructed attached residential houses. The seedy strip club, with its high posted neon sign displaying the contour of a naked woman bathing in a martini glass, served as a beacon through the night attracting adult men and women seeking to partake of the lewd pleasures available there.

This night, though, the outreach group with Mrs. Hernandez, stood outside the notorious gentleman's club, aiming to save souls, to reach out to the women working there, looking for a way out of the sex trade. Blocking their path at the club entrance were two strapping bouncers and the club's diminutive owner, a middle-aged, German-American man in a button-down Polo shirt, and loose fitting designer jeans. His name was Karl but everyone called him Mr. K.

"Look, none of my girls need prayer or blessings right now, ok, so find another spot, ok," the man said, gesticulating to the group of two men and three women. "Besides, this isn't no, no church."

"Sir, we not trying to mess up your business or anything but we know that some of the women in there could only benefit from prayer to help them; they work hard and need to know that there is hope for them," Mrs. Hernandez said, stepping forward to be the mouthpiece for the group.

"Look, I know what you're trying to do, and, and I respect that; I do. I believe in God myself but I take very good care of my girls in there. They not doing anything they don't want to do, trust me," Mr. K said, gesticulating more wildly, his two bouncers, one an ex-felon, the other an ex-cop, framing him and wearing screwed up faces, ready to pounce on the small group.

"Mr. we know that-that chu take care of your dancers but we just asking to pray for them and for the girl Peaches; we know she's in there," Mrs. Hernandez said, holding up a newspaper article about Peaches escaping from the hospital.

Now the club owner knew that more than a few of the girls in his establishment were under-aged, like Peaches. Men liked to see the young girls. He grew up with religious parents but started worshipping money once he became an adult. He didn't want this group of religious fanatics messing up his business by calling the police. He decided to let them have their way but on his terms.

"Ok, ok, Peaches, I think, is in the back, by the V.I.P.; But she isn't doing anything she doesn't want to do. You have seven minutes to get there, say your praying and leave out. And only the women can go in. The men have to pay," the owner said, glaring at Jameer and Deacon Bruer.

"Yeah, no free looks, on a religious tip," put in one of the muscled bouncers, flashing a menacing face.

"We'll wait outside," Jameer said, as he and Deacon Bruer walked back toward the car, watching the women walk into the club.

The club's brawny bouncers parted like the Red Sea to allow Mrs. Hernandez and the two women to walk unmolested into the sleazy club.

Pulsating music and flashing lights assailed the senses of the three women as they struggled to find their way through the darkness and the crowd of lewd men and partially nude and naked women.

With the exception of Mrs. Hernandez, none of the women had ever been in a strip club. They stared wide-eyed at naked young women winding, twerking and gyrating suggestively on the stage, playing to the gaggle of horny men who were serenading them with dollars bills, dancing under a shower of money raining down on them; there was no doubt in their minds they were in seventh corner of Dante's Hell.

"You can't tell me this isn't the Devil's playground," said Ms. Shirley Douglas, closing her coat, imagining eyes trying to peer through her clothes. "Just sinful, I tell you. Sinful. Just look at them," she said, aghast at the lecherous activity all around her.

"They are consenting adults, Shirley. Remember that. Don't judge," said, Mrs. Grace Johnson, the Sunday school teacher, similarly shocked by the bawdy scene but still saying a prayer for the men and women she passed by.

"We'll they aren't all consenting adults," shot back Mrs. Hernandez. "Some of these girls look sixteen or younger. But c'mon we only got like five minutes, remember what the man said."

The three women made their way to the VIP section at the back of the club, not unaware that one of the club's tall security men was trailing them.

"There she is," Mrs. Hernandez said, pointing to Peaches, attired in a string bikini with velvet peep toe wedge heels, sitting up on the stage counting her money, her head down, sweat glistening all over her curvaceous body.

"Peaches, my dear child, Mrs. Hernandez, said, "I found out that you were here. We come to pray for you. Let us pray for you," she said, over the din of the blaring Hip Hop music.

The three women quickly surrounded Peaches and began praying for her. Peaches kept her face down, steady counting her money, but not totally oblivious to the women. She was really happy they were here. She wanted to cry.

Then after a few minutes the towering security guard approached and spoke over the music and the prayers. "Ok, times up, ladieees!" He said, "We got a business to run here. She can go to church later. Come on, let's go!"

Peaches raised her face and even in the darkness of the club, and despite the heavy makeup caked on, the paralysis to the left side of her face caused by the gunshot made an obvious sagging and discoloration on that side of her face, like melted butter suddenly frozen in place, forever marring her beauty.

"Thank you," Peaches said as the security guard led the women back out the club.

"Oh my God," Mrs. Hernandez said horrified at seeing Peaches' face. "Peaches, what happened to y-your face?" she cried.

But soon, Peaches was hidden from sight as the music continued thumping and the crowd basked in the raucous, ribald atmosphere, seemingly unaware the women had passed amongst them, praying for them all.

Chapter 16

It was the First Sunday of the month, a hot day in July. Grace Baptist church was unusually crowded for the summer. Finding an empty pew was challenging. Church members and visitors sat too close for comfort.

Jameer proudly walked into Grace Baptist church with Passion on his arm. They made for quite the fashionable couple. Passion was striking in a powder blue, knee high dress with white low heel open toe shoes. She wore her makeup light and her hair was immaculately braided. Passion didn't look anything like the prostitute who worked Prospect Street. She was a vision of style and beauty. Only the tattoo on her neck and the gaudy, white gold chain hanging from her neck hinted of the life she had left behind.

Jameer was smartly attired in a navy blue three piece suit and matching silk striped tie, and polished wingtip shoes. He kept his head high and took measured confident steps. Walking together, Jameer and Passion looked like a celebrities.

Still, Passion was nervous. She didn't know what kind of reception she would get. Jameer had to convince her that she could walk into a church after living the past few years on the street as a prostitute. He made her believe that no one would know her past life unless she told them and even if they did, it didn't matter. She had turned a page and was living a different life, a life in Christ.

However, as they sauntered into the sanctuary, Passion immediately recognized more than a few familiar faces. Men she had known; johns who had picked her up on the street; those who had paid for her services, some more generously than others; they were all here in church, dressed in their Sunday best. Passion blushed as some of the men recognized her as well. Many of the men glared at her angrily, men like James McFadden, a hard working MTA track worker whose wife left him some years ago, and who, from time to time, took to the streets looking for sex and had the occasion of hiring Passion to satisfy his desires; he wondered what she was doing in the church, feeling that she didn't belong there, furious that anyone would bring her here. Other men, like Marshall Washington, a well-regarded banker who crept out in the twilight hours to have Passion do for him what his prudish wife refused to do, squirmed uneasily, struggling to avoid eye contact, fearful that she would expose him, bring to light his illicit nocturnal activities, here in front of his wife and children and church family. Still more, with fond memories of their time spent with Passion, like Jeffrey Williams, a self-proclaimed bachelor and shoe salesman, winked at Passion in appreciation, and anticipation of another clandestine rendezvous.

"Dominique, what's wrong?" Jameer asked, noticing Passion was uncomfortably distracted.

"Some of the men in here, I been with them," she said, embarrassed for herself and them. "I-I should go. This isn't right," she said. "I shouldn't be here."

Jameer stopped to comfort Passion, to assure her. "It's all right, they won't say nothing if you don't. Trust me. Anyway, that's all in the past now. It's all the past."

Jameer led Passion to a pew in the upper balcony section of the church and sat close to her. They opened the hymnal and joined in singing with the rest of the congregation.

Passion and Jameer were seated high up in the balcony section at a peculiar angle to the pulpit. The old Gothic style architecture replete with numerous cornices and naves posted a column obstructing their view of the pastor. They could only see the pastor's profile when he was seated. When the pastor rose to speak to deliver the sermon they couldn't see him at all, just the sound of his booming voice. The church being near capacity, there were no other seats available, at least not for them to sit together. They contented themselves to simply listen to the sermon and join in singing the hymns. For Jameer this was going to be the day when he would be exonerated, when the church would get to see how his faith and hard work had made Passion a new woman in Christ.

For Passion, meeting the church pastor was going to be another important step in changing her life from street prostitute to a woman of respectability. She was excited and nervous at the same time. Passion saw it as a coming out of sorts. She was coming out into the world of respectability and leaving behind a world of sin and shame. She wished her mother were here; she wished her father could share in this moment and find it in his heart to forgive her After a litany of church announcements and the singing of various hymns, it was time for the Communion as it was the First Sunday of the month. The pastor enjoined the church members and all those in the church to recite the Apostle's Creed. Then the ushers and deacons came to every pew and offered each person flat bread and a small cup of grape juice. Then when the ushers gave the signal to the pastor that everyone who was willing to partake in the Communion had been served, the pastor stood up and spoke from the pulpit:

"And Jesus said to his disciples, Take, eat, this is my Body, which is given for you. Do this in remembrance of me."

And everyone in the church did as instructed and took the unleavened bread and ate.

Passion suddenly felt the shame of her past life. She reflected on all she had done, all she had experienced and she started to cry. Looking around at all the nicely dressed church people, she felt unworthy. She didn't feel like she belonged. Again, she wanted to leave. Tears came down her face.

Jameer held her close and whispered in her ear, "It's all right, Dominique," he said. "It's going to be all right. Please Dominique, no one here is any better than you. They just found what you are looking for," he said. "Salvation and peace in God."

The pastor continued with Communion:

"Drink ye all of this; for this is my Blood of the New Testament, which is shed for you, and for many, for the remission of sins. Do this, as oft as ye shall drink it, in remembrance of me."

Passion began to gather herself, wiping her tears with the help of Jameer's assurances. She took the bread and ate it. She then took the cup of grape juice and drank it quickly. She smiled to Jameer, feeling assured.

"I'm all right; it tastes good," she said, winking her eye.

"Though your sins are like scarlet, they shall be white as snow; though they be red as crimson, they shall be white as wool," the pastor went on. "That is His promise to us.

The communion concluded, Jameer and Passion enjoyed the rest of the service. After a rousing selection by the youth choir, which included a dynamic call and response session which had many in the church catching the Spirit, the pastor signaled the end of the service by opening the doors of the church and calling out to the congregation for new candidates for Baptism as was his custom. The pastor stepped down from the pulpit, down several carpeted stairs and stood in the middle of the aisle, the red carpet beneath his feet, extending out to the church entrance some several yards. He addressed the congregation.

"As we open the doors of the church, are there any willing to give themselves to Christ, to turn their life over in His name, in His service?" the pastor said, holding his arms out to the congregation in invitation. "Are there any willing to be candidates for Baptism?"

No one stirred in the whole congregation. The pastor went on unfazed.

"Is there anyone willing to join and become part of the Body of Christ? Come on, don't be shy," the pastor went on.

Passion heard the pastor and felt an incredible urge surging up inside her to join the church and save herself. Her dream of burning continued to play itself out in her head and she was fearful. She saw her chance for complete salvation. She stirred.

On the main floor of the sanctuary, the pastor continued his plea for new members.

"In baptism, we demonstrate our hope in the resurrection and salvation. Is there anyone who is willing to take the plunge?" he said. "Joining the church, through the rite of baptism is like starting over in a new life, a new life in Christ," he said.

Passion got up from where she was sitting in the balcony section and headed downstairs to the main floor of the sanctuary, her nimble feet sprinting down the stairs. Her heart was racing with hope and excitement.

"Dominique, where are you going?" Jameer said. But then he knew. He followed after her. He couldn't believe she was going to do it. He was proud of her. He was proud of himself.

On the main floor, the pastor continued trying to prod new members to the church. Still, no one came forward.

"Remember, proclaiming yourself a candidate for Baptism is but the first step in your journey to Christ, not the end. But it's an important first step," the pastor said.

Still no one in the main level moved.

By now, Passion had reached the main level of the church and was making her way hastily to the sanctuary floor where the pastor stood. She was stopped briefly by the ushers at the entrance to the sanctuary, who smiled at her and encouraged her to go in.

"God bless you, my dear," a shiny black male usher said, his dark skin glistening under the lights of the church.

Jameer followed closely behind Passion bursting with pride. He couldn't be more proud of her. He was also pleased with himself to see Passion become a baptized member of the church. He felt that God had worked a miracle through him in getting Passion off the streets and he was seeing all his hard work come to fruition. Now the whole church would share in his accomplishment and the glory of God to transform a life.

Passion stopped at the red carpet which led to the sanctuary. She had to compose herself, ready herself to take this next step in her salvation. She was nervous but undeterred. She looked at the red carpet as it led to the pulpit and the pastor. He seemed a mile away even though it was only several feet. The pastor was standing by the pulpit, his towering figure resplendent in his black robe and gold and white stole. Passion couldn't make him out clearly as his back was turned to her as he was looking up at the balcony, exhorting the congregation but she saw in him her salvation. Soon her footsteps made her presence felt.

The pastor finally turned and saw her. He smiled.

"Ok, I see we have one who is ready to give her life to Christ. Come, my dear," the pastor said, smiling broadly. "Don't be shy."

He was exceedingly proud anytime he saw someone come to join the church. He opened his arms wide, invitingly, and took a few steps forward but then stopped, wanting her to come to him. The congregation all turned to see Passion on the main floor and showered her with applause.

"Baptism is the result of the work of the Spirit on the heart and mind through the Word," the pastor affirmed to the church.

Passion started crying tears of joy. She was like a statute now, motionless. She couldn't move forward. Jameer reached her and comforted her again.

"It's all right, Dominique. It's all right. Go ahead. Go to the pastor. It's all right. I'm so proud of you," he said.

At that, Passion collected herself, despite the potpourri of emotions bubbling up inside of her. She started slowly but inexorably walking down the carpet to the welcoming pastor. Applause continued to rain down on her. Then the clapping stopped as heads turned to see her find salvation.

"Come my, dear! Come to me!" the pastor continued walking to meet Passion as he saw her hesitation. "

But as they continued toward one another, both the pastor and the former prostitute felt an uncomfortable and unexpected sense of familiarity. Apart from the gown and stole, Passion began to recognize the pastor's heavy voice, his gait, and his face. And then his cologne. The pastor had a harder time recognizing Passion, dressed as she was, not in enticing and seductive pumps and ass-hugging shorts but conservative attire. Still there was no mistaking the familiar walk, immaculate, slender figure, the hypnotic beauty and cherubic face. A shudder went through him.

Passion began to remember the tall, heavy frame and the hands with the gold rings.

He started to recognize that flawless complexion and shiny, long black hair. As she approached closer, the pastor began to remember the soft freckles.

Then the pastor's smile disappeared and his eyes grew big like saucers and his feet slowed to a stop as if they had become mired in molasses. The good pastor was speechless, as if he had seen an apparition from an unspeakable past. His face grew ashen. Less than a few yards away, he recognized the woman before him as Passion.

And Passion recognized the pastor.

She couldn't believe her eyes, thought they were deceiving her. She wanted to believe she was seeing things at first and didn't trust her senses, what her eyes were showing her. She stopped hearing the voices around her, stopped sensing Jameer encouraging her on. The crowded church suddenly seemed empty. It was just her and the pastor now. Passion's hands grew cold. She was transfixed. Her face was a tangle of emotions. She took a step back.

Standing on the side, by the banister, Jameer noticed Passion had stopped and rushed the carpet to find out what was wrong.

"Dominique, are you all right?" Jameer asked, coming up to Passion now, joining her on the sanctuary carpet. It's all right. What's wrong?" he said, trying to encourage her on.

Passion wasn't moving. She just stood there just beyond arm's length of the pastor. She closed her eyes hoping that by reopening them, she would see something different. Someone different. But nothing had changed. There he was, still standing before her, a living reminder of a life she believed she had left behind. It was Roger! Roger the trick was the church pastor! Roger, the man in the Escalade. Roger the trick!

."Th-this is your p-pastor?" Passion barely managed to say to Jameer without looking at him but staring disbelievingly at the pastor.

"Yes, yeah, what's wrong, Dominique? You don't look well. I told you, it's all right. He's not here to judge you," Jameer said.

"Th-this is who you follow? Who sent you out to save girls like me?" Passion went on staring directly into the eyes of the pastor, feeling his shame, sharing his guilt.

"Yeah, this is the pastor of our church. What's wrong? What you know him? You changed your mind?" Jameer said, unable to discern why Passion was acting so strangely. "I told him all about you. Don't be scared," Jameer urged.

Passion remained transfixed a stone statute, like the woman who disobeyed God by turning back to see the destruction of Sodom and Gomorrah.

She just kept looking at the pastor, staring in utter disbelief, as if transformed into that pillar of salt.

The pastor stood staring as well, glaring at Passion, his once cheerful visage, a frightful frown now. His face was red like a plum. He didn't know how to proceed. But realizing where he was he then tried to play it off but the whole church was watching and he didn't know what to say. He would continue like nothing was wrong, he determined. He hoped that Passion would follow his lead and play it off as well, to save them both this utter shame and embarrassment.

"It appears our young candidate has second thoughts," the pastor said, recapturing his jovial manner. The congregation laughed as one.

"It's all right my dear. You don't have to do it today, here in front of everyone," he said, nervously. "We could go in the back and talk about it away from the crowd," he said, trying to give Passion a hint, a way out.

Sensing things going wrong, Jameer then tried to intervene. He would set things right. He approached the pastor.

"Pastor, this is the young lady I was telling you about who has decided to come to the church to change her life. She seems nervous and uncomfortable or something. I don't know. I didn't expect this. Let her know that she is welcome here," he said to the pastor.

But the pastor didn't hear a word Jameer said as he was preoccupied trying to think of a way to escape to the confines of his office or to anyplace except where he was standing right now.

Passion was unbelieving and confused, feeling a fury welling up inside of her, a surge of anger. She felt like screaming at the top of her lungs and then crying her eyes out all at the same time. But the confusion in her mind left her mute, angry, unable to speak; she was rendered dumbfounded. She was stranded between the urge to flee and run from this humiliation, and the desire to remain and confront this charlatan pastor, expose him for all to see. Passion resolved to be strong, keep whatever dignity she had left and excuse herself. She caught on to what the pastor was trying to do. She would depart from the church.

Passion turned to leave, when Jameer grabbed her by the hand to stop her.

"Dominique, where are you going...?" He said. "Don't leave; you can do this," he pleaded, wondering if he was doing it more for her or himself.

Passion recoiled violently against him. "Don't-Don't touch me," she said more like a growl. "Let me go! Let me out of here!" she shouted, confused, her usually cool demeanor completely rattled. She was a volcano of emotions about to erupt.

"Dominique, what is it? Tell me what's wrong," Jameer said trying desperately to understand. He expected every reaction but this one. "Don't you want to be baptized? Don't you want to be saved?"

Passion stared long and hard into Jameer's eyes, taking the time to understand that he really didn't know. She would tell him then. She couldn't keep her emotions bottled up anymore. She had to share her pain.

"I-I, you-your, your pastor, I-I know him," she finally said. "I mean, I know him," she forced herself to say, stammering, and her voice starting softly, barely above a whisper than rising.

"What do you mean? You know him?" You met him before" Jameer said trying to wrap his mind around what she was trying to say, afraid to grapple with her hidden reference.

"He, he, he used to see me. He used to date me, me!" she continued on boldly, not whispering anymore, tears coming down her face. "Y-your pastor...I know him...he used to pick me up on the street and paid me to have sex with him in cheap hotels! You, your pastor is a fucking trick!" Passion said loud enough for people to hear, now pointing her finger right at the man in an accusatory manner. She then turned directly to the pastor in anger, tears of pain and hurt coming down her face, horrified at his duplicity, disgusted by his dishonesty.

A loud, collective sigh came from the church as her words traveled through the congregation. Ushers and deacons left their posts and rushed to the pastor as if to protect him from her accusations, shield him from her vitriol as if they were bullets from an assassin. Others went to remove Passion from the church.

"What's the matter Roger or Pastor Emerson or whateva your fucking name is—you don't know me now? You don't want me now?" Passion said, mocking the pastor, shouting at him, her face red with rage, tears streaming down her face. She felt the grape juice and unleavened bread that was communion, turning in her stomach, making her feel she was about to regurgitate. "What's the matter? Nothing to say to me now in front of your big fucking church?" she hollered. "Nothing to say?"

The pastor didn't respond. He was completely embarrassed, mortified. Her words hitting him like daggers, cutting him down, piercing him. Soon he was surrounded by his army of deacons and church ushers.

Passion turned back to face Jameer. "Let me go! Let me out of this fucking church! All of this is a fucking joke!" Passion said, walking and then running, running as fast as she could, past the startled congregants. In a moment, Passion was gone leaving, Jameer standing incredulous, dumbfounded—speechless.

Rising whispers and murmurs could be heard among the astonished church crowd. One elderly woman rose to her feet, let out a loud gasp then fainted outright, only to be caught by another parishioner. Some wondered if Passion was really talking about the very same pastor that just presided over the morning service but there was no denying who she was pointing to. It was obvious that she was accusing the pastor. The pastor's acute silence in all of this was troubling to the congregation. They wondered why he didn't say anything.

Jameer stood staring at the floor. He was still trying to grapple with what Passion had said about the pastor, his pastor. He was trying to process it all but he couldn't. His mind and faith wouldn't let him. He finally found the courage to look up at the pastor, waiting for some explanation, for clarity, that it was all some big misunderstanding. He caught the pastor's eyes before the pastor turned away; shame and guilt were all over the pastor's face.

Jameer watched as the pastor retired to his office, his throng of deacons surrounding him, leaving without so much as a word of explanation.

The associate pastor and musical director stood up quickly took control of the service, both dumbfounded. The choir master directed the similarly stunned choir to close the service by singing one refrain of Amazing Grace.

Following his direction, the choir raised their voices to sing the closing hymn. But their once renowned harmony was replaced by disharmony and the dissonance of unfocused and confused voices. After one painful verse, the choir concluded and doors of the church were opened letting everyone out. The only sounds heard now were the whispers and murmuring of a rattled congregation.

PART 3

CHAPTER 1

After the scene caused by Passion that First Sunday, Grace Baptist Church was hardly the same. Word had spread like wildfire through the church and the community, regarding the accusations a former prostitute had made against their beloved pastor. Many had thought it was Jameer's attempt to discredit the pastor so that he could restore his own name; that he was jealous of the pastor and was looking to see him fall by having a woman accuse him falsely of being a trick. Others simply thought the young woman was crazy out of her mind and had mistaken the pastor for someone else, another hapless trick and that she was doped up on some mind altering drug.

Still some thought that it was true. Eyewitnesses, who were there, remembered how the young woman seemed so distraught and upset and couldn't possibly make up something like that. People had already heard rumors of how the pastor had been seen driving around Prospect Street in the wee hours of the night and early morning and now this confirmed it. It would explain why the pastor was almost always late for the sunrise services. It would also explain why the church was always short of money, because the pastor was tricking it away. It started to make sense to some. They speculated that the handsome pastor, a widower, was simply being a man.

A few hypothesized that Jameer was an undercover pimp and was giving the pastor discounts on his prostitutes.

Shocked church mothers pulled their children out of the Sunday school, afraid their children would get wind of what the pastor was accused of. Some stopped coming to the church altogether, ashamed to know that their pastor was a hypocrite, preaching against sin during the day while sleeping with prostitutes at night. People who had never come to church before, came to see this well-known pastor who had one foot in the spiritual world and the other in the world of whores. They felt good in knowing that for all their own sins they had something in common with the mighty pastor of Grace Baptist Church. They delighted in seeing a purported man of the Cloth still be more than willing to partake of the sins of the flesh. They flocked to the church to see how the mighty had fallen, knowing that the pastor of the church was no better than they. They were ready to forgive him, hoping their own transgressions would be forgiven as well.

The single women of the church who weren't turned off by the talk of their beloved pastor sleeping with prostitutes, decided to offer him their prayers; the more enterprising among them, looking to have the pastor as their own, offered him more than that. Like, Joy Grant who traded in her conservative floral dresses coming to church instead in miniskirt, spandex tights and form fitting tube dresses; like, Sheila Jones who now wore long braids and stilettos; and Candace Martin who came to church in camisoles, open- toed pumps and party derby hats.

Through it all, through all the talk, the pastor remained silent. He would come to service but would sit quietly behind the pulpit while a parade of visiting pastors, from other churches would come and deliver the Sunday sermon. No longer would the pastor stand at the close of the service at the receiving line, welcoming new visitors and guests to the church as well as old members. After the Sunday service, the pastor would simply retreat to his office study and stay there until everyone had left the church.

The Associate Pastor, Reverend Richard Eisley, took over the primary duty of running the church and holding down the service. He was a balding, brown-skinned man in his late fifties, from North Carolina given to wearing unremarkable brown and grey, three piece suits and wingtip shoes. He had a large nose that spread across his face. He always spoke with a southern drawl as he was raised in the south. He wasn't a very articulate pastor but he spoke plainly and with conviction and people generally liked him.

Still everyone longed for the Pastor Emerson and the associate pastor could in no way replace the pastor who had served Grace Baptist church for the past 15 years. Seeing him sitting behind the pulpit made them miss his voice, his words, and his smile. They wondered when and if he would ever get back up on the pulpit and deliver the Word. Even more wondered what he had to say to explain away the wild accusations made against him, to stamp out the dirty rumors that spread like wildfire throughout the community.

Then one Sunday morning, the pastor wasn't sitting behind the pulpit. In fact, he was nowhere to be found. He was gone. His absence hadn't been announced in the morning program but it was apparent to all. The chair where he sat was empty. Murmurs could be heard throughout the morning service as people arrived, hoping to see him sitting up there. Many expected him to arrive late, as was his custom, but more than an hour into the service there was still no sign of the pastor.

During the reading of the announcements at service, the Associate Pastor Eisley interrupted the speaker, Ms. Moses, a longtime member. He came to the pulpit and read a letter from the Pastor Avery Emerson, himself putting to bed all the rumors.

"It is with great sadness and out of great respect for my office that I, Reverend Avery Emerson, senior pastor of Grace Baptist Church, announce my resignation from the church I have served faithfully for the past 15 years."

At the word 'resignation' a great hush came over the congregation. Crying and sobbing could be heard among the congregants as well as snickering and laughter. The associate pastor raised his hand for silence then he continued reading.

"I am resigning my office due to a moral crisis of faith that I must address and meditate on in solitary communion with my Lord and Savior. Please keep me in your prayers."

The associate pastor then retreated to the pulpit seat and the organist began to play.

"Let us rise and sing from Hymn 345," said the Deacon Anderson. "Onward Christian Soldiers…" he started to sing and the congregation followed along.

Chapter 2

An unmarked police cruiser carefully followed Lavender's car for several city blocks, up and down Prospect Street in the cool October night. Snow from the night before sat in large mounds on the street. It wasn't long before the police cruiser's red and white lights started flashing and pulled Lavender's car over on an obscure side street. The police car sat behind Lavender's car for some time. Two white plainclothes police officers finally emerged from out the cruiser and approached Lavender's car, one on either side.

Lavender was sitting in his car, calm and cool. Riding shotgun was Ivana, a twenty-one years old Russian-American prostitute with a fondness for black men and hip hop music. He found Ivana at the Port Authority, after her boyfriend-pimp was arrested for assaulting her in public. She found Lavender charming and loved his smooth talk, pimp swagger not to mention the marijuana he promised her with. She needed little coercion to work for him after that.

As the police officers approached, Lavender told Ivana to just relax and she did.

The detective on the driver's side spoke first.

"Hey, Lavender, how you doin?" It was the same two plainclothes detectives that were in Lavender's apartment.

Lavender rolled down the tinted window. Cigarette smoke quickly escaped into the cool night air. Lavender smiled showing his yellow stained teeth unmistakable from his two front gold teeth.

"Yo, what's up Steve? You got something for me?" he said in his raspy, deep throated voice.

"Yeah, we got a lead on who mighta offed your girl, Desire. Two guys in a BMW got pulled over with marijuana in the car about a week ago. They had the same BMW you had told me about. They had some blood stains inside the car. We're trying to get a match," the detective said. Steve Mack was a veteran detective, on the Force for eleven years. He had established a mutually beneficial relationship with Lavender over the years. He provided Lavender with protection for his girls from getting arrested for solicitation and Lavender in turn provided him with information on the street, from drug trafficking, and rival drug dealers and pimps. He also provided the detective and his friends with prostitutes for their pleasure.

"Where are they now, still in lockup?" Lavender said.

"No, they posted bail a few days ago, got some lawyer to get them out. They are some young rich kids, I guess." Detective Mack said. "They live over there on Crescent Avenue. Here is the address." He handed Lavender a plain white paper with an address. "Handle your business," he said.

"Thanks, Steve, you all right with me." Lavender said, smiling a smile so full of menace that the veteran officer became fearful. The grinning pimp then put his car in drive and pulled off.

The two detectives returned to their car and after looking around got in and went the other direction, knowing that they had just given evil free reign.

Lavender felt a rush of excitement going through his body. The prospect of revenge and violence had the adrenaline flowing in his veins. He had what he wanted, the guys that murdered his baby mother. He was going to handle things his way. He salivated at the thought of surprising the punks who think they got away with taking out Desire. He could only imagine the look on their faces when he comes face to face with them. The element of surprise was his now and he had every intention of taking full advantage of it.

Lavender drove his car back up to Prospect Street and turned to his Russian prostitute Ivana. "Listen, sweetheart, go make that money. I got some business to take care of. I will catch up with you later. Aight."

Ivana smiled and gave Lavender a kiss on the lips. She knew what 'business' meant. Lavender had a score to settle. Ivana got out of the car and Lavender drove off, headed north.

Pelham Parkway in the Bronx was one of the better neighborhoods in the borough. It was primarily a residential neighborhood composed mainly of working class and middle class families. Dominated by 6 and 7-story elevator apartments and coop buildings, the residential streets were lined with a vibrant blend of housing types including detached houses and larger Art Deco and Tudor Style apartment buildings. It was in this enclave of the Bronx, nestled between the extremes of poverty and middle class life that Lavender came to exact his revenge.

In one of those Tudor Style apartment buildings three young men, two African-American, the other Puerto Rican were enjoying NBA2K15. It was midnight. What was left of a Dominoes pepperoni pizza pie sat in the box on the kitchen table. Empty bottles of Hennessey Black and Grey Goose were placed around the pizza.

The apartment was wall to wall plush carpet except for the kitchen area which had expensive white and black tile on the floor. A large, black leather sectional filled the entire living room furniture, aside from matching glass end tables and the large glass coffee table in the center of the room. A 56 inch Plasma flat screen TV was mounted on the wall. The lights in the apartment were off, plunging the room in darkness to heighten the enjoyment of the video game.

"Man, I wish we could go pick up some hoes tonight. Feel like getting my dick sucked!" said Herman Rios, a twenty something Hispanic young man who was furiously handling the game controller.

"Yo, we gotta lay low for a few. They still got my Beamer, remember. I think I owe parking tickets on that bitch, too," said Stefon, who orchestrated Desire's death. He still had the bruise above his left eye from his encounter with Lavender the pimp.

"Nigga, you worried about parking tickets? You need to be worried about them finding evidence in your car of that bitch we got rid of for you. You know, that white hooker? You betta hope they not doing any of that forensic shit to your whip," said his college friend Jeff Styles who was standing up and smoking a cigarette.

"Yo, that was almost three years ago, they ain't worried about finding who killed that ho. She's just another dumb bitch that got made in the streets. I ain't worried about that. Anyway, I got a lawyer; I'm going to get my beamer back. I ain't worried about that shit," Stefon returned.

Stefon enjoyed life as an only child to two correction officer parents. They gave him anything he wanted, including his own apartment and late model BMW, while working hard to pay his college tuition. He attended college full time only to look busy and convince his parents that he was doing something with his life; they had no idea he was on academic probation. Smoking marijuana and picking up prostitutes was his favorite areas of study.

"Yo, we outta weed. Time to go on a weed run. Stefon, call up yo, man." said Herman, his college friend.

Stefon tried to call his supplier on his iPhone 6, but no answer. "Yo, he is not answering, I think I gotta holler at him; he's just downstairs. Let me go downstairs. C'mon, Jeff let's make a run," Stefon said. "He's in apartment 2F, right below us," Stefon said. "I just hope he doesn't remember I owe him from last week."

Stefon and Jeff got up and went to the door to go downstairs leaving their friend Herman behind to play the video game.

Meanwhile, Lavender was lurking in the building, having gained access to the privately owned residence by breaking the door lock with his gun. Lavender was hyped up on coke, having indulged himself in his car minutes early in order to get psyched for what he was about to do. He normally didn't travel by himself but he counted this a personal vendetta. The cocaine in his system made him feel strong and confident that he could take out ten college kids.

Lavender just missed Stefon and Jeff as they went down the stairs and he got into the elevator to the third floor. In no time at all, he was at the apartment he was looking for, 3F. Lavender paused, his eyes red and intense. He was in a killing mood.

Herman heard a loud knock on the door. He wondered why Stefon didn't just open the door with his keys. Then it occurred to him that it might be their weed connection, that maybe he finally answered Stefon's text and came straight to the apartment. Herman put the game controller down and got up to answer the door but not before putting the game on pause.

"I'm coming, yo. Just a minute," he shouted.

When Herman opened the door, the large figure of Lavender, wearing his three quarter black leather coat and Lavender Timberland boots, stood right in the doorway. His large bug eyes were filled with hate and revenge. Herman was startled but wondered if this was the weed connection Stefon called.

"Stefon called you? You looking for Stefon," he said, nervously.

Lavender didn't even answer him. He squeezed his large fist and smashed the young man in his face so hard that the man fell back off his feet onto the living room table glass table, smashing it into a million pieces.

Herman didn't look much like Stefon. They were maybe the same height and had the same styled hair. But as hyped up on drugs that Lavender was, he didn't take much notice. Also, the lights in the apartment were out.

Lavender charged into the room, closing the door behind him, believing that he was alone with the object of his revenge.

"Now muthafucka, what! What! You killed my bitch, and now I'm gonna kill you!" Lavender said, grabbing Herman off the shattered glass, picking him up and slamming him against the plasma TV on the wall, cracking the screen. He commenced to punching him mercilessly about the body and face.

Stefon and Jeff returned from their weed run, eager to smoke their illegal bounty; they found the door ajar and hearing the noise went to open the door. "Yo what the fuck is Herman doin in there?" Stefon said. "He knows he going to have to pay for it."

Stefon opened the door and saw the hulking figure of Lavender assaulting their friend. Fear gripped his heart. Even though it was years ago, Stefon instantly remembered the man who pistol whipped him within an inch of his life.

"What the fuck! Who the fuck is this dude!" shouted Jeff. "He's fucking up Herman?"

"Yo, that's the muthafucking dude who almost killed me! That's that pimp, dude," Stefon said. "Who the fuck cares! Yo, he's killing Herman, now!" shouted Jeff. The two young men, startled as they were to see violence in the home, quickly sprang into action.

Jeff instantly jumped on Lavender's back, trying to get him in a choke hold, while Stefon searched the apartment for something heavy to hit him with. But Lavender, at six feet four was too big for the five foot nine, Jeff. Lavender simply straightened himself up, bent over and flipped Jeff off of his back onto the kitchen floor. Lavender looked down and punched Jeff hard in the sternum, causing Jeff to fold up in excruciating pain. Lavender then turned his attention back to Herman who was bleeding profusely from the nose and mouth.

Lavender slugged Herman in the nose, effectively breaking it. He then grabbed him in a choke hold ready to end the man's life with his bare hands. "I shoulda killed yo ass the first time nigga. But I'm gonna do that right now. That was my baby mama, nigga and my ho! You gonna pay for that shit!"

Herman was turning blue, as Lavender had the man's esophagus closed off. Herman was fading in and out of consciousness. He was feeling the life being drained from it.

Stefon seeing his friend dying quickly ran to the kitchen and grabbed a six inch knife from the knife storage block. He screamed as he plunged the knife into Lavender's back. "You got the wrong one, bitch! I'm the nigga you looking for," he shouted.

Lavender recoiled in pain, letting go his choke hold on Herman. He was in such a cocaine induced rage that he didn't realize that the man who just stabbed him was the man he was looking for. But he didn't care. Enraged by the pain, Lavender reached inside his leather coat and pulled out his Glock .45 caliber pistol. He aimed it at Stefon and fired two rounds that missed their intended target. Stefon dropped to the ground for cover.

Herman regaining his wind swung weakly and punched Lavender in the back. Lavender turned his attention back to Herman and quickly unloaded two more rounds, blasting Herman in the chest. Herman fell back against the wall. He was dead before he hit the immaculately tiled floor.

Jeff, no stranger to violence, having grown up in The Zone and seeing his older brother, a fledgling drug dealer, shot dead before his eyes, hurriedly grabbed the PS3 tower and tried to knock the gun out of Lavender's hand with it. But Lavender's large hands held firm the gun and aimed it now at Jeff. He fired the gun at Jeff, catching the young man in his right leg. The bullet went through his leg but Jeff was only wounded. Still, he managed to scramble behind the kitchen island. His friend Herman's dead body shielded him from Lavender.

Stefon took advantage to jump on Lavender from behind. They both fell forward on the kitchen floor but with Lavender on his back now and Stefon straddling him.

Lavender tried to point his gun at Stefon but the quick thinking man quickly knocked it from his hands with all his might. The Glock pistol slid across the floor to Jeff. Jeff grabbed the gun and pointed it the large pimp.

Stefon's eyes lit up and straddling the pimp, he punched Lavender in the face several times but with no effect as the unyielding pimp just glowered at him. Then he called out to his friend Jeff.

"Gimme me the fucking gun, now! He shouted. "Gimme the gun now!"

Jeff, having never fired a gun in his life, gladly threw the gun up in the air to his friend. Stefon snatched the gun out of the air and aimed it quickly at Lavender's head.

"No!" the fearsome pimp yelled, realizing the end was near.

Holding the gun with two hands, Stefon calmly squeezed the trigger and emptied the clip of its remaining rounds directly in the face of the notorious pimp, splattering blood and brains all over Stefon and spread across the kitchen and living room floor, a horrific mixture of blood, brains and bone. Gun smoke filled the apartment mingled with the smell of blood.

Jeff and Stefon sat silently by the gory scene. The adrenaline was still pumping in their veins. They both sat speechless for some time, traumatized by the carnage. Jeff finally spoke first.

"Yo, who the fuck is this muthafucka? Yo, did he come by himself? He came in here like some fucking fake ass Batman!" Jeff said, still staring at the bloody, disfigured body.

"That's, that white ho's pimp. The dude who fucked me up the first time, I told you," Stefon said.

"Word?" Jeff said. "Yo that's a big muthfucking dude! He killed Herman, yo! Herman's dead!"

"I know, man. I know," said Stefon. "This is crazy! Are you all right?"

"Yeah, he caught me in the leg but I think the bullet went through. Yo, how the fuck did he find you? We a long way from The Zone." Jeff asked, holding his wounded leg. "You sure they ain't more goons waiting for us outside, yo?"

"I don't know, man; I don't know. He slept on some on college niggas, that's for sure. But I bet it was one of his ho's who saw us pick up that white ho. This ain't over!" Stefon said. Stefon started rifling through Lavender's pockets, finding car keys and a gold plated money clip full of cash. Steve's eyes lit up at the sight of all that money.

"Yo, we could cop some serious weed with this here," Jeff said, looking at the cash. "That looks like two grand in that clip."

"Yo I'm taking his gold rope and watch," Jeff said as he removed Lavender's jewelry. "Damn, this shit is heavy! I could probably get some serious paper for this shit."

"Let's clean this shit up and then we gonna take this pimp's ride and find the ho that ratted us out," Stefon said.

"But how are we gonna know which ho ratted us out," Jeff asked.

"We gonna go through all of them one ho at a time, that's how," Stefon said. "Now come on, there's a lot of blood on this floor. Grab a fucking mop! We got two bodies to get rid of," he said. "Come on."

After a few hours cleaning up the blood on the floor, Jeff and Stefon handled Lavender's body. They wrapped it in the carpet and then carried him out of the apartment and into his own car. They then went back for the body of their friend Herman. Fearful to call the police, they wrapped his body in garbage bags and also put it in the car. Both bodies fit in the trunk. They drove the car to the Long Island Sound where they dumped first Lavender's body under the cover of darkness.

"No one will ever find that fake ass pimp, muthafucka," said Stefon, talking about Lavender.

They then took their friend Herman's body out of the trunk and dumped it in the Sound.

"God rest your soul, my brother," said Jeff as he pushed their friend Herman in the river.

In memory of their friend, Jeff and Stefon lit up a joint with the weed they had coped earlier. After several minutes passed and feeling the high take over them, they knew what they had to do.

"Now let's find some hoes," he said. The two of them jumped back in Lavender's car and sped off.

Chapter 3

Passion was masterful at her craft, her technique was astounding, and her skills were unmatched, so the hapless john didn't stand a chance. The middle aged john, a married father of three, was all a-flutter, bubbling with excitement, anxiety and pleasure, all at once. He had never been with a woman as pretty and sexy as Passion, at least not since his army days overseas. Trolling "the Zone" in his Honda SUV, he found Passion standing idly on the corner and solicited her for oral sex.

His rail thin body tensed before he released himself in a fit of explosive pleasure. He exhaled a loud sigh of relief before relaxing completely followed by a succession of rapid panting, as if he was chasing after his own breath.

Passion stopped performing on the man as soon as she made him come. This was an easy and quick job; it only took about five minutes, she thought to herself.

"Man, that was great!" the john proclaimed, suddenly feeling stress free.

"Listen here, Passion, can I get your number? We gotta do this again. I wish my wife could do me like this. We haven't had sex in six months, just fights and arguments" he said regretfully.

"Sure, here, baby," Passion said as she wrote her cell number down on a piece of paper for the john. "Just call me anytime." Passion winked as she prepared to get out of the man's Honda SUV.

"Ok, baby, sure. I'ma come out here next Friday, for sure," he said, already planning how he would meet up with Passion again. The married father of three let Passion out at the corner and peeled off, headed back home.

Passion returned to Prospect Street and the stroll with a vengeance. After leaving the church that First Sunday, months ago, she was intent only on making money. She was turning tricks at a rapid pace. Over the past few months, she was trying to make enough money so that she could get back in good graces with her pimp Lavender. Passion thought that if she could go back to him with a stack of money to somewhat make up for the time she was away, it would go a long way in smoothing things over with him. He wouldn't ask so many questions, like where she had been and what she was doing and with whom. And why she wasn't answering her phone. More importantly, she was hoping to avoid a vicious beat down.

Passion was also working hard to forget what had happened to her. She was struggling with feelings of betrayal and confusion. She felt Jameer and his church and the pastor were frauds. Passion felt like she was being made fun of; that she was being ridiculed by all of them somehow; like they had played her. There was no redemption or saving a girl like her, she thought. She was a prostitute, and when the time came she would pay for her sins, burn in hell. But now she didn't care. She was trying to survive the best way she knew how. She wasn't going to follow any pastor by day and freaky whoremonger by night, that's for sure. He was a fake, a phony, a hypocrite, like those hypocrites Jameer talked about in the Bible. She never wanted to see either one of them again.

She found it hard to think about Jameer and the feelings she had for him. She was sure she was in love with him and she couldn't get him out of her mind. She enjoyed the time they spent together but now she was confused. She wondered if it was all real. She resolved to put it all out her mind. Still, what she had learned and studied with Jameer stayed with her.

Passion needed a place to stay. For the past few weeks, she slept on park benches, roof tops, abandoned buildings, anywhere that seemed safe and isolated. She washed up in gas station bathrooms. It was during these times that she prayed remembering the Bible verse, "Cast thy burdens upon the Lord and He shall sustain thee."

Passion pawned her gold chain for a huge, diamond studded crucifix she wore on a long gold chain down to her midriff, to protect her from the evil on the streets and the evil-minded. She still carried the small Bible Jameer had given her, reading those passages from the Bible she and Jameer had read together, trying to understand what they meant in the context of her life. She also said a prayer from the Bible each time she went out to work the street and when she finished for the night, thanking God for bringing her home safe and in one piece.

Passion had most recently been staying at a hot sheet motel, using some of the money she earned working the streets, before she finally decided to find Mercedes, hoping she would allow her to stay with her until she could get on her feet, whatever that meant.

Passion made her way by cab to the North Bronx and found Mercedes at her stylish co-op, her Louis Vuitton bag slung over her shoulder. Mercedes was busy matching clients with girls on her rhinestone studded Apple laptop, tapping furiously on the keyboard.

Mercedes was stunned to see Passion at her door; she thought Passion was dead, a victim of the streets. Passion appeared gaunt, her face ashen, her clothes dirty like she had been living on the streets. It still didn't dim Passion's natural beauty, something that didn't escape Mercedes' discerning eye. Mercedes was vexed.

"Girl, where you been? We been worried sick about yah. Yah not answering your cell phone or noting. You been M.I.A for months. I thought yah dead, somewhere, baby girl. You ok? You look like somebody stole someting from you." Mercedes said, rushing to give Passion a hug after letting her inside her plush apartment.

Passion entered the aroma filled, air conditioned living room with the Persian rug. She felt like she could fall asleep right then and there on the expensive carpet. She thought how she would enjoy living with Mercedes in her nice, clean co-op.

"I'm fine, M," Passion said. "You wouldn't believe what I've been through. I think I was played. By the way, could you give this to Lavender?" Passion said, pulling out a wad of money and giving it to Mercedes.

Mercedes handled the money. She was impressed and envious all at the same time. It was five thousand dollars.

"Looka here, looka here! It seems like somebody been putting in a little overtime. It must be about four to five thousand dollars here," Mercedes said out loud, judging the amount by the weight of the money, a trick their pimp taught her. Mercedes quickly put the money to the side. "I will be sure to pass it on to Lavender," she lied.

Passion then told Mercedes everything about Jameer and the church and the pastor. She told her how she really started to believe that there was another life out there for her and how she was played because the church pastor was an old trick of hers.

"Girl, I told you those preaching people ain't shit. You got a hell of a lot more going on for you than them sorry asses. Don't worry, yah came back to the right place," Mercedes replied.

"I know, I know," Passion said, feeling comfortable with Mercedes. She felt confident in asking Mercedes to let her stay with her. "Listen M, I really need a place to stay. I was basically living on the street ever since Desire was killed. Can I stay here with you until I get on my feet?" begged Passion.

Mercedes looked at Passion without a shred of sympathy or compassion in her eyes.

"No, it wouldn't work for you to stay here with me because I have so many things to do," Mercedes lied, unable to really come up with a good reason. She secretly enjoyed seeing Passion in the predicament she was in. She would be the last person to help her out of it. Besides, she worked too hard to get her place and then have to turn around and share it.

"But yah could stay at 1385," Mercedes said. "It's free rent with a bed and working light and gas, and heat," she said, trying to make it sound appealing. "I will just put the word out to all the other girls that you'll be staying there and not to bother you."

Passion's heart sank. She felt betrayed again. She thought Mercedes was her friend, or someone she could count on to help her out. She realized that she was wrong. She couldn't believe that Mercedes would send her there when she had so much space in her own co-op. Passion had no other options however. She didn't want to stay in that foul place, but where else? She was literally homeless. Passion knew that going to a shelter wasn't an option either because she wouldn't be able to work and abide by any curfew the shelter would try to impose. The thought of going back to Jameer never even entered her mind.

"Ok, I'll stay there," she said, resigned to her situation.

"Good, here's the key to the pad, so yah won't have to depend on the super to let you in," Mercedes said, smiling, finding a spare key in her small purse. Mercedes delighted in being cruel. "I will let the other bitches know not to go there when you're there. And if they have a fucking problem with it call me. "

Passion unhappily went to stay at the crash pad at 1385 Prospect Street. She forced herself to try and clean it up, sweeping the dirty floor and throwing out the broken down furniture. Incredibly, she made it look habitable if not decent, but two weeks later after some of the other prostitutes complained that Passion was messing up their business by staying there, Mercedes went back on her word and told Passion that she couldn't interfere with the flow of customers that other girls brought there, even if it meant having to get up all hours of the night and wait outside until they finished their business. Passion was upset. Passion started to see why Desire hated Mercedes but couldn't find it in her to hate anybody. She had agreed to stay at the crash pad despite her misgivings and now she was regretting it.

In the meantime, Passion went out on an assignment for Mercedes, a request for a stripper girl in the housing projects of the South Bronx for a bachelor's party. It was a high paying job. Passion arrived at the crime ridden housing projects, stunning in a black fur waistcoat over a black mini dress with hood, fishnet stockings and black Manolo Blahnik pumps; a Marc Jacobs bag hugged her shoulders. As arrived at the entrance of the building lobby, Passion noticed luxury SUVs and beamers parked outside.

Passion was keyed up off cocaine Mercedes had given her to give her confidence. Passion used the drug more and more to help her along, to get her in the right mind frame to do what she had to do. Mercedes encouraged her in this way, supplied her with the best stuff money could buy. Mercedes was dealing directly with Lavender's own supplier Bump, a midlevel drug dealer and ex con. Mercedes recouped the price for the drugs out of Passion's earnings unbeknownst to her.

Passion took the stairs to the second floor as the elevators were stuck on the 26th and 14th floors. Once she arrived at apartment 2G, the metal apartment door was littered with magnetized flyers from upcoming rap concerts and night club productions. Rap music blared from inside. Passion knocked hard on the door.

"Well hello, Ms. Stripper, right on time," said a light skinned young man with a bald head and faux diamond earrings in both ears as he opened the door. "Come right in, come right in with yo fine self," he said, grinning from ear to ear.

Passion stepped inside the two bedroom apartment, the smell of K2 marijuana overwhelming her. The apartment was dark but she could still distinguish at least eight African American young men sitting in the dark living room, their heads turning immediately to Passion as she entered the room. A heavy cloud of smoke clung to the ceiling. Even in the darkness and smoke-filled atmosphere, the men's lecherous intentions were clear.

"Who is that coming in my house this late?" a middle aged woman's voice could be heard shouting from the bedroom over the music.

"Oh, it's Kayshawn, Ma. He just got off work," shouted back the young man who answered the door. "You could go back to sleep now, Ma."

"Come in, come in my dear," the man pulled Passion inside by her hand. "We been waiting for you. 'bout to get this party started," he said.

"Do you have my money?" Passion said, getting right to business.

"Hold on, hold on, now," the man said. He went to everybody in the room and collected money before returning to Passion and handing her a wad of bills. Passion counted the money quickly. It was two thousand, five hundred dollars in all.

"You can go to the bathroom over there and get ready," the man said, pointing to the bathroom in the back. "That's my mother in the bedroom over there. She's bedridden with swollen legs and can't get up. She won't bother us," he said.

"Ok, give me a minute," Passion said as she went toward the bathroom.

"Ok, baby with yo fine self," he said. "We waitin' on you. I'm the best man by the way; my name is Derrick. What's yours?"

"Passion."

"Passion, I like that. I like that. Well go on ahead and freshen up. We'll wait."

Passion went inside the dark, dirty bathroom and closed the door behind her. A putrid scent from the bathroom threatened to make her puke right then and there. She plotted her next move in the fetid atmosphere. She had no plans on staying here and entertaining all those sex hungry young men in the living room with a sick woman in the bedroom. They already paid her so she got what she wanted. She just didn't know how she could get out the apartment.

"Yo! Hurry the fuck up in there, bitch," a voice shouted from the living room.

Passion was tense. She opened the bathroom door and went into the other bedroom, crawling on her hands and knees in the dark. The bedroom had a foul smell, of someone who hadn't bathed in weeks.

"Is someone in here?" a woman's voice came from the bed.

Passion said nothing until she reached the window by the bed. Standing up now she could see a gigantic, obese woman laid out on the bed.

"Is someone in here? Is that you Derrick," the woman said.

Passion said nothing as she unlocked the window quietly and opening it wide, deftly put one leg then another outside the window until she was sitting on the ledge, measuring the height she was from the ground. She was one story above the ground.

Just then the door to the bedroom bust open and three young men charged into the bedroom.

"Hey, what the fuck, you doing in here?" the man named Derrick shouted.

"Yo! She trying to run with our money! Get her!" Another man said.

"What? What? What's going on? Derrick," the bedridden woman said. "Who opened the window? It's cold in here!" Close that window!" she begged.

Seeing the young men coming at her, Passion removed her designer pumps and saying a quick prayer, jumped out the window onto the frozen ground, falling on her knees.

"Yo! she got my money!" One of the men said, pulling a handgun out of his waistband and firing random shots out the window in the vicinity of Passion.

Passion quickly got up and ran for dear life before disappearing in the darkness.

Yousef drove Passion back to the crash pad later that night. Her heart was still pounding from the gunshots. She thanked God for her life. Despite her best efforts, the studio apartment was still dirty and reeked of smoked crack cocaine and illicit sex.

Passion decided to sleep on the couch as it was cleaner and comfortable. She laid out a borrowed spread sheet after removing most of her clothes. Passion took a swig of alcohol from her flask. She then threw herself carelessly on the creaky sofa and in no time was sound asleep.

"Passion, wake up! Wake up! I need the room," an urgent voice said, interrupting Passion's sleep. Passion looked up to find Ebony, a heavy-set light skinned prostitute, known to rob her customers, staring down at her. Standing behind her was a young man wearing a black Polo Lacoste shirt, True Religion jeans hanging off his hips and high top Jordan sneakers.

"Passion, it's me, Ebony. I got a date. I need to use the room for a few," Ebony said, urgency in her glazed eyes.

Passion jumped up and immediately covered herself as she was seminude, topless, wearing only her panties.

"What time is it?" Passion asked tired, and wondering how Ebony and her date got into the pad.

"How did you get in here?" Passion said.

"Its 4 'o clock. The super let us in," Ebony said trying to answer all her questions. "C'mon Passion, give me a few minutes."

Passion remembered that the super always let in the girls that didn't have a key to the apartment which were more than a few. Passion got up and putting on some jeans walked outside the apartment. She stood just outside in the hallway while Ebony handled her business. Twenty minutes passed before Ebony came out the apartment.

"Thanks Passion. Good lookin," Ebony said, counting her money as she walked, then suddenly darted out the building. A few minutes later, came the young man she was with.

"Hey! hey! That bitch stole my money!" shouted the duped trick, come running down the street after the prostitute Ebony, pulling his pants up.

Just as Passion started heading back into the studio apartment, another prostitute, Sydney, a black male transvestite with short red hair and wearing tight slim jeans and heels, came up the stairs with a tall, lanky, thug teenager in a hoodie trailing behind.

Sydney the transvestite whispered to Passion, "Passion, listen, girl, I need to use the room for a few minutes. Can you wait outside? It will just be for a quickie, ok. This is my last date before I turn in. He's cute right?" Sydney said, a naughty look shaping his face.

Passion didn't protest. She just wordlessly stood to the side and let the two of them pass. Passion thought to herself how they would be more hoes coming in with last calls. It was going to be a long morning.

⌃

Mercedes hadn't heard from Lavender for some time after he got out of jail, couldn't reach him by phone and didn't know he was dead. And, she didn't care. She was too busy running the business like a pro. In Lavender's absence, she managed his girls, some ten of them, forcing them to bring in more money under pretense that that's what Lavender ordered and parceled out the money to the girls but kept most of it for herself. Mercedes used the extra money she made off the girls to pay her college tuition and buy new shoes and expensive clothes for herself. The few times she did step out on the stroll were just for show, so that the other girls wouldn't suspect anything.

Meanwhile, she continued arranging dates online for her girls through her growing escort website.

With Lavender out of the picture, Mercedes started the practice of using a high end limousine service to ferry some of the girls to meet with their clients. She hired, Yousef, a 34-years-old Guyanese immigrant livery cab driver, to escort her best girls to their clients in a white stretch limousine. This way she evaded police by having fewer girls standing on the corner. She employed the limousine service for the more well-heeled and well-to-do clients who valued their privacy. She selected the best looking girls to be escorted to and from their clients. The starting price for such service was a thousand dollars because the livery driver had to be paid in addition to the girls.

This Saturday night she arranged a limousine service for Passion. Yousef, the driver was scheduled to pick her up at 10pm and take her to see a married, businessman on the Upper East Side.

The client, a successful entrepreneur, shared a luxurious brownstone in Manhattan with his socialite wife. He indulged his sexual fantasies with prostitutes whenever his wife left to attend her high society meetings. The man estimated that his wife wouldn't be back until 3am, which she normally does, as her girlfriend group often got into heated discussions about what to wear to the next affair and who would and wouldn't be invited. He would have time to be with Passion, he figured.

Passion arrived at his home wearing a sexy Vera Wang strapless black mini dress, black fishnet stockings and black suede red bottoms, all courtesy of Mercedes who let her borrow her outfit for the evening. Passion wore her hair in curls.

"Hey, Boo," she said as she entered the apartment, her angelic smile lighting up her face.

"Well hello," the man said as he opened wide his front door, letting Passion inside.

The married man was aroused from the moment he saw Passion in his living room, standing all sexy like. He immediately opened his black leather billfold and pulled out eleven hundred dollars cash. He was accustomed to spending that and more on prostitutes, money being no object to him. He put the money on the mahogany table by the door. Passion looked down and immediately snatched it up and put it in her purse after counting it.

"Ok, lover boy, let's get to it, my will is your command," Passion teased.

Passion's words were music to the man's ears. He deliberately moved toward Passion and started feeling her up, putting his sweaty, urgent hands under her dress and palmed her ass. He then moaned as he squeezed hard on Passion's perky breasts.

"Careful now, boy, take your time. What's the rush?" said Passion coyly, uncomfortable with his urgent groping.

The man ignored Passion and continued to fondle her. Overcome with desire, he then tried to kiss her. Passion recoiled.

"Please, let's just keep this professional, ok?" she said annoyed. "No kissing. I don't…"

The man stopped himself, feeling frustrated that he couldn't get Passion to reciprocate but he was really excited, attracted to her as he was.

"Let me," Passion said, putting the man at ease and holding his hand; she led him to the leather couch in the living room. The man complied mechanically. He sat down on the living room couch as he removed his trousers. He was already aroused. He showed his readiness through his cotton briefs. Passion paused to consider his size. "I see, someone is ready for me," she said. She grabbed him, quickly looked around the room and positioning herself on the couch, began performing on him, taking him slowly in her mouth. The man gasped as her warm mouth engulfed him. He was so excited, he wanted the feeling to last forever. Passion was good at what she did, a true professional. She performed on him, starting slowly then more energetically, giving the impression that she was enjoying it. The enraptured man could feel himself losing control. He grabbed Passion's head with his hand, patting it softly.

Just then, the key turned in the lock. It was his wife. She had unexpectedly returned home early from her night out with her friends. She was taking out loud to herself.

"Honey, I'm home. Betty got sick; maybe food poisoning. She had to go to the hospital," the man's wife shouted, putting her keys on the keypad and resting her bag down by the small table by the door. His wife quickly walked into the living room, expecting to find her husband still up watching one of his science fiction movies or a sports documentary. She wasn't prepared for what she saw, instead. Her mouth dropped as she took in the sight of Passion performing oral sex on her husband in their living room.

The startled man lost control at the sight of his wife and started coming as Passion, seemingly oblivious to the man's wife having just entered the living room, continued doing what she was paid for.

"James!" shouted, his wife, her eyes wide as the moon. "What the hell is going on here?"

The man stood, ejaculating involuntarily. He tried hurriedly to get his pants back up from his ankles but fell back on the couch.

"Honey, I can explain!" he said. Passion calmly stood up and straightened herself as she turned to look at the man's wife.

"Oh shit," Passion said, feeling sorry for the hapless couple.

"What! The fuck?" the man's wife said, incredulously. She then quickly lunged forward at Passion, aiming to scratch her very eyes out. But Passion quickly took the woman's measure and pulling a razor from her waistband, slashed the wife across the face. The woman fell forward, clutching her face as blood streamed and spurted from her face.

"James! James!" the woman screamed for her husband as she was lying on the carpet, writing in pain.

"Liz!" the man said, stunned by the sudden violence tried to grab at Passion but he stumbled as his pants were still undone and he was weak in the knees. Passion took advantage, and swinging down also slashed the man in the face, twice with the razor. Blood came down his face. He fell back in sudden pain.

Passion then clutched her bag and ran toward the door. She quickly let herself out and running down the stairs and out the building as fast as she could. She texted Yousef, her driver the code to let him know it was a bad situation. Once she got to the street, the car was ready and running. Passion jumped into the waiting limousine. They sped away and was across town in minutes.

The next night Passion found herself in lower Manhattan in the Meatpacking district. She went to a swanky loft, the residence of a trendy, young white couple looking to spice up their sex life with a threesome. Mercedes responded to their online request for a girl they could act out their erotic fantasies. She sent Passion.

Passion arrived wearing a sexy red laced outfit complemented with black stiletto heels and fishnet stockings. Passion rang the bell casually.

"Hi, you must be the girl we asked for," said a very perky, barefoot brunette female, who answered the door in a see-thru black negligee and silk robe. The woman extended her hand to Passion as she opened wide her apartment door. "Come in, come in," she said, ushering Passion into the loft and closing the door behind her.

Very expensive burgundy leather furniture, a sofa, loveseat, ottoman, matching end tables, were spread out across the spacious loft. Large antique vases could be found in every corner of the apartment. A huge silk rug was placed in the center of the floor. Naturalistic paintings hung on the walls. A curio bust of a naked man stood in the very back.

Passion had never seen such a large apartment and felt dwarfed by the sheer size of it. She spied a large, brass king sized bed at the back of the loft near the very large windows. A slightly built but very pale, effeminate, dark haired man was sitting on the bed, sipping on a glass of red wine. The persistent smell of marijuana wafted through the air.

"Come, come my dear, let's get this show on the road," said the brunette. She brought Passion to the bed where the bare chested man was sitting patiently, wearing only silk blue boxers.

"Jim, this is the girl they sent us. Isn't she pretty?" the woman said excitedly. "She's perfect for us, isn't she? Great ass," the busty brunette said, simultaneously tapping Passion lightly on the behind. "You people have such nice bodies," the woman carelessly remarked.

"Yes she is," said the man, eyeing Passion with lust in his light blue eyes. "She is very pretty. What is your name my dear," he said, in a deep musical voice.

"My name is Passion. And yours?" Passion said, offended by the woman's racial remark.

"Oh, I'm so sorry; my name is Karen and this is my fiancé, Jim. Where are my manners? Anyway, it's my fiancé's 30th birthday and I want to give him a threesome for his birthday. It's something he always wanted. Ok? It's fine. You don't have to be nervous. Do you want some wine or a joint to relax before we get started? We already started smoking one," the woman said, eager to put Passion at ease. "You are so pretty. I'm so excited!"

The woman went to the open kitchen area and returned with a bottle of Chardonnay and some wine glasses on a silver tray.

Passion could hardly keep up with how fast the woman was talking. She was very high strung and Passion wondered if she was high on drugs or that was just her way of talking. She could see how excited she was to give her fiancé this experience. Passion wondered how long they had been together.

"Here, this is for you," the woman said, quickly pouring Passion a glass of wine. "Now just listen to me and I will tell you everything you need to do. You won't have to think at all. I'm sure you've done this before in your profession."

Passion accepted the glass and quickly took a sip of the chilled wine before gulping it down. The chilled liquor passed over her tongue and down her throat, a tart taste. Passion took another drink and another drink until she felt at ease. Passion smiled easily as she sat on the edge of the bed.

The woman named Karen removed her silk blouse to reveal her slim shapely nude body with the most perfectly sculpted breasts. Her skin was the color of alabaster. A small tattoo of a colorful lizard was just above her midriff. Passion was unexpectedly attracted to the woman. The woman smiled a naughty smile and came at Passion, taking her face in her hand and planting, a slow, deep kiss on her lips. Passion responded in kind, reluctantly at first but then kissing the woman back, letting their tongues intertwine in their mouths. The woman slowly started removing Passion's clothes as they made out.

The woman's fiancé, Jim, smiled impishly, turned on by the two women making out. He took the wine bottle and downing it in one deep motion tossed it aside to join the two women, one his fiancée, the other a prostitute. The man went for Passion first, helping his fiancée remove her clothes. In no time, Passion's own perky breasts were exposed as well as her curvy body. The man gently cupped Passion's breasts before putting his mouth on her nipples, licking them voraciously. He did so for what seemed like hours as the wine made Passion feel light headed and woozy. He then kissed Passion softly then hungrily, pushing his tongue into her mouth. They kissed for what seemed like an hour before his fiancé gently but forcefully pushed them apart.

"Here put these on," Karen said, handing out colorful baroque style masks that only covered their eyes. Passion took the black mask and put it on. The man and his fiancé followed suit, making them all look like rejects from a Halloween party.

"C'mon, let's get this started," the girlfriend said from behind her purple mask. They converged on Jim, who was already laying prone on the bed, on his back, his legs spread wide.

Karen gently brought Passion along with her until they were bending down on either side of her fiancé. Karen playfully removed his silk boxers, letting them lightly fall to the floor. His manhood was exposed. Following Karen's lead, Passion began performing fellatio on the woman's masked but naked fiancé, taking turns on him. He began to moan lustily, deep heavy breaths. Satisfied that he was ready for them by virtue of his notable erection, Karen carefully mounted her fiancé, straddling him, taking him inside her. She then directed Passion to sit on his face. Jim wrapped his arms around Passion from inside her thighs and commenced stimulating her with his large tongue. Passion inhaled as his warm, wet tongue invaded her and slowly brought to the peak of arousal by its incessant lapping.

Karen reached forward and grabbed Passion by the face and kissed her ravenously.

After an hour, the attractive couple and Passion were exhausted and spent from the erotic activity. They relaxed on the bed, with a large joint Karen passed amongst them. Passion soon roused herself from the bed and started putting on her clothes, her job done. She began heading in the direction of the door, giddy from her high.

"Hey, suga, wait a minute, I almost forgot," Karen said as she bounded from the bed, in the complete nude, her pert breasts barely bouncing. She headed for the large black refrigerator in the corner of the loft. Reaching inside, she brought out a small, immaculately designed strawberry shortcake. She returned to the bed and broke into an impromptu song.

'Happy birthday to you, happy birthday to you…" she sang to her fiancé, begging Passion to join in which Passion did with a vigor that surprised even her.

'Happy birthday to you! Happy birthday! Dear baby, happy birthday to my lovely Jimmy, happy birthday to you! I love you, baby!" Karen said, and then she punctuated the serenade with a wet kiss on the lips of her soon to be betrothed

"I love you too, Karen, baby" the man returned with a big smile. "Thank you, baby!"

They then turned to Passion.

"Thank you so much, Ms. Passion,' said the woman. My fiancé and I really enjoyed this night. Your money is in the envelope on the night stand. And thank you again from the both of us."

"You welcome," Passion said enthusiastically. "Good night, and happy birthday to you both."

Passion found three thousand dollars in crisp thousand dollar bills on the table near the door. She quickly pocketed the money and let herself out.

Passion took a few steps toward the elevator before she could hear glass smashing and a voice screaming from behind the door of the loft she left.

"Why the fuck were you kissing her like that? She's a fucking whore; that's what she is!" Passion could hear the woman named Karen going on. "I can't believe you embarrassed me like that? How could you?"

Outside, on the corner, Passion's driver greeted her with a smile. "Everything alright?" he said. "Why are you crying?"

"Yeah, everything is all right, Passion said, tears coming down the side of her face. "Everything is fine. Get me outta here."

CHAPTER 4

It was the middle of winter in the city. Jameer returned to leading the street ministry, more in an effort to find Passion than anything else.

The subject of the pastor was still on everyone's mind.

"Do you think the pastor was really with that prostitute?" asked Deacon Bruer. "And if he was what are we doing out here?"

"I don't know, and it doesn't matter if he were; it doesn't change the fact that what we are doing out here is important, more important than who our pastor is sleeping with," returned Mrs. Hernandez.

Jameer stood silent about the subject, feeling it was his fault for bringing Passion to the church.

Though it was cold, prostitutes still littered the streets of the Zone, desperate to make money before the bone chilling weather invited frostbite. Jameer peered in each woman's face, hoping to see Passion's angelic visage. Each woman they approached, Jameer wouldn't fail to inquire about Passion and if they had seen her. Star was one of the prostitutes they encountered that night, walking the stroll in slut heels and tight designer jeans and a black Northface waist coat.

"Hello, dear. Hello. How are you? Listen, girl, you don't need to be doing this. You are a beautiful young woman who has her whole life ahead of her," Mrs. Hernandez said, pleading with Star to consider changing her life. "Let us pray for you. Can we do that?"

Star looked at Mrs. Hernandez and the group and didn't know how to respond to them. Star was cold and just wanted to cop but needed a trick to make money. She looked away from Mrs. Hernandez before saying, "Go away, you're messing up my hustle," and started to mind her smartphone, her genial personality taking a back seat to her heroin craving this night.

"Do you know a girl named Passion?" Jameer eagerly interjected.

"Yeah, I know Passion." Star said, hoping the man could be persuaded into having a three some. "Why you want to date her?" she asked naïvely.

"No, I'm looking for her," Jameer said. "I-we want to help her. Have you seen her?"

"No, I haven't seen her," Star said, matter-of-factly, now thinking Jameer was a cop or something and only pretending to belong to the church. Star went back to her smartphone.

"God bless you, young woman. I pray that you will turn your life around. There's nothing out here for you. It's not too late to make something of your life," Jameer returned, noticing the track marks on her arms. "Think about the people who care about you. I know someone wouldn't want to see you out here."

Jameer's words touched Star, and for a moment she forgot about her gnawing drug addiction. She thought about how she had betrayed so many people in her life, especially her grandmother. "Could you pray for me?" she suddenly said to the ministry group.

"Of course, of course," Jameer said, encouraged by her plea. "Come on y'all." He motioned to the rest of his ministry group and they made a semi-circle around Star and started praying for her. Pretty soon, other prostitutes in the area saw what was happening and came forward, curiosity in their eyes. Prostitutes and streetwalkers named Delicious, Ebony and Fantasia, Remy and Diamond, Nasty and Envy, all gathered around Star and the outreach ministry forming a small crowd.

Peaches arrived on the street from working in the club, heavy makeup still unable to completely mask the paralysis to her face. "Pray for me, too, please," she begged from among the crowd.

"Would you pray for me, too?" said a tall prostitute named Robin. "I want to be with my daughter again. She's only five years old. I haven't seen her since I gave birth in the hospital."

"Can you pray for me, too? I want to get off of drugs and go back to my husband. But my pimp won't let me. I need help. Please pray for me. " offered up Alize, a blond haired, flat-chested prostitute.

Suga, a veteran 40-years-old prostitute and her pimp/husband of 10 years, Miguel saw the small crowd gathering and approached too, out of curiosity. They expected to see they were giving out free food. They were pleasantly surprised to see it was prayers, instead.

Suga worked the streets alongside her husband with a singular purpose: turn enough tricks to keep them high on drugs every night.

"Can you help us turn our lives around?" Suga's plea carried above the crowd. "Can you pray for us too," Suga said.

"Come, come," said Mrs. Hernandez, crying tears of joy to see how many of these lost women and men came asking for prayers. She gave out as many care bags as she could before running out, then with the help of the other group members gathered everyone in a circle, performing a mass prayer group on the corner of Prospect Street under the circular pool of light cast by the street lamp.

After the prayers, the prostitutes and junkies, street walkers and pimps all thanked Jameer and Mrs. Hernandez and the street ministry and went back to work, looking for the next trick or their next fix, all except Peaches. She stayed behind.

"Can you help me?" Peaches asked. "I don't want this anymore," she said, a tear coming down the warped side of her face.

Mrs. Hernandez ran to embrace Peaches.

"Its gonnabe all right, my dear," Mrs. Hernandez said, tears in her eyes. "It's gonnabe all right now." She enveloped Peaches in her arms and kept saying, "It's gonnabe all right."

Chapter 5

Star pondered Jameer's words long after she walked away from the group. She wondered if she could ever leave this life of drugs and the sex trade behind. Just then she looked up and saw Lavender's black Dodge Charger coming up the block with its customized out-of-state license plate. Star assumed that Lavender either wanted to see how much she was making or he had a special customer in mind for her. She wondered why he just didn't text her where to go like he usually does. She began to think it strange that he would come up to his girls at peak working hours when police could be lurking anywhere. Still as cold as it was, she was happy to get in his warm car for a spell.

The black Charger pulled up to the block. Star quickly went to the car and opened the car door and got inside. She was startled and surprised to see that it wasn't Lavender her pimp driving the car but two young men she had never seen before.

"Hey, what the fuck is going on? Who are you two and why are you driving Lavender's car? "Where is Lavender?" she said. "Are you working for him or something?"

"Don't worry about your pimp, bitch. We gonna be your pimps now," Stefon said. Stefon was driving the car while his friend Jeff rode in the backseat. They were both high off weed.

Star started to panic. Her adrenaline started to flow making her forget her drug craving. She began to fear for her life. Star had been raped twice before by tricks. It wasn't an experience she wanted to relive.

"Look, let me out! I'm not feeling this. Let me out! Is this Lavender's car? Are you working for Lavender?" Let me out," Star started to scream. "I don't have money."

"Listen bitch, your small time pimp is dead! We run things now! We need to know if you done told him where to find us," Stefon said, driving the car to a deserted area on the outskirts of the Zone.

Hearing that Lavender was dead, Star's heart started to racing. She noticed that the man was wearing Lavender's gold rope and diamond watch. She believed them. She was scared to death. She reached for her smartphone to call the police but Jeff snatched it from her.

"Where are you guys taking me?" Listen, just let me go and I won't say nothing. Just let me go and I won't say nothing. Please let me out. Please," Star begged.

"We gonna let your ass out of the car when we are done with you, bitch," said Jeff, a menacing look on his face.

Star started crying. She had been in this situation before. She knew what was going to happen.

Stefon quickly pulled the car over and parked it on a dark, isolated street. "Now bitch, we going to find out if you the one who ratted us out or not. Let's get this show on the road."

Jeff and Stefon grabbed Star and started pulling off her clothes. "We gonna take turns on this bitch," Jeff shouted. Star screamed but no one could hear her.

Star was found the next morning, having been raped and badly beaten, bruised and unconscious lying half naked in the street. She was found by local police and quickly taken to Lincoln Hospital by police. She was treated for rape, assault and frostbite. She stayed in the hospital almost a week but despite aggressive questioning by authorities refused to give her name or identity. She refused to make a police report. When Star was able she promptly walked out of the hospital, in clothes donated by the hospital.

Star walked up Prospect Street in the midafternoon, looking for a ride, desperate to get to Mercedes and get out of the cold. She didn't wait long before a familiar john she dated in the past spotted her on the street. He stopped for her and Star quickly got inside, begging him for a ride. The familiar john gave Star a ride across town to Mercedes apartment but not before demanding a sexual act and paying her handsomely for it. He was ugly but he always paid her well, Star mused. She would use the money to cop later.

In no time at all, Star arrived at Mercedes co-op. She knocked frantically on Mercedes door, as if her life depended on it. Mercedes came to the door and saw Star standing there in mismatched borrowed clothes with bruises on her face.

"Oh my God, look at you!" Mercedes said. "Are you alright? Come in, come in! I hope no one followed you here," she said, looking out into the hallway to see if any crazy john followed Star to her stylish co-op. But also, if any of the tenants saw Star coming to her apartment, afraid they would report her to board for socializing with vagrants.

Once inside the luxurious co-op, Star collapsed on the leather couch. "You wouldn't believe what just happened to me," Star said.

Mercedes worked the streets long enough to know what happened to Star. She just wanted to know the details.

"So tell me what the fuck happened to you. You look like shit," Mercedes said, matter-of-factly.

"I-I was raped in Lavender's car, M," Star said.

"You were raped in Lavender's car?" Mercedes asked, not expecting to hear that, not quite understanding if she heard right. "Lavender raped you?"

"No, no it was two guys, M. I didn't really get a good look at those muthafuckers," Star said. "I mean I was scared. I thought it was Lavender coming for me. Then they wouldn't let me out of the car. The one driving punched me in the face so hard---and then all I remember is them pulling off my clothes and raping me, taking turns on me with their little dicks---well one, he wasn't so little. But they fucking raped, M!"

"They raped you in Lavender's car?" Mercedes asked, still puzzled as to how they could be driving Lavender's car. She wondered if they were Bump and Spirit, two of Lavender's drug dealer friends. They were always looking to get freebies with Lavender's girls.

"Fuck yeah; they raped me! I'm still in pain; my ass hurts," Star shot back, a tear rolling down her face. "I swear I can't do this no more, M. I mean it; I'm done working the streets. This is the third time I been raped in this fucking business. The next time I'm going to end up dead. Maybe those religious fanatics were right. Maybe it's time for me to turn my life around," she said. "They prayed for me, too."

"Fuck those Bible thumpers," Mercedes said, annoyed that they continue trying to convert her girls. "Look bitch, I feel for what happened to you. But what are you gonna do for a living? How are you going to support yourself? I'm not telling you to go back out on Prospect right now, but you gotta be realistic. You gotta eat. Look, you're one of my...er, Lavender's best girl. You can't let this side track you. You knew it's one of the hazards of the job," Mercedes said.

"Where the fuck is Lavender anyway?" Star interjected. "Why were those niggas driving his car? Have you heard from him? I tried to call him on his cell but the motherfucker aint answering him. That's not like him. Have you heard from him?"

Mercedes thought carefully before answering. Since Lavender has been missing for the past few months, she has been running the show. She has been collecting money and setting up the girls with clients, making more money than when Lavender was here. She didn't want it to end.

"He's out of town, trying to recruit more girls. I tink he went down south. That's what he said, anyways," she lied.

"Ok, well, tell him I'm out of this. Can I crash here with you until, I figure out what to do? I have an uncle that lives in Brooklyn. Maybe he would let me stay with him," Star said.

"Ok," Mercedes said. She then went into her Coach bag and retrieved a small clear bag of heroin.

"What's that?" Star asked, knowing full well what it was.

"Just a little sumthin, sumthin" Mercedes said with a smirk on her face. "Want some?"

"You know that's my shit, M!" I aint got much money, just this," she said, handing Mercedes the money the john gave her,"

Star started scratching her arm; her addiction was like fire in her veins. She was beyond thirsty to cop.

Mercedes counted the money Star gave her. "This ain't enough, girl not for this shit right here. This is that good shit," Mercedes teased. "But you can get it providing you do this job for me, girl." Mercedes said, gently putting the heroin on the table.

Star stared at the bag and then started to cry. She knew what Mercedes was doing. "M, please I can't do that no more. I can't go out there again. Look at me; do you know what those dudes did to me? They both raped me, over and over. Please don't make me go out there. Please M."

"I'm not *making* you do anything," Mercedes said, "I guess you don't want this," she said, about to put the heroin back in her Michael Kors bag.

Star started to go into panic mode. She was a heroin addict and that's why she worked the streets, why she was in the sex trade. She needed heroin like a drowning man needed air. Star was known for exchanging sex for drugs if she was in desperate need of a hit. She couldn't resist her urges. She had a newfound hatred for Mercedes. Heroin was her kryptonite. She would do anything for it.

"Ok, ok, M. I'll go back out there. I hate your fucking ass though," she said. "Now give me my shit, you devil-bitch!"

Mercedes laughed. "That's my girl," she said, handing Star the bag of heroin.

Star held the bag like it was her life raft. "M, do you have a needle?" she begged.

Mercedes smiled. "Sure do, girl. I also got a customer lined up for you who likes some real freaky shit," Mercedes said with an evil grin on her face. "You won't even have to go out in the street just hang tight at 1386 and he will come there. I already set it all up. Just dress sexy. You know what to do. Alright, girl?" Mercedes said. Star wasn't really listening. Star had already started shooting up. Mercedes watched with glee as Star's eyes rolled up into her head. In an instant, Star was in heroin heaven.

Mercedes brought Star back to the crash pad later that evening. She encouraged Star to take another hit of heroin before her customer arrived, giving her another a small liquid bottle of the drug. She didn't have to ask her twice.

"Are you sure this isn't some crazy ass that's goin to rape me, M?" Star asked as she drained the bottle with a used syringe and after flicking it she plunged it into a taut vein. "I'm not used to doin' this shit over the internet. I like to know who I'm dating, see them face to face, y'know?"

"That's the old way, girl. It'll be all right, Star. Trust me, doing it this way is much safer than getting picked up on the street. Anyway, he should be here in a minute. I'm goin' to leave you two alone. Aight," Mercedes said. "Try and look nice and sexy for him. Alright, alright," Star, hiking up her miniskirt to show more of her behind while she sat on the bed. "Is this good?" "Yeah," laughed Mercedes as she headed out the door. "Take care," she said to an already nodding Star.

⋏

"C'mon, Peaches, you could do it," said, Mrs. Hernandez as she stood watching over her. "It's not that hard. Just flip it over. You did everything else. But be careful."

Peaches was struggling with the cheese omelet. She had done everything, scrambled the eggs, diced the onions and peppers and tomatoes, and poured the mixture. The final step was flipping it up onto the plate from the frying pan. She was nervous and didn't want to mess it up. She had never done anything like this before. Making the omelet ready to eat was part of her training in helping her get off the streets. She was learning how to cook.

With one easy motion, Peaches picked the omelet up on the skillet off the frying pan and flipped it onto the plate. She burst into a smile.

"Hey, you did it girl! You did it!" shouted Mrs. Hernandez. Months ago, Ms. Hernandez and Jameer found housing for Peaches at the Castle, a residential recovery center for sexually exploited teenage girls, located in Forest Hills, Queens New York. Among other things, the program teaches life skills, including culinary arts to many of the girls to instill in them a sense of confidence. Peaches thrived in the program.

ᐱ

Mrs. Hernandez jumped up and hugged Peaches tenderly. "I'm so proud of you, Peaches. How do you feel?"

Peaches smiled a big awkward smile. The persistent paralysis on the left side of her face which distorted her smile was a stark reminder of her life on the street. Having been abandoned by her mother at the age of three and never having known her father, Peaches wasn't accustomed to smiling anyway.

"I, I feel good, Mrs. Judy, thank you. I didn't think I could ever cook for myself," Peaches said, gushing with pride.

Mrs. Hernandez felt so proud to have Peaches off the streets and receiving the help she needed. Mrs. Hernandez knew firsthand how degrading and empty life was on the streets. She also knew how hard it is to get a prostitute out of the business. She saw in Peaches, her own self, living a life that would only end in destruction and death. Mrs. Hernandez came to the drug rehab center on her own time to help encourage and monitor Peaches' progress. She also volunteered to assist in the life skills training program to help Peaches in her rehabilitation. The last thing Mrs. Hernandez wanted was for Peaches to get discouraged and fall back into the street life, like most of them do, like she did herself.

"Do you want me to make you an omelet, Mrs. Judy?" Peaches asked, all innocently.

"Sure, why not. I had a small breakfast this morning," Mrs. Hernandez said. "I still have room in my stomach for more," she smiled.

ᐱ

The worn mattress springs creaked and groaned in rhythm under the weight of the middle-aged man humping on Star's dark limp body. The heroin-addicted prostitute was laid out naked on the bed, passed out from the heroin flowing through her veins. It didn't matter to the client Mercedes set her up with. The professional window washer by trade, paid Mercedes handsomely to live out his pseudo rape fantasy. He was excited when he entered the crash pad and found Star, lying there passed out on the dirty mattress, wearing only a camisole, waiting to be ravaged. He gave Mercedes specific instructions that he didn't want any interaction with the woman; he wanted her to be completely under when he had sex with her. Mercedes followed his instructions to the letter. She made sure to have Star in a doped up trance, a deep drug induced state. She even asked Lavender's drug dealing friend, Bump to make sure to give her a strong heroin dose. Bump simply mixed the heroin with more acid but warned it could put her out. Mercedes didn't care; she wanted to make her customer happy. When the man finally concluded his business, he raised his sweat soaked body off the unmoving prostitute. He gathered his clothes, dirty denim pants, simple, red, plaid shirt and Fruit of the Loom underwear and dressed himself quickly; putting on his soiled snow boots, he made his way toward the door. He looked back only momentarily at Star and her sexy dark body. He smiled to himself before leaving, satisfied that he had indulged his perverse fantasy. He was completely oblivious to the fact that he had actually finished having sex with a corpse. Star had died moments earlier from a heroin overdose.

Chapter 6

Jameer heard a knock on his door in the late evening. He wasn't expecting anyone and was getting ready to turn in for the night after reading his Bible and praying for Passion. He went to the door and was surprised to see who was standing on the other side of the door after looking through the peephole. It was the Pastor Reverend Emerson, former senior pastor of Grace Baptist church.

Jameer paused before slowly opening the door. A flood of emotions, from anger to confusion to pain went through him.

"Pastor, sir, how, how are you? What brings you here so late at night?" he said wide eyed as he greeted the pastor.

"Good evening, Jameer," the pastor said in a soft, humble voice. "May I come in?"

"Of course, by all means, come in, come in." Jameer stammered, feeling bad that he didn't think to invite him inside. This was the first time the pastor of Grace Baptist Church had ever come to his home since his adopted mother died. Jameer had asked him several times before, but the pastor was always too busy.

Jameer looked at the pastor and couldn't help but be amazed at how much thinner the pastor had got in the last few months since he went into seclusion. He must've been fifteen pounds lighter. His face had lost its color and he was gaunt-looking. The pastor wasn't smiling either his trademark smile. His face was dour, his visage grim.

He sat down on the couch in the living room.

"May I offer you something to drink, pastor?" Jameer said.

ᝰ

"Just some water," the pastor said softly. Jameer went into the kitchen and poured chilled water in a glass. He brought it back and handed it to the pastor. He sat down across from the pastor. He watched as the pastor swallowed the entire glass of water in one motion. It seemed like the pastor had the weight of the world on his shoulders. And it was more than he could bear.

"My son, I have come here because I believe I need to express my deepest apologies to you. My wife, when she was alive, had nothing but hope and praise for you. She saw past your anger and saw a young man with a lot of potential to do good things," the pastor said. "Before she died, my wife, she made me promise to guide you, to help you reach that potential. I watched as you grew in the church to become one of the most dynamic and promising members of the church. I marveled at your progress. I could see my wife smiling down from heaven at your development. You have become a shining example to the young men and women in the church. You are testament to the glory of God."

"Thank you, pastor, sir," said Jameer, tears welling up in his eyes, thinking about the pastor's dead wife, thinking about his adopted mother, overwhelmed by the pastor coming here to apologize to him, feeling sad that the man he looked up to was somehow less than what he had always thought him to be.

The pastor continued. "I thought you were way over your head when you decided to head the outreach ministry. I feared you would falter like I did, so many years ago when I was still grieving the loss of my wife. But you were solid and steadfast. You saved that little girl and I want you to know that I am a proud of you. You have earned ordination to deacon hood as far as I'm concerned. Where is that young lady, Jameer?" he asked.

ᝰ

Jameer was speechless. He was humbled by the pastor's words. He was even more humbled to hear the pastor admit to faltering. He couldn't deny the truth about what Dominique had accused him. He could hardly look at the pastor now, knowing that he had taken advantage of Dominique, the woman he was now in love with.

Nevertheless, Jameer gathered himself enough to answer him.

"After that day in church, I never heard from her again. I think she went back to the streets, back to her pimp," he said. "But I'm in love with her, pastor. I need to let you know that and I couldn't tell you that before but I'm in love with her," Jameer confessed.

"You're in love with her?" the pastor said, not sure he heard correct.

"Yes, yes I am," Jameer responded.

"Are you sure, its love?" the pastor asked. "And not lust."

"I'm sure, sir" Jameer said. "I do love her."

The pastor looked at Jameer and knew that he was sincere.

"Oh my, that poor little girl. Then we must go find her, you and I. She needs to be found. Let's go now," the pastor said, getting up off the couch with a suddenness and vitality that took Jameer by surprise.

Jameer didn't expect to go out looking for Dominique tonight, especially with the pastor. He reached for his coat, without thinking.

"We'll take my car," the pastor said. They both left the apartment together and in a hurry.

⚔

Passion arrived at the crash pad exhausted. It was three in the morning. The livery cab driver was polite as always.

"If that's all Ms. Passion, I hope you get some rest," he said letting Passion out and flashing a smile before peeling off.

"Thank you, good night." Passion said.

Passion mounted the steps to the building and opened the front door. Walking up the stairs, she turned to start down the corridor to the apartment. She flirted with the idea of spending her money to stay in a hotel but resolved to give it one more night here. She had been secretly putting money aside to rent an apartment.

Passion arrived at 1B and put the key in the door. As she walked inside the apartment, she wasn't prepared for what she found. Sprawled on the dirty, sheetless mattress in the middle of the floor was the dark, lifeless body of Star, completely nude except for a black camisole.

Passion tried to scream but the sound got stuck in her throat.

She crept slowly toward Star's body; it was cold to the touch. Passion recoiled in terror. She was horrified. A shudder of fear shot through her body. She couldn't tell the cause of death. The body seemed unharmed, save for the needle tracks up and down Star's arms. Passion grabbed her crucifix about her neck, saying a prayer to herself. She then turned to run out of the apartment which was now a morgue. Frantically, she called 911 to report her friend's demise.

"Hello! Hello, please come quick! My friend, this girl is dead! She's lying here dead! Please send someone!" Passion screamed into her cellphone as she ran out the building.

It was four in the morning, when police cars converged on the building where Star's body was found. An anonymous call was made reporting the corpse. Yellow police tape cordoned off the apartment 1B, leaving a narrowly prescribed path where building residents could enter and exit the building without coming near the crime scene. Detectives and forensic specialists in suits and white gloves scoured the crime scene and determined the cause of death was heroin overdose.

Most of the tenants in the building were questioned by police and detectives about the vacant apartment and if they knew it was being used by prostitutes to entertain their johns. Most tenants knew, but many denied knowing.

The building super was arrested and deemed a Person of Interest. The building landlord was being sought for further questioning into what he knew about what was going on and his involvement in the illegal use of the apartment.

Passion wandered the streets aimlessly. She was hysterical.

She felt a cold shudder come over her, to match the frigid temperatures outside. She didn't know where to turn. She was fearful and afraid and confused. Death seemed all around her. Her first thoughts were to go to see

Jameer but she hated him, felt that he made a fool out of her or was a fool himself. She wanted to find Mercedes but didn't trust her; after all, it was Mercedes who made her live in the filthy, crash pad. She realized she still had money on her and would use it to go somewhere, but where? She made up her mind to go to Lavender. But where was he? No one had seen him in months. He wasn't answering his phone. Passion decided to go back on the streets in the hope that she would spot him or his car on the street.

As it started to rain, Passion felt more lost than ever before, like her world was coming apart. She was lost and afraid and homeless again. And very cold. She felt like she couldn't make it without Lavender; that she couldn't survive without her pimp. She felt that she needed him.

Just then, Lavender's black Charger drove up the street. Jeff spotted Passion first on the corner as they rode around.

"Look, look that was that girl who was with that white ho we burned," Stefon, said. "The real pretty one. I know that's her."

"Yo, she's a dimepiece fo sho." said Jeff, staring admiringly at Passion's long legs and pretty face.

"Yeah, I remember her. Let's get at her. Get her in here," he said.

Jeff and Stefon had been terrorizing the working girls on Prospect Street for the past few weeks. They used Lavender's car to sucker his girls into getting in by pretending to be their pimp or working for their pimp and then they would rape and rob them. They saw Passion as another victim.

They slowly drove up to Passion and stopped just in front of her so that she would know to get in.

Passion saw the black Dodge Charger, coming up the street with its glistening rims and vanity license plates and she couldn't believe that Lavender had finally come back. She was elated. Her eyes grew wide. Desperation seized her. She couldn't resist the need to get back with her pimp. She saw Lavender as her salvation.

Jameer and the pastor turned the corner in the escalade and saw Passion standing on the corner. Jameer's heart skipped a beat.

"Look! There she is," Jameer said. "Drive faster. She's getting in that car."

Passion jumped into the street and reached for the car door of the Charger. She was smiling, anxious to see Lavender and redeem herself to him. Eager to tell him about what happened to Star, knowing that he would get to the bottom of it. Then at the last minute, something made her stop. She felt something wasn't quite right. She hesitated. She got back on the curb and waited to see if Lavender would open the car door. She didn't know what it was but her intuition made her back off.

"Yo, she's not getting in!" What we gonna do?" Jeff said from inside the car. Stefon decided they had to act. "Fuck it, grab her ass! They ain't no PoPo around, anyways!"

At that, Jeff sprang into action, opening the car door and lunging at Passion. Passion was confused, not knowing who it was coming out of Lavender's car, a man she had never seen before. Passion stood frozen. Jeff, using the element of surprise, grabbed Passion about the waist and quickly pulled her into the car, and with such force, caused Passion to bang her head against the roof of the car, knocking her dizzy in the process. Still, once inside the car, Passion tried to resist. She looked hard at Stefon. She remembered Stefon as the man who picked up Desire, before she was found burned to death. Passion immediately started screaming for help.

"Yo! Shut her up with this," Stefon said, handing Lavender's gun to Jeff. Jeff took the gun and smashed Passion across the head with the butt of the handle, opening a nasty gash on her forehead, knocking her unconscious.

"Hey, hey!" some passersby yelled when they saw the apparent kidnapping. The black Charger ignored the voices and peeled off.

The pastor and Jameer had just turned the corner onto Prospect Street when they witnessed what just happened to Passion being pulled into the black Dodge Charger.

"That was her! That was Dominique!" Jameer shouted. "Somebody is trying to kidnap her," he said. "I think that's her pimp. Did you see that? He pulled her into that black car."

"Yes, I saw that, poor little girl," the pastor said. "Call the police, while we follow them."

Jameer called 911 on his cell phone and kept his eyes trained on the black Dodge Charger racing ahead of them.

"Faster, faster, we can't lose them!" Jameer screamed. His heart was pounding. He was anxious and feared for Passion's life.

Jeff and Stefon quickly noticed the pastor's Escalade following them. "Yo, is that fucking car following us? Go faster!" Jeff shouted to Stefon "Let's lose those muthafuckas!"

Stefon put his foot on the accelerator and the car started racing down the street.

"We're going to lose them! Go down Carroll Street and cut them off, "shouted Jameer. He knew the streets all too well and where they intersect. The pastor did as he was told and made a sharp right off Prospect Street to Carroll Street. He sped down the empty street until he came back on Prospect Street and saw the Black Dodge Charger bearing down on them. He swerved but it was too late. The Charger rammed the side of the Escalade, almost making it tip over but pushing it up on the sidewalk. Both cars crashed to a violent stop, waking the whole neighbor as people opened their windows to look down at what caused the sudden collision.

The two young men Jeff and Stefon stormed out of the crashed vehicle. Jeff was holding Lavender's gun.

"Yo! Who the fuck is you chasing us? You ain't no fuckin' po-lice!" Jeff shouted, holding the gun and pointing it at the passenger side of the Escalade.

Jameer stared down at the gun and the man holding it. He felt an anger welling up inside of him he hadn't felt in years. He hated anyone to point a gun at him unless they were going to use it. He felt like they were disrespecting him in the worst way.

When Jeff just kept talking and not actually about to pull the trigger, just walking closer to him, Jameer saw his opportunity. Feeling the adrenaline rushing through him, he unlocked the passenger door and pushing it open so fast, he managed to knock the Jeff's arm down with the gun. He then lunged forward out of the SUV and grabbing Jeff's wrist, he forced him to release the glock. The gun fell to the icy ground. Jameer followed his daring play by pummeling the young man with his fists. One punch sent Jeff sprawling to the ground, the other punch put his head into the concrete sidewalk.

Stefon saw what was happening and screamed, "Jeff, Jeff!" He jumped out the car leaving a shaken and dazed Passion reeling from the car crash.

Stefon ran up from behind trying to catch Jameer unawares but he was met by the solid fist of the pastor smashing across his chin, dropping the young man to his knees.

"No, young man, your wild ride ends tonight," said the pastor, standing over Stefon.

Stefon looked up at the large pastor and thought to himself how he hit harder than the pimp Lavender. He still wasn't going to be deterred. He jumped to his feet and swung at the pastor.

The pastor managed to catch Stefon arm in midswing and twisting it behind him, brought the young thug to his knees. He then planted a left hook across the back of Stefon's head. Stefon was laidlow and unconscious. Having taken care of the young thug, the pastor went to assist Jameer.

Seeing the pastor about to join his friend and double team, Jeff scrambled to find the fallen gun. Seeing it under the car, he lunged for it. He came up on the other side of the black Charger with the gun pointed at the pastor and Jameer, from a kneeling position. He fired a single shot from the gun.

The pastor pushed Jameer to the ground and took the slug in his arm before going down. The bullet exited out the pastor's shoulder. Jeff sprang to his feet and moved in to finish the job.

Two police cars suddenly arrived on the scene, their bright lights and sirens blaring. But, Jeff, the adrenaline in his veins flowing was filled with fear and anger. He was aiming to kill the pastor and Jameer. He was oblivious to the police arriving on the scene. He also didn't hear the police shouting at him.

"Freeze! Drop the gun!" one of the police officer shouted, his gun drawn. The other officers positioned themselves strategically behind their cars, their guns also drawn and trained on the gunman. "Drop the gun!" they shouted.

Jeff seeing the pastor lying prone on the floor, an evil smile creased his face. He pointed the gun down at the pastor and squeezed the trigger. But the clip was empty. There were no more rounds in the gun.

At the same time, four police officers immediately opened fire as one, riddling Jeff's body with a hail of bullets, dropping him where he stood. A mass of blood formed under Jeff's body. He was dead.

Jameer stared at the bloody scene before running to the pastor, fearing him dead. He was relieved to find him still alive with only the bullet wound to his arm. "Pastor, you've been hit! Are you all right," Jameer shouted.

"Don't worry about me, my dear boy," the pastor said, as he lay prone on the ground, unable to feel his wounded arm. "God spared me tonight. The police are here. Go to the young lady."

Jameer immediately went to see that Passion was still in the Dodge Charger. He found Passion dazed but coming to. She was as beautiful as ever.

"Dominique, are you all right?" he said, softly. "I love you."

Passion looked up and saw Jameer's soft brown eyes, his face full of genuine concern. "We're you been?" she said. "I'm alright now."

Passion was treated for her head injuries at Jacobi Hospital in the Bronx. Standing at her bedside early Sunday morning was Jameer, excited to see her wide awake now.

"How you doin' baby," he said.

"My head is still ringing a little but I'll be all right," Passion said.

"Listen, somebody is here to see you. They came a long way to," Jameer said, a sneaky smile on his face.

"Oh really?" Passion said. "Ok, let them in."

Jameer left the room and came back in with a much taller, darker man behind him, whose warm brown eyes Passion could never forget.

"Hi Dominique, it's been a long, long time, but I finally found you. It's good to see you," the man said in a deep but familiar voice.

"Dad, Dad?" Passion said, unbelieving. "H-How, how did you find me?"

"This young man here contacted me some time ago and told me you were here," Passion's father said, his broad frame barely contained in his sheriff's uniform. "I missed you so much. Trust me, I will never let you go again." Passion's father smiled warmly.

CHAPTER 7

Grace Baptist Church was filled to capacity on this Easter Sunday for the pastor's recommissioning ceremony. There were no empty pews and those unfortunate enough to arrive late found themselves fighting for standing room only. It didn't help either that local news station vans or members of the press and media took up parking spots and front row church seats usually reserved for long time members. Once word had circulated that the pastor would be delivering the sermon this Easter Sunday, every church member, past and present, lay members and community people familiar with the scandal that brought down the well-known pastor, flocked to the church to see how the disgraced pastor would give an account of himself.

The church mounted two 50 inch flat screen televisions high up on either side of the pulpit so that all could witness the joyous occasion. Elaborate floral arrangements adorned the stage around where the ceremony would take place. Huge votive candles ringed the pulpit and entire sanctuary. The 20-member church choir was stunning in their red gowns with gold stoles and trimming.

The Pastor Emerson arrived at the church on time. He was dressed in a sharp, Ralph Lauren gold pinstriped suit with high lapels and matching gold colored shoes. He wore his wounded arm in a white sling like it was a badge of honor. The pastor held his head high, ready to meet the challenge of recommissioning.

When the pastor emerged into the church sanctuary, the congregation rose as one and started clapping. After a lengthy ovation, the congregation settled down and took their seats. Silence pervaded the church. The pastor walked toward the pulpit and looked up at the Associate Pastor Richard Eisely.

Mr. Eisley calmly walked up to the pulpit ready to read from a prepared statement. He looked down at the former senior pastor. The full complement of the churches deacons lined the rails around the pulpit. The associate pastor opened his mouth and spoke from the epistle:

'To Whom It May Concern, we the undersigned serve as committee of counsel for the restoration of the Reverend Avery Emerson. Throughout the restoration process, Reverend Emerson has been honest, forthright, vulnerable and fully cooperative as we sought to apply discipline and restoration to Pastor Emerson; we have been met with genuine repentance, seriousness and enthusiasm about what God is doing for him. We, along with other pastors and church officials, laid hands upon and recommissioned the Reverend Emerson during the annual camp meeting of the National Association of the Churches of God in Washington D.C.; therefore we release the Reverend Avery Emerson to any and all ministry to which he has been called; rejoice with us and we rejoice for and with the Reverend Avery Emerson."

With that declaration the entire congregation rose again and applauded as one, happy to have their beloved senior pastor returned to them. There were a scattering of boos in the congregation, by those who felt that he had betrayed the trust of the parishioners by laying with a prostitute and that he was a hypocrite, but those jeers were drowned out by the calls of appreciation and rejoicing by those exhilarated to have the pastor back leading the church.

"Now we will hear from the senior pastor of Grace Baptist Church, the Reverend Avery Emerson," the associate pastor said. Applause again filled the sanctuary. The pastor rose and climbed the stairs up to the pulpit. He took in the hand clapping for a good while before waving his hands for the congregation to be seated. Then he opened his mouth and spoke.

"God is good!" proclaimed the pastor to the congregation. The congregation exploded in applause and laughter. The pastor screamed again,

"God is good…" he called out to the congregation and this time waited for a response.

"….All the time!" the congregation returned as one. The pastor laughed a hearty laugh. "Yes, indeed, all the time! All the time! Yes indeed!"

The pastor was beside himself with joy and happiness. The congregation had never seen him so animated and full of rejoicing, not since before his wife died so many years ago.

"Preach, preach!" random voices in the congregation screamed.

Emboldened by the hearty reception he was getting, the pastor was grinning appreciably. He was beaming. He had prepared a sermon for this moment and would deliver.

The pastor started off speaking in a deep, conversational tone, letting the cluster of microphones carry his voice.

"Paul the greatest of all the apostles…Paul spoke about turning our weakness into strength. And the Lord said unto Paul, 'My grace is sufficient for you, for my power is made perfect in weakness.' And then Paul understood, not to be ashamed of his weaknesses or his inflictions or shortcomings. 'Therefore I will boast all the more gladly about my weaknesses, so that Christ's power may rest on me.' And, Paul said, for 'Christ's sake, I delight in weaknesses, in insults, in hardships, in persecutions, in difficulties. For when I am weak, then I am strong.'" The pastor stopped as if in reflection. He then opened his mouth to continue.

"Preach," someone shouted from the congregation.

"God's grace helps us work through our shortcomings. When we become dependent upon God's grace to buttress our own weaknesses, we are more sensitive to the needs of others. God's grace helps us work through our fears, our disappointments and discouragements. For when I am weak, then I am in strong through Christ."

"Go on!" another congregant shouted out.

"If we confess our sins, he is faithful and just and will forgive us our sins and purify us from all unrighteousness,' our beloved disciple John said," the pastor said.

"And now, I'm brand new, and old things have passed away!" he shouted proudly. "On this Easter Sunday, I am made brand new in Christ! I am a new creation in Christ! Always know that no matter where you are in your life, God's grace will find you," he said, pointing emphatically at random members in the church.

The congregation exploded with warm cheers and applause. Many in the church were crying tears of joy. Many more stood up clapping. He was restored to the church. The pastor was back. The applause continued to shower down on him as the congregants showed their thankfulness for his return to service.

The organist began playing the celebratory music followed by the drums and lead guitar and tambourines banging. The music saluted joyousness of the moment.

Having finished his sermon, the church started singing "Amazing Grace." The pastor was moved to tears at what he had done and now how the church was willing to forgive his transgressions. He was overcome with emotions to the point where the associate pastor had to comfort him. Having composed himself, the pastor walked back toward the microphone.

"But we still have more important business to attend. Now at this time, as my first task as your pastor, it is my honor and privilege to introduce to you our very own Jameer Creston, a real servant in God and a giant in the faith. Come forward, Jameer."

From his front row seat, Jameer walked up toward the pulpit and stood on stage, immaculately dressed in a cobalt blue suit, crisp white shirt and paisley azure tie. Gucci black shoes completed his outfit. Jameer was serene. He had always looked forward to this day as being one of the biggest days of his life and it was. Just not in the way he thought. He listened to his pastor.

"Now before I ask the Deacon Drummond to proceed with our church devote, I would like to ask Mr. Jameer Creston before the presence of Lord and before this congregation, your church family and the people that you love, that as the Lord has called you out to serve as a deacon in this ministry, that you will serve Him with your whole heart, your mind, your body and your spirit and that you will exemplify the biblical qualifications of Acts

Chapter six; being a man full of the Holy Spirit, a man who is a servant in the body of Christ," the pastor said.

"I do, I do," Jameer said, speaking loudly but reverently for the whole congregation to hear him.

"Very well then. God bless you, my boy, it's an honor to welcome you," the restored pastor said, smiling abundantly. "Now, Aaron, would you please present to the congregation, the recommendation from the deacons.

Deacon Chairman Aaron Drummond came forward on the pulpit dressed very businesslike in a heather brown suit with Hershey brown shoes. He turned addressed the congregation and said:

"Church, do I have a motion to accept this man as a deacon in our body. All in favor say, 'Aye'"

The church responded with a rousing "Aye".

"Opposed?" the deacon chairman said. Not a word was heard in the church.

"Welcome, Jameer," the deacon chairman said and walked over and politely shook Jameer's hand. "It's a pleasure to have you in our ranks," he said.

A brief silence pervaded the church. The Pastor Emerson stepped down onto the sanctuary red carpet and made a declaration.

"Finally, let us welcome our newest member, having completed the sacrament of Baptism...please welcome Ms. Dominique Glavin. She was lost but now she has accepted Jesus in her life."

Dominique Glavin stood up from the front pew and walked up to the pulpit. She was dazzling in a full figured mahogany dress with a plunging neckline. A gaudy, glittering engagement ring sparkled on her finger. She stood beside Jameer, smiling and crying tears of joy. The congregation rose as one to shower her with thunderous applause.

The pastor approached gleefully and eagerly shook Deacon Jameer's hand, giving him a very impassioned hug. He then turned to Dominique and planted a kiss on her forehead, grabbing her hands together and grinning in her face. He then stood between them, bringing all three of them in a great wide embrace. The pastor's smile stretched across his face, crying tears of exultation.

Applause filled the congregation as the church members scrambled again to rise to their feet to welcome the praise the pastor, the new deacon and Dominique. Live music played as the young band members pounded the drums and keyboards. The choir clapped and broke into song as the service came to a close. Church members eagerly filed downstairs to the church's reception area where a huge banquet was prepared in honor of the reverend's recommissioning and his triumphant return to the church. Member eagerly sought to shake hands with the pastor and their new deacon and his fiancée Dominique. It was a new day in the church.

EPILOGUE

Dominique completed her recovery and detox at the church's new Gloria Emerson Residence, a remodeled and expanded rehabilitation program for Sexually Exploited Women, named in honor of the pastor's late wife. Her father James Glavin attended her graduation from the program. She then went on to obtain her high school diploma in night school.

Dominique enrolled in college but continued to work at the Gloria Emerson Residence as a counselor and mentor to other young girls trying to escape a life of prostitution. She also volunteered her time to the street ministry to reach out to those women still on the streets, looking for hope and a way out, giving her own story as living testimony.

⋏

Stefon Grey was taken into police custody. After a lengthy confession, he was charged with possession of a stolen car, weapons possession, assault, attempted kidnapping and the murder of Yvonne Cassidy aka Desire. He cooperated with authorities in telling them where they could find Lavender's body and the body of his friend. The bodies were eventually recovered and forensics confirmed the cause of death. Stefon was sentenced to ten years in prison, with the top charge of murder in the first degree for Desire, the prostitute.

Mercedes was arrested after Peaches and Passion turned state's evidence and testified about Mercedes' involvement in running a prostitution ring from her "Lonely Hearts" escort website. Mercedes was charged with sex trafficking and promoting prostitution. She served a three year bid.

After she was released from jail, the 30-years-old Mercedes went back to the streets to work her hustle. Mercedes had gained considerable weight while incarcerated. Still, her curvy, full bodied shape was appealing to those desperate johns looking for a cheap thrill. Outfitted in dated designer outfits, Mercedes was determined to reclaim her status. The other girls on the stroll looked at Mercedes as washed up. Many kept their distance so as not to mess up their own flow.

Mercedes' new pimp was Lavender's drug dealing pal, Bump who provided her with crack cocaine and protection as long as she brought in money. He often gave Mercedes special treatment than the other girls only because she used to be Lavender's bottom girl and she never tired of reminding him of that. He was also infatuated with her and often let her keep a day's pay if she satisfied his sexual desires, much to her disgust. Mercedes counted the days when she would get back to running things her way.

A broken down, grey Ford Explorer pulled up to the curb on Prospect Street just before the break of dawn. The truck stopped just in front of Mercedes, who was dressed in white spandex tights and leather and silver stilettos. She wore a platinum blond wig that complemented suntan complexion. Spying a potential trick, Mercedes put away her crack pipe, tucking it in her clutch purse. She quickly walked to the passenger side of the car and solicited the man.

"Hi, honey! Looking for a good time? It'll cost you a buck (a hundred dollars)," Mercedes said,

"I ain't got that much, baby; help a brother out," the man shot back, matter-of-factly, screw facing her.

"What you got?" Mercedes leaned into the man's SUV, desperate for another hit from her crack pipe, eager to negotiate. She vaguely recognized the man but couldn't place him.

"I only got forty," the man shot back; it was Derrick Strong, his face ashen and drawn, his clothes disheveled, looking forlorn. Since his encounter with Mercedes years ago he had made patronizing prostitutes an expensive habit. "Take it or leave it," he said.

"Ok," Mercedes said reluctantly, still trying to remember the man, and sure she had went out with him before. Nevertheless, she grabbed the passenger side door and jumped in the car. The dilapidated SUV sped off in the night.

End

ACKNOWLEDGEMENTS

Special thanks to those who helped make this book possible: God for the inspiration; Mom; Glenn Owens; Sonia; Jada; Robin Rollan; Nicole Nugent; Shekeena Nugent; James Nugent; Seth Ewell; Andre; Morgan R; Tyler Johnson and Andrew Clarke; Mary McBeth; Larry James and the Wellhouse; and all who fight against human trafficking and the sexual exploitation of women.

About The Author

Jaye is an urban fiction writer living in Connecticut.

www.ingramcontent.com/pod-product-compliance
Lightning Source LLC
Chambersburg PA
CBHW030917120626
46554CB00001B/183